Shattering the Glass Slipper

D1256581

Other Anthologies Edited by:

Patricia Bray & Joshua Palmatier

After Hours: Tales from the Ur-bar
The Modern Fae's Guide to Surviving Humanity
Temporally Out of Order * Alien Artifacts * Were-
All Hail Our Robot Conquerors!
Second Round: A Return to the Ur-bar
The Modern Deity's Guide to Surviving Humanity

S.C. Butler & Joshua Palmatier

Submerged * Guilds & Glaives * Apocalyptic
When Worlds Collide * Brave New Worlds

Laura Anne Gilman & Kat Richardson

The Death of All Things

Troy Carrol Bucher & Joshua Palmatier

The Razor's Edge

Patricia Bray & S.C. Butler

Portals

David B. Coe & Joshua Palmatier

Temporally Deactivated * Galactic Stew
Derelict

Steven H Silver & Joshua Palmatier

Alternate Peace

Crystal Sarakas & Joshua Palmatier

My Battery Is Low and It Is Getting Dark

David B. Coe & John Zakour

Noir

Crystal Sarakas & Rhondi Salsitz

Shattering the Glass Slipper

Shattering
the
Glass Slipper

Edited by

Crystal Sarakas
&
Rhondi Salsitz

Zombies Need Brains LLC
www.zombiesneedbrains.com

Copyright © 2022 Crystal Sarakas, Rhondi Salsitz, and
Zombies Need Brains LLC

All Rights Reserved

Interior Design (ebook): ZNB Design
Interior Design (print): ZNB Design
Cover Design by ZNB Design
Cover Art "Shattering the Glass Slipper"
by Justin Adams of Varia Studios

ZNB Book Collectors #25
All characters and events in this book are fictitious.
All resemblance to persons living or dead is coincidental.

The scanning, uploading, and distribution of this book via the Internet or any other means
without the permission of the publisher is illegal and punishable by law. Please purchase
only authorized electronic editions of this book, and do not participate in or encourage
electronic piracy of copyrighted material.

Kickstarter Edition Printing, June 2022
First Printing, July 2022

Print ISBN-13: 978-1940709482

Ebook ISBN-13: 978-1940709499

Printed in the U.S.A.

COPYRIGHTS

"Two for the Path" copyright © 2022 by Bryn Neuenschwander

"A Bracelet of Blood and Hair" copyright © 2022 by Lucia Gressani Iglesias

"Not the Youngest, Nor the Prettiest, But Someone Else" copyright © 2022 by Alyse Winters

"#BeYourSelfie" copyright © 2022 by Rebecca A Demarest

"The Twenty-Fifth Bean" copyright © 2022 by R.J. Blain

"The Crane" copyright © 2022 by Jane Pinckard

"Time Is a Secret Door" copyright © 2022 by Rachel Swirsky

"Harvest" copyright © 2022 by Angela Rega

"Dear Auntie Star" copyright © 2022 by Alethea Kontis

"Bride of the Blue Manor" copyright © 2022 by Y.M. Pang

"Goblin King" copyright © 2022 by Patricia A. Bray

"The Six of Them" copyright © 2022 by Cat Rambo

"The Seven Princesses and Two Dukes" copyright © 2022 by Rhondi Salsitz

"Ashes of a Cinnamon Fire" copyright © 2022 by Rhiannon Held

"The Tale of Jordan and Atheny" copyright © 2022 by José Pablo Iriarte

Table of Contents

SIGNATURE PAGE

Crystal Sarakas, editor:

_____

Rhondi Salsitz, editor:

_____

Marie Brennan:

_____

Lucia Iglesias:

_____

Alyse Winters:

_____

Rebecca A. Demarest:

_____

R.J. Blain:

_____

Miyuki Jane Pinckard:

_____

Rachel Swirsky:

_____

Angela Rega:

_____

Alethea Kontis:

_____

Y.M. Pang:

_____

Patricia Bray:

_____

Cat Rambo:

_____

Rhondi Salsitz:

_____

R.Z. Held:

_____

José Pablo Iriarte:

_____

Justin Adams, artist:

_____

Two for the Path

Marie Brennan

The proverbial "message in a bottle" is supposed to wash up on a seashore. The one I receive comes by river instead—by river and by ally—and both of those are strokes of luck. The sea has relatively little a bottle can get caught on except a shore, but a river through a forest is full of bends and stones and the roots of trees, all of which might stop a bottle before it got very far. And although few go into that dark, trackless forest, "few" is not "none," and someone else could have found it. Someone who would not have recognized the handwriting on the message inside; someone who would not have brought it to me.

To whomever may find this, the message begins, *I beg for your help.*

My ally, the man who found the bottle, stands silently as I crumple the message in my fist. It's written on a rag instead of paper, with greasy charcoal that rubs off on my fingertips. The rag doesn't have room for much text, but the writer has crammed in enough. Information on the plight from which she hopes to be saved…and directions on how to find her.

I do not know my way through the forest. My ally is a royal huntsman, and he does.

* * *

The years have not been kind to either of us, but she's fared better than I. A glance is enough for me to recognize her; old and decrepit-looking as

I am, and with the excuse of selling scissors, I manage to get close before she recognizes me.

Then her work-chapped hands tighten on the broom, and a spark of fire flares in her dull, weary eyes. "It may not be much of a life," she spits, gripping the broom like a weapon, "but I won't let you take it."

I would lift my hands to show I mean no threat, but they still hold scissors, pointed and sharp. "I haven't come to kill you. The huntsman found your message—the one where you asked for help."

"You, helping me?" Her laugh has the sound of disuse. I doubt there's been much cause for laughter in her life since she came here. "Leave before *I* kill *you*."

I don't doubt her resolve. I leave as ordered.

But I come back.

* * *

She's weeping when I approach a second time, sitting exhausted atop an overturned bucket. At the sight of me, she scrubs away the tears, but more come in their wake. "The queen herself, come twice to visit me. How lucky I am."

"Queen no more," I say. "Not since I lost my beauty. Your father has a third wife now." I doubt she's found any more joy in it than I did. My former husband is a huntsman, too. But his bait is a crown, a golden castle his cage.

My step-daughter is so tired she doesn't even flinch when I stroke her hair—an affectionate gesture from the days before I let my jealousy consume me. Now that jealousy has spat me back out again, I find I miss the old habits. There's a comb in my pocket, and I begin drawing it through her hair, gently teasing out the tangles that caught my fingers before.

"This is a trick. You want me dead."

"I did," I admit. It isn't a pretty thing; I was ugly on the inside when beautiful without. I'm not sure I've received the inner sort in trade for the outer, but I've gotten more honest. "That's past. I'm not asking for you to forgive me—only for you to come with me. I can help you get away."

A long silence, long enough for me to almost unsnarl her filthy hair. I wonder if she's fallen asleep, despite the tugs I can't fully avoid. But then she speaks, barely above a whisper.

"They'll never let me go."

"They aren't here," I say—but I'm wrong. Noise in the forest resolves into *them*: the men who have kept my step-daughter as their slave for all these years. And despite my resolve to stand fast, to confront them with all the dignity and authority of the queen I used to be, they have mining tools and the strength to swing them.

"*Go*," she says, low and urgent.

I don't test their ruthlessness. I flee to safety.

But I come back.

* * *

Our first day in the forest, the huntsman slapped some berries out of my hands before I could put them in my hungry mouth. "Don't eat those," he snapped, impatient and curt. "One will make you sleep. Two will make you seem dead. And three will make you dead in truth."

Now, slowing my flight, I come across another bush. For one brief, vengeful moment, I think about picking a basket of those berries and leaving them for the men. But they haven't been feeding my step-daughter well; unwarned, she might eat the berries herself.

I pause, thinking of the deer's heart the huntsman brought to me in place of my step-daughter's. For years I lived with horror and regret, thinking it was hers. Thinking she was dead, at my command.

Now I bend, my old back aching, and I begin to pick the fruit.

* * *

"Do you trust me?" I ask, cradling the berries in the palm of my hand.

She wavers. She isn't sure. I can't blame her.

I have another in my pocket. I take it out, show it to her, and eat it.

She takes the ones in my palm and eats them.

* * *

I wake up first. The huntsman starts swearing at me when I do. Apparently, his numbers were not as precise or reliable as I assumed; I've taken a far greater risk than I know.

But not in vain.

The men don't bother with a coffin or even a pauper's shroud. They dump her body far enough away that it won't attract scavengers to their home, and then they go back to the mines. They'll continue on without their slave, as they did before she came, and their house just won't be as clean, their meals ready when they get home. It's better than they deserve.

She's unconscious for three days. I dribble water between her lips and massage her throat to make her swallow it. When she wakes up, she's dizzy and disoriented, vomiting up the food she hasn't eaten—and then after that, she's grateful.

It isn't the same thing as forgiveness. Once I asked the huntsman to kill her; once she considered any refuge, no matter how brutal, better than living with me and her father. But she's free now, and that's what matters. I may no longer be beautiful, I may not be queen, but for the first time in years, I will sleep well at night.

She makes me show her the bush where the berries grow. She plucks one and studies it, held gently between finger and thumb.

"A third wife, you said."

"When last I heard, yes. There might be a fourth by now." Another pretty thing, to be cast aside when her youth and beauty are gone.

My step-daughter says, "I'd like to meet her."

One for sleep. Three for death. And two for the path to a new life.

I don't question her intentions. I help her pick berries.

And we go back.

A Bracelet of Blood and Hair

Lucia Iglesias

I am an uncommonly good sorceress, but I used to be an even better dancer.

On the eve of Prince Sigson's birthday, all I wanted to do was practice so that every step would be perfect, but my siblings wouldn't stop pestering me for new clothes.

"So you want a dress made from starlight?" I sighed. "And you, you want a doublet of moonlight? And you, a cloak lined with thread spun from new sunshine? Very well. But you must dance with me first, every last one of you."

I have many siblings. We danced throughout the night and I was still awake making their clothes when first light split the horizon like a sour orange. Their wishes were simple enough. I had a closet of starlight and moonbeams. Their wishes bored me. When all the new clothes were hung, I sat on the wide window ledge, sharpening my shears and letting my leg hang over the sill. It was just past sunrise, dew lifting in a sweet haze off the flax fields. Soon the sun would crisp their leaves and we would have to put on our wide-brimmed hats, but the early morning was still cool as the tip of a cat's ear.

I studied the scene below me, looking for something to steal. But I'd already done a dew dress; I had a suit of flax-flower blue; I'd even cut a hood out of a particularly luscious sunrise. There was nothing left, nothing new. I gave up and crawled into bed, thinking I'd just have to wear the flax-flowers after all. Those gorgeous flounces of sunshine tended to wash me out—at least in the blue I would glow.

When I woke up, my siblings were squawking around the closet, doing up each other's buttons and tying each other's bows. They were disappointed when I pulled out the old suit. They'd hoped I would have something fabulous and new.

"Of course I will," I promised them, like a fool. "You didn't think I'd wear something new just for tonight's dancing, did you? I'm saving it for tomorrow night, the Queen's ball." And then, because I'm the oldest and they all look up to me, even the ones who are already much taller, I couldn't help but add, "It's like nothing I've ever done before. I think Prince Sigson might fall in love with me tomorrow."

Some of my siblings laughed at that, but more of them demanded to know what I'd done. I told them they'd have to wait until tomorrow to find out.

That evening, I danced badly. All I could think about as I spun around the palace courtyard was the masterpiece I'd promised my siblings. It was lucky I'd spent all night practicing or I'd have maimed a fair few of my partners in the blade dance. No one asked for a second dance, except for Sigson's friend Benno.

After the first few dances, I collapsed on a bench between some of my siblings and one of them handed me a mug of cider. They were all a little drunk and silly, so I slung my arms around their shoulders and looked up at the night sky. The moon was a ripe quince, all golden and almost round, with a shimmer to it like very fine fur. With my arms locked around my siblings I could lean very far back, far enough to see all the constellations of the summer sky spread out like a game of jacks. I was warm and my collar was tight and the cider was very good and for a moment I felt as if I were looking down at the sky instead of up. I started feeling sick to my stomach and was about to say so when the music stopped with a wet, sideways sound. I sat up fast, stars tumbling past my eyes. The musicians were all staring at the palace's red marble steps. And there was the Queen, in one of her better but not best gowns, descending with a train of autumn oak leaves rustling down the stairs behind her.

She gave the barrels of cider a heavy look, but didn't say anything. Instead, she turned to Sigson and wished him a happy birthday. Then she gestured at a pair of small boys who had followed her down the steps. They were carrying a heavy crossbow between them, dark walnut wood with fastenings in silver.

"I had this made for you," said the Queen, as Sigson caressed the barrel with the back of his hand. "You're all that a man should be now, except you have no one with whom to share your throne. I am old and you are getting older. Tomorrow at my ball you will tell me whom you wish to wed."

Sigson's fingers tightened around the silver fastenings. "Mother," he murmured, "I'm not ready."

"I know," she said, "that's why I've given you until tomorrow." Then, with a flick of her whispering train, she paraded back up the palace stairs.

After that, the night became like a bad dream. The prince was swarmed by a flock of aristocrats, handmaidens, and knights, fluttering around him in a rainbow of velvet, silk, and satin, all stepping on each other's hems and crushing one another's crinolines. It was awful. A few of my siblings tried to shove me into the frenzy but I shook them off.

I hate to give him credit for anything, but it was Benno who put an end to the pandemonium. He fought his way through the thick of the mob and towed the prince out with him.

"Listen everyone," he bellowed, "let's not suffocate him. A bevy of swans just passed overhead not long ago. It's out of season for swans, but I say, let's hunt!"

So Sigson and about half his suitors called for their horses and rode off into the Queenwood still in their dancing clothes. As they galloped off, they looked like a meteor shower come down to earth, all those gold and silver hems trailing behind them. My siblings do not hunt, so they stayed to help finish up the cider. I told them I fancied a midnight walk and headed after the hunters into the wood. I thought perhaps I might find something there that would make a good costume for tomorrow's ball. The stakes had been raised. If I could find something in the woods that Sigson had seen as he cantered past, something that would remind him of the tender summer nights and the fresh air on his face, perhaps—

I walked for a long time, fingering the shears tucked into my belt. I found many things that I could have made into suits or gowns: the shadow of the weeping willow, black against the river's silvery sand; feathery halos of cattails going to seed; birch skin, chalk white dashed with stripes of gray. Any of them would have made a fine frock for the ball, but I never had a chance to make my decision because with no warning, a white mist unfurled from the roots of the trees, rising as high as my knees. I could no longer see where I was placing my feet. I walked through a dry and restless sea, unsure of where I was going. As the mist twined up my legs, I came to a clearing in the trees and saw a lake the same shape as the lumpy moon. The lake was white with swans.

Breast to breast, they moved as one, slow ripples fanning out across their ranks like waves on water. I was so absorbed in their dance that I didn't notice Sigson until he stepped from the shadows, crossbow cocked. He must have become separated from his hunting party, lost perhaps in the same mist that had obscured my way. I watched, helpless, as he took aim. Then, from the midst of the flock, a woman stepped out lightly, wading through the lake towards Sigson. I am an uncommonly good enchanter, but even I cannot tell you where she came from or how she came to be there.

The Prince, too, was taken aback. The crossbow twitched in his hands—I think, for a moment, he was frightened enough to shoot, but then the bow drooped and he dropped to one knee.

She seemed to be about our age or a bit older. She wore only a light slip, plain muslin and very white. She was tall, taller even than Sigson, I thought, though it was hard to tell with him still kneeling in the mist. Her shoulders were quite broad and ribbed with muscle, like the fibrous bands that run the length of a redwood's trunk. The grace of her movements flowed around her, finer than any silk I had touched. Crouched in the shadows, I felt clumsy as a child. She did not step out of the lake but instead seemed to drift up and onto the bank like the mist itself.

I do not know what passed between them. I was too far away and heard only an owl's nervous cruing. But soon, the two of them were dancing along the lake's shore, mist spiraling out around them. I knew I was watching something I was not meant to see, so I turned and walked back the way I came. As the mist sifted back into the underbrush, I found an owl feather sticking up between two stones. I decided it would make a dress and worked the whole gown out on my walk home. I made it complicated to keep myself from thinking about what I had just seen. It had a high, tufted collar and hoops over the shoulders that fanned out over my scapula like wings. My arms and collarbones were bare, and there was an outer corset boned with more feathers. The skirt was long and full, split down the middle to reveal petticoats of frothy white feathers scattered with black specks. The outer skirt trailed out in a train that was half as long again as the skirt itself. All along the edges were feathery ocher eyes.

When my siblings found the gown tossed over the foot of my bed the next day, they woke me up with their noise. They demanded I try it on and I was too tired to bully them out of my bedroom. Once their curiosity had been satisfied, there was nothing for it but that they should have feathered vests and caps and capelets to match. They seemed very certain that the Prince would want to marry me and didn't want to miss out on any attention that might be bestowed on the lucky family. After what I had seen on the lake last night, I did not think there was any chance of that, but I could not bring myself to tell them. Perhaps it had all been a dream brought on by cider and the moon.

So, bristling with enchanted feathers, my whole family processed up the palace steps and into the ballroom. Then I was glad that I had dressed all my siblings so well, for truly no one in the palace looked less than radiant that night. I couldn't rest my eyes anywhere, overwhelmed on all sides by extreme beauty. I lingered over cheekbones daubed with crushed roses, hair twisted into the shape of a sleeping dragon, a dress slit up the side to reveal a glittered thigh. I paused over elegant wrists emerging from a voluminous cape, a red beard oiled so that it glistened like fire, an earlobe encased in a fragile silver blossom.

Then I saw Sigson. But before I could even begin to savor that spectacle, I saw her. They had dressed her in a white gown, hardly more intricate than the shift she had worn out of the lake—the same, sharp white, only longer, brushing the tops of her feet, which were still bare, and gathered slightly at the shoulders so that the linen poured down her back in two wide bands. Her hair was too short to put up. It seemed she'd done nothing but comb some water through the white-gold strands and slick them back so that they formed a sleek cap. I had to get closer.

Leaving my siblings to fend for themselves, I drifted through the dancers. Sigson had his hand over hers, but they were not dancing, just nodding slightly to the sway of violins. When I reached them, I inclined my head to the Prince, but couldn't think of a single word to say to him. It was as if we had no common language. Instead, I turned to look at the girl.

"May I have this dance?"

She nodded and placed her hand in mine. Before I could remember how my legs worked, she had slipped her other arm around my waist and spun me around. I was a very good dancer in those days, but with her, I was perfection. She did not lead like other dance partners. Instead of indicating where she wanted me to go with a slight pressure on the arm or waist, she made small movements with her head. Her head was never still. It was always fidgeting, twitching, twisting slightly on that long, agile neck. And her skin! I had thought her simply pale, but her coloring came not from the skin itself but from the thin sheen of feathers that covered it, as fine as the hairs on my own arms and legs. Her eyes were a deep orange, the pupils small and unreadable.

It wasn't until after the first dance that I realized I hadn't even asked her name. Benno had spun her away from me and I brooded from afar as he tried to lead her in the waltz. With any other partner, Benno was a capable dancer, but he didn't seem to see the movements of her head. They careened around the dancefloor, both trying to lead, leaving a trail of flattened hems behind them.

I danced with her twice more that night. After Benno and a few of Sigson's other friends had their turns, she sought me out and asked for another dance. She told me her name was Odda and she was to marry the Prince within the week. When I asked where she had come from, she smiled and cocked her head twice very quickly, as if trying to shake water out of her ear.

"From magic," she said.

"Can you tell me more about this magic?" I asked. "I am an enchanter."

"I am not," she said, ducking her head. "So I cannot."

"Are your kin from this place? Are they near?"

"Yes, but they are a shy and meditative people. I do not think they will come to court. But tell me—" Here she met my eyes. "—are *you* often at court? For I should like to see more of you when I have wed the Prince."

"I suppose you will," I said, but I had bitten my tongue when she spoke of marrying the Prince and the words did not come out very clearly. "I am often here, because the Queen is very fond of the clothes that I can make."

"Then you must be the very best!" she exclaimed. "Will you make me a wedding gown?"

I said that I would, but the words seemed to cut my mouth.

After our third dance, I lost her in the gorgeous crowds. I saw her again later, dancing with Sigson. Like Benno, he did not seem to read her head movements and made a horrible mess of the dance. Then they must have gone away somewhere together because I did not see her again that night.

The next day, I was woken by a hoard of my siblings all piling into my bed.

"Pela!" they screeched. "Pela! Pelageya! Wake up! You're wanted at the palace. You're wanted right now!"

I pushed them off me and rubbed my eyes. They told me that a messenger had arrived with a letter—*stamped by the Queen's own ring!*—inviting me up to the palace to begin work on Odda's wedding gowns.

"Get up! Get up!" they cried, hoisting me out of bed and dragging me to the wardrobe. I let them dress me in a light tunic and trousers and buckle me into my work belt. How could I say no? To my siblings or the Queen? I let them cram my feet into boots and push me out the door. "Tell us everything!" they shouted at my back.

The red marble steps of the palace had been swept clean, and the columned halls were quieter than the woods on a moonless night. I could not even hear the echo of my own footsteps because the marble was covered in plush carpets the color of spilled wine. I met with the Queen in her day parlor and we talked about colors and textures and what was beautiful in the world at midsummer. Throughout our conversation, I kept hearing a sound blowing in from the open window: hissing, intermixed with sharp cries of pain. On the pretext of getting up for some fresh air, I sauntered over to the window and leaned against the casement.

"Be still!" someone grunted from above—Benno, I thought. "Still, I said!"

"Please, Odda." That was definitely Sigson. "It's like plucking eyebrows. Plenty of people have survived that!" He laughed then, but the laugh was empty as a bell without a clapper.

I wanted to call out to Odda—but the Queen was staring at me now. I looked down at my hands, knuckles white on the hilt of my shears.

As soon as I could make a polite retreat, I bowed to the Queen and promised sketches by morning. I hurried into the hall, but I couldn't find any stairs and I could no longer hear anything.

Even in the quiet, I could tell I was being followed. A shadow slid from column to column, always one behind me, never closing the gap. I thought it must be one of the Queen's little serving boys playing a game, and when I decided it had gone on long enough, I turned and said, "Very well then. You're quite good at keeping quiet. You can come out now."

The shadow froze on the wall.

"You can come out now," I said again.

But there was no response from the shadow behind its red marble column.

I brushed my thumb over my work belt, lingering on the shears. Then I walked to the edge of the carpet and peered around the column.

Odda looked back at me, her hair sticking out at all angles, blood drying in a grim mask over half her face.

"Oh!" I sucked in the sound, afraid someone else might hear us.

"I do not think I will marry the Prince after all," she said very calmly and very quietly. "Can you help me leave this place without anyone noticing?"

I glanced up and down the hallway, choosing my materials. Then I nodded.

Getting her out was easy enough. I made her a hooded cloak, cutting some red from the marble. She darted from column to column and when we reached the doors, I engaged the guards in a short conversation about last night's ball, angling myself so that their attention would not follow the marble blur moving through the doorway. When we reached the foot of the palace steps, I paused, studying the gravel drive ahead.

"Where do you want to go from here?" I asked, scooping up a handful of dust from the road and casting it over her.

"The woods." And she was already off, a faint shimmer on the drive, like a heat haze drifting through the palace gates.

When we reached the woods, she peeled off her mantle and pressed a hand to her bloody face. She flinched and drew her fingers away, reopening the wounds.

"What did he do to you?" I asked.

"They plucked me," she said, and now there was a tang of anger to her words. "Or they tried to. I didn't make it easy for them. But then they wrestled me down and Sigson sat on my chest with his knees around my ears so I couldn't move my head."

"How did you get away?"

"Sigson tried to stroke my face, and that gave me just enough room to turn my head and snap at Benno's hand. I think I may have broken some fingers," she reflected, ducking her chin.

"Why?" I asked, twining my fingers through the handles of the shears. "Why were they plucking you?"

"The Queen thought I should look like a real Princess for the wedding day."

I looked at my feet. "Well, you're away from all that now. What do you want to do next?"

"I don't know." Odda's eyes were very wide, head ticking nervously to the left. "I can't go home. Sigson knows how to find the lake. Oh, Pelegeya! He knows how to find my family. If he can't find me, he'll come for them. I know he will." She shook herself, like a bird straightening her feathers. "There's nothing for it. I'll have to go back to him. I can't let him hurt them."

I stared at her. "You can't mean it, Odda. How could you go back? You'll be a slab of raw meat when the Queen is finished with you!"

"Wouldn't you do the same for your family, Pele?"

My hand had gone numb around my shears.

"There's nothing else we can do. I told you. I don't know magic."

I took her hand and placed it on the pommel of my shears, covering it with my own. "I do."

This is how magic was explained to me when I was very small.

You see a wave coming towards shore. You can take its measure, its length and depth. You can see light bending through it. Then the wave breaks on the sand and is gone. There is no wave. But the water is still there. The wave was just another way for the water to be, for a while.

Enchantment is like making a wave. I take something in the world and coax it into another shape, for a while. Sometimes for a very long while. To make snow, you need a bit of ice, something to teach the water in the air how to form a crystal. To make a gown of starlight, you need a starry night, to teach the air how to shine just right. But I can't make something from nothing. A pattern is necessary to guide my shears.

Slipping the shears from my belt, I drew a thin line over the bone of my wrist where the skin was thinnest. I caught three drops of blood in the air. They slid down the blades into a new shape.

I cleaned the shears in the wet grass. Then I stepped back to study my work.

Amongst the clover and shiny oak leaves was a woman, curled up as if asleep. I had shaped her from my memories of the ball last night. In length of limb she matched Odda like a twin. But her skin was smooth and red as rosehips. Odda and I both looked at her for a long time. I cannot say what passed through Odda's mind, but I thought that I had finally outdone myself. If only my siblings could see the beauty I had made. The woman glowed like the eastern sky in a cold, clear dawn of late December.

"You're going to hand her over to the Prince?" hissed Odda, kneeling now to brush the ice-blond hair off the woman's brow.

"She'll go herself," I said. "I was in love with the Prince once. I've given her all of that."

Odda looked up at me, eyes narrowed.

"He won't hurt her," I said. "She doesn't have any feathers. She can tell him she plucked them out herself."

"That would explain the color," murmured Odda, running a finger down the woman's bare arm.

"Wake her," I said.

The woman, we decided to call her Odile, woke slowly, like a small child in the middle of a dream. She smiled up at us, her wide eyes orange as egg yolks. We helped her sit up and explained that she was to marry the Prince. As soon as she heard his name, she shut her eyes and said in a dreamy voice, "I feel as if I've always known him. I think I love him."

"You do," I assured her. "But you cannot ever tell him about the two of us because he promised he would only ever love Odda, and if he knew that you are not her, he would leave you."

Her face crumpled like a rose petal and she promised she would never say anything about us, and begged us in turn to remain hidden in the woods. Then I snipped a loose thread from Odda's white shift and shaped a matching one. After we had dressed her, Odile hurried away towards the edge of the woods, skipping happily on every third step. The skip worried me. Though in shape and form she was twin to Odda, she moved like a child.

But before I could decide what to do about that, Odda had slipped her hand into mine and was pulling me deeper into the woods. I knew where she was taking me. I was afraid that if she found out I already knew the location of the lake, she would lose trust in me, so I told her what I had seen that night she met the Prince. Odda laughed.

"I knew you were there, Pele! I can see in the dark. Why do you think I agreed to dance with you? I wanted to know more about the enchanter I'd seen in the woods."

I followed her back to her home. There was no mist on the water now. In daylight, it looked like an ordinary lake. The swans were no longer swimming in formation, but diving and fishing and resting each to their own fancy.

"Come on!" said Odda, stepping into the water, head bobbing with excitement. "It isn't deep."

I left my boots on the shore and followed her in. The day had grown warm and there was no shade from the sun, which glared straight down on the lake with a hot, metallic light. But the water was pleasantly cool and the sand was very fine, swirling up in little clouds around my feet.

In the middle of the lake, Odda opened a door. This was no magic I had ever seen before. She reached out and twisted something in the air, and as her arm drew back, it was as if she were pulling aside a curtain that had been there all along. Air and water made room for the new place. I followed Odda inside and she closed the door behind us.

"Do you think a message will be able to reach us?" I asked, looking around the airy little cottage of white walls and high windows. We had told Odile that if there was any trouble, she must go to one of my siblings. They would get a message to me, for they all had some small magic of their own.

"I think so. The cottage is somewhere near the lake. The seasons are the same, and the weather, and sometimes I can even hear the trumpeting of the swans. But I've walked all over the woods and never found it. Would you like something to eat?"

She fixed us a crisp, juicy salad of watercress and cattail stems sliced into papery half-moons. There was bread, too, a dark, greenish loaf that tasted a little brackish but was nice enough with butter.

My head kept nodding. Odda took my bowl when my head nearly ended up in the salad. I woke in a cloud of white linen and down pillows. The sun had set and the sky beyond the windows had darkened to the luminous purple-blue of flax in bloom. I was about to get up and find Odda when a turtle dove landed on the windowsill and cooed at me.

In the voice of one of my brothers, the bird said: "You must go back to the place where you left Odile. She is coming to find you. She says she danced with the Prince."

Rubbing my eyes, I shambled into the kitchen calling for Odda. As soon as I had explained what the turtle dove had told me, she pushed open the door to the lake. We splashed back to shore, apologizing to the swans, who ruffled their feathers at us and said nothing at all.

The woods were very dark now and the moon had not yet risen above the trees. Odda clutched my hand, leading me along paths only she could see. The shadows stuck to our feet, dragging silently over the leaves behind us.

We heard Odile before we saw her. Deep, gulping cries oozed through the undergrowth from the place beneath the oak tree. We sat in the leaves and wrapped our arms around her shoulders, rocking her gently between us. Gulping back sobs, she told us that Sigson had wanted to practice their dancing in preparation for the wedding.

"I don't know how to dance!" she wailed. Odda looked over her head at me. Her eyes were all pupil; there was no anger there, only a hollowness. She was not even surprised.

"It's alright," I said, trying to stroke Odile's head. But my hands were sticky with sweat and I only pulled her hair, making her yelp.

"It's not!" she cried. "He knows something is wrong with me. He's been asking all sorts of questions about where I went this afternoon and how come my skin is so smooth."

"Don't worry about that," I said. "You're everything he wanted."

"But I don't know how to dance!"

"You will when you leave these woods."

Odda, whose hands were always dry and cool, nudged my hand away and stroked Odile's hair. All the while she looked at me, head cocked, waiting.

I pressed the heels of my hands into my eye sockets, trying to block everything out so I could think. To make a gown of owl feathers, I had needed only an owl feather. To make Odile, I had needed only blood and memories. And to make her dance better than anyone, I would need to outdo myself once more.

I knew what I had to do. But I couldn't make my hands move. I wanted to rest, I *needed* to rest—just a moment, just a moment longer, in the dark, in the stillness.

I don't know how long they let me rest there with my hands pressed against my eyes, but I was dimly aware of Odile slipping out from under my arm, her ragged breaths settling into the rhythms of sleep. I heard an owl—perhaps the same one I had heard only two nights ago—*cru-crrru!* he called, *cru-crrru!*

When I opened my eyes, Odda was still watching me. Odile slept, head pillowed in Odda's lap, one hand wrapped around the swan-woman's knee. I brushed my hand over the sleeping woman's knuckles, following them over the curve of Odda's knee and down over her calf, stopping when I reached her ankle. She was warm through the silvery buzz of her feathers. They hadn't plucked her here. She did not move under my hand. I could feel a tendon pulsing there under the thin skin.

Without saying anything, I drew the shears from my belt. She drew in a short breath but said nothing. She didn't move. The tendon vibrated softly as a purring cat. So much of dancing well comes from knowing when to be still.

Then I rolled up my right trouser leg. Taking my hand from her ankle, I found the matching tendon on my own. I opened a slit in the skin, the length of my hand, and peeled back the edges so that the tendon was laid bare. Carefully, as if pulling out a row of stitches, I picked at the tendon with the point of my shears, until the threads came undone and I could peel up a thin fiber from the toughened plait. My fingers were steady, but the rest of my body was shaking so hard I was afraid the shears would slip. The pain was like nothing I'd ever known before. It radiated up my leg, pounding through my spine with every beat of my heart. I knew I would lose consciousness soon. My life would be in Odda's hands then.

I opened my eyes and found Odile's right ankle, nestled in the clover and green oak leaves. I didn't look at Odda.

"I need a lock of your hair," I said. My voice sounded as if it were coming from somewhere under the leaves.

She didn't hesitate, just pulled a strand right out and placed it in my bloody hand. Without looking, I tied the hair to the flesh and joined them together around Odile's ankle. I tied them very tight, so that they pressed up against the skin. The bangle tightened around Odile's ankle, and then it began to dissolve, sinking into the woman's rosy flesh.

After that there was a darkness that lasted a very long time and I could not find my way out.

I woke up to swan feathers fanning out across my cheek and a sharp peck on the ear. When I opened my eyes, I found myself propped against a sway-backed willow on the shore of the lake, with several swans nestled comfortably around me and one blowsy little cygnet nibbling my earlobe. Before I could do anything, Odda swept down and picked him up. She clucked something at him and tossed him into the lake.

"You're back!" she said.

So she had decided to love me. I could see it in the crinkles around her eyes. I could see it in the knots of white linen bound around my ankle, and the sprigs of yarrow she'd placed between the folds.

"How long have I been gone?"

Odda settled beside me in the crook of the willow tree, nudging some swans out of the way. They fluttered up into the air and settled back down in her lap.

"Long enough for the Prince to marry his Swan Princess and dance throughout the night. Long enough for the stories to reach all the way into the wood. *And if they haven't died, then they are still living today.*"

I looked at my ankle again. "Thank you," I said.

"I couldn't leave you to bleed. I need a dancing partner! You're the best I've ever had."

"I do not think I will ever dance again."

She laughed, a great honking sound that startled the swans off her lap. They tumbled up in a white flurry, like laundry on a windy summer's day.

"I know what I'm doing, Pele. It wouldn't matter if you had cut both your legs off. You have me to lead you now."

She was right about the dancing. My leg healed well enough. But my shears were ruined forever. I couldn't make them cut so much as the green from a blade of grass. Odda said it wasn't the shears that were ruined but my will. I believe she was right about that too. As soon as I drew the shears from my belt, I would begin to wonder whether the green wouldn't be happier staying on that blade of grass, turning gold with the larch in autumn, and sleeping the winter away under a thick quilt of snow. Then the shears would slip from my fingers, sinking hilt-deep into the soft mud of the lake shore.

We danced every night that summer. And the swans flew in wide rings around us, filling the air with the low, rushing music of their wings.

Not the Youngest,
Nor the Prettiest,
But Someone Else

Alyse Winters

Else was bicycling home when Odd and Harald stopped their cart to tell her of an unusually large white bear headed towards her family's farm.

"Oh, damn it," Else said, for her plans for the evening had been to clean the mud off her new bicycle, take a long bath, and read until dinner.

Now this would all have to be thrown out the window. Either the bear was simply an unusually large white bear, in which case it would have to be chased off by the family's dogs, Solveig and Vigdis (unlikely), or shot by her father, whose vision had never been all that good (exceedingly unlikely).

On the off chance it was not an unusually large white bear, but some sort of spirit or god in disguise (extremely unlikely) or some sort of purloined duke or prince (slightly more likely, but still quite uncommon, in these days), her evening would be ruined, because the household would be thrown into chaos over what said miscreant wanted and which of their daughters would have to save his soul.

Else, who craved reading material the way a drunk craves a nightcap, was very familiar with these scenarios, and some small part of her was in fact hopeful to one day encounter one, so that she might treat it to the full, acerbic commentary she felt it truly deserved.

"Want a ride?" asked Odd, who was looking with bemusement at the runs in her stockings (sheer, to her mother's horror) and her rumpled walking skirt (a demure navy blue, to Else's horror). "Assuming you prefer to reach home before nightfall…"

"How impossibly clever you are," Else said with saccharine sweetness, dismounted her bicycle, and thrust it at the hapless Harald. Both brothers were engaged with self-conscious courting of her elder sister Birgit and so had to be obliged, as Else's family was rather poor, and Odd and Harald's rather rich. Or at least, what passed for the rich in the farming country. Birgit was not so much sought after for her great beauty (that belonged to Inger, the youngest), but her strong sense of practicality.

A tall, commanding-looking young woman, Birgit was neither elegant nor beautiful. But no one could deny that if you wanted anything done quickly and efficiently, Birgit was your woman.

"Birgit got all the sense in the family," their mother was fond of saying, while at the same time implying said sense derived from her line, and not their rather absent-minded father. Yes, Birgit was the practical, sensible one, Else the bookish, prideful one, and Inger was beautiful and artistic, Else supposed. And dreadfully spoiled.

Rumbling along in Odd and Harald's well-oiled cart, pulled by two stout chestnut draft horses, Else watched as the family farm gradually appeared. While she saw no signs of an invading bear, she could hear the dogs barking from some distance away, never a good sign. Then again, they could be barking because a weasel had gotten into the chicken coop again, as opposed to because the family was being held hostage by a robber in a furry pelt.

"Expect we should come investigate," said Harald, hoisting up the rifle the brothers were fond of traveling with.

Else tossed him a look of practiced scorn. "I really don't think that will be necessary," she said, though part of her felt she rather would like some sort of weapon in hand as they trundled down the road to the farmhouse. "Are you sure it was a bear you saw? And not a lost sheep? Or a big white dog?"

"I think I know a bear when I see one," said Odd, while Harald now seemed uncertain.

Rolling her eyes, Else waited until the cart came to a stop and alighted from it gracefully, though the effect of her calf-length skirt belling out around her suffered from the spot where she landed—namely an unusually deep puddle, spattering her clothes with mud.

As she sputtered and wiped at her spectacles, Harald handed down her bicycle and shushed the horses, who seemed somewhat out of sorts, as if smelling something foul. Else peered around the farmyard, noting the peculiar silence. In fact, she could not hear the barking at all anymore. A claw mark she was certain had not been there this morning gouged the center of the front door.

"Oh," she said, faintly. "Perhaps there really is a bear come to call."

As if in response, a piercing shriek echoed from inside the house.

"Now is the gun necessary?" Odd demanded, hopping down from the cart, rifle in hand, and leaving a dejected Harald to calm the horses.

Marching ahead like a soldier, he kicked open the door and stalked indoors, calling out gallantly, "Birgit! Where are you, darling?" Evidently the rifle was doing wonders for his ego, Else thought as she followed behind, as he would never have dared address Birgit so in her parents' hearing otherwise.

Assuming they were still alive to hear it.

For this reason, she was gladdened, upon stepping into the dining room behind Odd, to find her family alive and well. In fact, gathered around the table for their evening meal, lit by candles, rather than the new electric lights favored by the wealthy, they seemed rather sweet and cozy. Excluding, of course, the massive white bear crouched at the head of the table, whose furry head nearly brushed the ceiling rafters.

"Odd, put that toy down," Birgit snapped; it would not have been her who screamed. In fact, she seemed more annoyed with the intrusion than anything else, and Else saw now that the bear seemed to have been welcomed, in a sense. A place was set for him, with a platter instead of a dinner plate, and his white snout was red with raspberry preserves. Or blood.

"We heard a cry," Odd said, lowering the gun slightly and casting a dark look at the bear. "Did this villain threaten his way inside?"

"No, he knocked, only with a bit more claw than we are used to," Else's father chuckled nervously. Nearly all his chuckles were nervous, even in the best of times. "Prince Sverre, this is my middle daughter, Else."

The bear's beady black eyes flickered over to Else, who was torn between triumph that one of her hypotheses had been right and alarmed at suddenly being in the middle of said hypothesis.

"Pleased to meet you, Your Majesty," she said, and imitated a curtsy, picking some dried mud off her sleeve.

"I was the one who screamed," Inger volunteered, somewhat sheepishly. "Prince Sverre almost trod on Solveig."

Evidently, peace had been made, for Solveig, curled up on her cushion in the corner, chewed on what seemed to be a freshly bloodied bone.

"Well," said Odd, sounding disappointed that there would be no epic clash with a real bear, as opposed to an enchanted prince. "I suppose I should be headed home, then." He glanced at Birgit, clearly an invitation for her to interject and insist he stay, but she merely nodded decisively.

"Thank you for escorting Else, dear," Else's mother said, attempting to soothe any ruffled feathers.

Odd grunted in reply and meandered out with his gun, leaving Else framed in the whitewashed doorway.

"I should change for dinner," she said, but her father had already drawn out a chair.

"No, no, sit," her mother insisted, and so she did. What passed then was a good thirty minutes of stilted chatter and intense looks. While it was obvious Prince Sverre could approximate the human tongue, he clearly had no interest in speaking any more than necessary, and it seemed rude to talk over royalty. So they sat there, picking at their meals, cautiously watching him scarf down his, which appeared to be a great quantity of fresh fish and berries.

"I picked those berries this morning," Inger said at one point. "I use them for my paintings."

Prince Sverre huffed in response and continued eating.

Finally, when their food had been cleared away by a now rather sullen Else and patient Birgit, their father gathered up his nerve.

"To...to what do we owe this pleasure, Your Grace?" he ventured.

"Are you in any way a relation?" Else's mother wanted to know. "My mother's step-grandmother was once a grand duchess, before the revolution, you see..."

"No relation," said the Prince. He coughed, liquidly, spattering the table with droplets of berry juice, and licked his chops. Else had never realized quite how long a bear's tongue was until now. Inger appeared both fascinated and repulsed. "I come here for marriage."

That did make a certain amount of sense. One heard about very few princes these days, but if one did, they were always marrying the wrong sort of women or starting wars or going mad and being committed to asylums. As no one would come here to start a war, and they were not a sanitorium, it thus followed he would be seeking a bride.

"Marriage!" said Else's mother, trying to sound aghast, but failing to hide the mercantile gleam in her eyes. "Oh, we couldn't possibly consider..."

"Well, Aslaug, let's hear the fellow out," said Else's father, quavering.

"Give me the hand of your youngest and most beautiful daughter," said the Prince, who looked around with one swivel of his great head to reassure himself, and then settled on Inger. "In return, I will make you rich beyond your wildest dreams."

Now, what followed for Else was a profound sense of anger, for she fancied herself something of a reformer and considered the principle of exchanging brides for material wealth as in need of reforming. Yet also, for the briefest moment, she glimpsed a house that was not cold and drafty nine months out of the year, where the pipes did not freeze and burst. Where one did not need to use an outhouse in the yard half the time, where the candles were replaced by electric lights, and where bill collectors did not come to call with alarming regularity.

Electric lights in exchange for Inger, she thought, disgusted with herself, and tossed down her napkin. "Father, we can't—"

"Not without a prenuptial agreement," Birgit nodded soberly.

Inger gazed down at the frayed tablecloth and said, mournfully, "I'll do it."

"You're a child," said Else, though Inger was nineteen. "You don't know what you're saying."

"Inger, darling, you mustn't sacrifice yourself for us." Else's father took Inger's delicate hand in his. "We've almost paid off the mortgage!"

"If by 'almost,' you mean 'almost half,' Roald," Else's mother sniffed. She looked the bear up and down. "How do we know you are, in fact, a prince? And not some bandit with a charm up his sleeve who intends to make off with our youngest child's virtue?"

"Mother," Birgit said reproachfully, though she seemed quite interested herself.

As if he'd anticipated this question, the bear slid out of his broken chair and padded out of the house, the family following. A leather pack was hanging from a tree in the yard.

The pack was so large and heavy it would take two strong men to carry, or one very large white bear. With a swipe of a massive paw, he knocked it to the ground, where a great sum of gold, silver, and precious jewels spilled out. They appeared like exotic, glittering insects from far away, contrasted with the familiar muck of the farmyard.

Else gasped despite herself, and Inger gave a little cry, her hands flying up to cover her mouth. Only Birgit squatted down to inspect the wealth, while their father and mother looked at the Prince in awe.

"After I marry your youngest daughter," the bear said, "I will give you thrice that amount. I trust this will suffice for now, if I may leave with her tonight."

Else looked at the silver coins gleaming in the last rays of sunlight from the west, and then at Inger's face. Her sister looked frightened, but also had that pensive, stubborn look she occasionally got just before undertaking some grand project.

Else knew then there was no hope for it. If Inger agreed, no one could stop her, least of all their parents, who, given some of the men in this world, might be inclined to see an uncommonly polite bear as a bonus for a son-in-law.

"I will go with you," said Inger to Prince Sverre.

"Will you always be a bear?" Else's mother inquired, as he went back down on all four legs.

"Perhaps."

Inger timidly touched his fur; so thick her fingers sank in to the knuckles. She gave a nervous chuckle, the one she had inherited from their father.

In that moment, Else loved her fiercely, and wanted nothing more than to sit Inger on her bicycle and flee, or offer herself instead. But she was not the youngest and most beautiful daughter, and like all aristocrats, he had been extremely specific as to his preference.

"She can come back and visit, can't she?" she asked instead, sounding more childish and fearful than she would have liked, rather than the proud girl who had ridden into town on her new bicycle.

"Yes," said the bear, though he made no mention of when. He nodded his head at Inger. "Climb onto my back."

"With no support? Do you want her to fall off and break her neck when you run?" demanded Birgit, who rushed into the stables to fetch their largest saddle, the one they'd used for their old plow horse before he died. Even so, it did not quite fit the bear, but with the addition of a few belts, Inger had something to hold onto besides his oily fur.

As she sat there, looking unfairly regal for someone with paint on her cheek and boots with holes in the toes, Else, Birgit, and their mother rushed in and out of the house, gathering as many of Inger's things as possible into a basket for her to bring with her.

"She will have many fine things at my castle," said Prince Sverre, but nor did he protest the additional luggage, or Inger's insistence they go back in and fetch her paints and brushes.

Finally, they appeared settled. The moon appeared overhead, the sky a velvety shade of indigo. Else wrapped her arms around herself to ward off the chill and watched as the Prince pawed at the ground, ready to be off.

"Goodbye, darling," her mother said, kissing Inger on the cheek. Her father did likewise. "Do try to write ahead of time when you return. And send us postcards if you have a honeymoon!"

"Where would they go?" Else asked, waspishly. "The Oslo Zoo?"

The bear did not seem to notice the barb, though Inger smiled waveringly and waved to Else and Birgit. "Goodbye! I'll visit soon! And I will write, Mama, if the post goes through!"

"I expect it will be delivered by swan at midnight," Else said loudly as the bear raced off into the night, rapidly turning into a white blur in the distance, Inger a mere speck on his back. But she only said it because Birgit, practical Birgit, was muffling her teary face in her apron, as her father and mother sadly gathered up their newfound wealth.

* * *

Else found herself in a strange sort of limbo after the bear prince carried her younger sister away. Word soon got out and for a few weeks it was as if they had suffered a sudden death. Well-wishers kept flocking to their doorstep, often bearing gifts of food and speaking in hushed voices, refusing to reference Inger's absence directly.

On the other hand, most of these well-wishers also gave furtive, sweeping glances to the farm itself, for word had also spread of their newfound wealth.

Not being much in favor of banks, Else's parents had only deposited a small amount of the treasure in town and hidden the rest in the root cellar. Fortunately, they did not have to worry about either Birgit or Else getting carried away and going on shopping sprees. Neither sister felt much like purchasing frivolities when Inger's bed lay empty and her easels and canvases were tucked away in the corner of their shared room. Else indulged in a new pair of gloves and some fur-lined boots. Birgit purchased a hat and some appliances for the kitchen meant to save time.

Even their mother and father, for all of their swift agreement, seemed loath to actually revel in their reward. It didn't feel like much of one, with Inger gone. Else had expected to feel at least some measure of cool triumph at Inger's easy abandonment of the family—proof that her scatterbrained little sister was just as flighty as she'd always suspected—but of course it hadn't been easy at all. Inger had done it for all of their sakes, and now she was God knows where, perhaps locked up in some spindly tower deep in the wood, or the dungeon of some stormy seaside castle.

No mail came from her, certainly not delivered by swans at the stroke of midnight.

With home far from comfortable, Else took to bicycling even more than usual, and one day, a month and a half after Inger's departure, had the misfortune to crash into the hedgerows outside Odd and Harald's well-manicured home. While extricating said bicycle from the thicket, cursing under her breath all the while, the elder brother came out, followed by a lazy black sheepdog.

"What did my mother's gooseberries ever do to you?" he asked, as Else finally wrenched the handlebars free of the brush.

"This road needs paving," she informed him instead, adjusting her cap. "It slopes badly to the left."

"Go and pay for it, then. You're quite comfortable now," he retorted, but seemed to regret it at the look that crossed Else's face.

Red and angry as a berry fit to burst, she straddled the bicycle once more, ignoring the way her skirt hitched up around her knees. Unsurprisingly, her mother had had little and less to say earlier about improper attire, what with one daughter married to an animal.

"I'm sorry, Else," said Odd, and seemed like he might reach out to stop her, but she was already pedaling away, along the sloping road.

Her ride took her into town, still displeased, given the townies' habit of gawking and whispering about her family's scandal, but there wasn't anywhere else to go, unless she intended to pedal until she miraculously stumbled upon her ursine brother-in-law's manor.

In town, she parked her bike near the gymnasium and spent an inordinate amount of time using the rowing machines, then trudged back out a few hours later, her anger and grief more or less exhausted. When she went to retrieve her bicycle, she was surprised (and not in a pleasant manner) to find Gunnar there. Gunnar was often aptly described as the town rake, with a shock of black curls (rather exotic in a location dominated by pallid blondes and watery brunettes) and a so-handsome-it's-almost-grotesque grin.

Else had, in truth, been hopelessly infatuated with Gunnar for most of primary school, but the attraction had passed around the time he began to make crude remarks about girls' breasts (or lack of them, in her case). Now she felt nothing but weary irritation but ignoring him was impossible when he was leaning on her bicycle like that. If he broke it…she didn't know what she'd do. Find an unenchanted, utterly ordinary bear to feed him to in pieces, perhaps.

"May I help you?" she asked sharply, shifting in her sweaty clothes.

"Else," he said, grin widening. "You look ravishing."

"Famishing, actually," she said. "If I don't leave now, I'll miss dinner entirely, so if you don't mind…"

"Come to dinner with me," he suggested, rather than moving off. "My treat. A toast to your good luck!"

It's not luck, she thought suddenly, sourly. It had been a sale. My sister in exchange for a few creature comforts. She wished Inger were here now, so she could giggle over Gunnar's tousled hair and too-tight trousers while Else teased her for it.

"Thank you, but I really do have to go," she said.

"Alright," he huffed, getting off her bicycle, to her relief. "But it's getting late. Come on, I'll give you a ride home in my governor's auto."

By "my governor," he meant his father, a high-ranking councilman known for his annual attempts to outlaw "loose dancing," something Gunnar made an art of.

"I prefer to bicycle," said Else, though dusk was rapidly approaching. She felt a jolt of annoyance; if not for Odd's snide little comment, she would have gone home hours ago. Now she wouldn't be back until dark, even if she accepted Gunnar's dubious offer of a ride.

"Nonsense," he said, and waved at two approaching figures. "Here's Hans and Jon. Don't be silly, we'll give you a lift."

Else recalled Hans and Jon from her school days, too. Bullies and imbeciles, if you asked her, who tooled around with their family's money and went to university in the nearest city on a fairly erratic basis. Birgit had once memorably laid Hans flat with a single blow when he pulled her braids one time too many on the playground.

Suddenly this felt rather like a set-up.

Else glanced around the deserted avenue, the now closing gym, and drew her bicycle closer. Running would do her no good, and while she could probably escape them if already on her bicycle, at the moment she wouldn't get the chance.

"Alright," she said, suddenly grateful for the small wrench in her pocket, which she always rode with in case of hasty repairs. It wasn't much, but it was enough to crack a man's skull open, if used correctly.

The automobile ride did venture toward her homestead, which she supposed was better than any sinister alternatives. However, as she sat in the backseat wedged between Jon and Hans, it occurred to her that this had likely been the plan all along. Gunnar's running commentary about how flush her family was now, how shocked and overwhelmed they must be by their newfound wealth, only contributed to this sense.

"You were always the clever one, Else," he said, jovially enough, as the cool evening breeze ruffled at their hair and the sky turned slate gray, almost pale lavender, overhead. "So, I suppose I might as well come out and say it. Your father's a good-hearted man, and I'm hoping he could provide me with a small loan. I've gotten into a bit of nasty scrape with some trollish fellows in the city."

Gambling debts, she surmised. Perhaps his own papa had finally cut him off. Her country bumpkin family must have seemed like easy targets with no strong sons and rather useless guard dogs.

"It'll be nice to see your sister, too," Hans added darkly, in a tone that implied he had not forgotten the infamous playground knockout. "I've been meaning to pay her a visit."

"It's high time you girls were married, with Inger settled," Gunnar said, over the roar of the sputtering engine. "What do you say, Else? How do you feel about being Mrs. Gunnar Gunnarsson?"

She laughed, poorly, in response, and then realized, from the malicious look in his eyes in the rearview mirror, that he was not joking in the slightest. That, too, made sense. Gunnar was certainly sleazy enough to consider intimidating some mousy girl into marriage just for a permanent cash flow. Else had just never assumed said girl would be her.

"Gunnar," she sighed, as if considering the matter. She could see the farm in the distance, and distantly hoped Harald and Odd might be on the road themselves, but at this hour, it seemed unlikely. They were good boys and always home on time for dinner. "I'm flattered, truly…"

"No buts, Else!" Gunnar chortled, as he began to turn onto their drive. "I'm not taking no for an answer. You've stolen my heart."

Else slid the wrench from her pocket into the palm of her hand, wedged under her thigh. As soon as the motorcar stopped, she assured herself. Then she'd hit at least one of them so hard he splits his crown. That might scare the others off, and the dogs—please, please bark.

But this night, like the one six weeks ago, the farm was unusually quiet.

As the automobile pulled up short in the farmyard, Else noted the lack of chickens once again. And the half open front door.

"Good evening!" Gunnar cried, kicking open the driver's door and strutting out into the yard. "I've brought your darling Else home! How about some dinner, Mrs.—"

The door swung open slowly, revealing not Else's admittedly formidable-in-her-own-right mother, but a hulking white presence.

"Bear," Gunnar gasped, his crowing transfigured into a whimper.

Hans screamed, and Else easily clambered over the cringing, sniveling Jon and out of the car herself.

"Brother!" she greeted Prince Sverre merrily enough, wrench gleaming in her hand. "Have you eaten?"

"I could," the Prince rumbled.

Gunnar scrambled back into his vehicle; if he'd had a tail, it would be between his trembling legs. Else was not sure which was louder; the roar of the engine, or the one that emanated from Sverre as he ambled out of the house, followed by her wide-eyed family.

"Else!" Her satisfactory view of Gunnar and company in flight was interrupted by a familiar pair of warm arms locked around her.

"Inger!"

There her sister was, in perfect health. If anything, Inger stood a little plumper and richer than she'd left, her hair grown out of its formerly fashionable bob, her clothes the richest of forest green silk and trimmed with gray ermine. "I've come home for a visit!"

"I can see that," Else said, trying not to sniffle. Birgit was already doing enough for both of them, wiping at her eyes with a kerchief.

Inger, heartsick, for all the wonders of her lavish new home, had begged for a visit home. Her beastly prince had acquiesced—on one condition. She was not to speak to her mother alone.

But of course, he had not accounted for sisters.

"I swear to you, it is a man with me in bed every night, or at least something like a man," Inger said in a hushed voice, sitting cross-legged on her childhood trundle bed, while their parents made polite conversation with their son-in-law below. "Do you suppose he hires one to be my bedwarmer?"

Birgit snorted at that, while Else said, "Are you certain it is a man? I mean, have you seen him?"

"Of course not! He insists I put all the lights out before he comes to bed. And I know the shape of a man," Inger added defensively, while Else turned quite pink.

"Well, you will know one way or another, depending on how much hair your first child has," Birgit said, reasonable as ever.

"Mother thinks he could be a troll," Inger picked at the faded quilt underneath her worriedly. "Do you suppose she could be right? They can take on the guise of men."

"They can," Else agreed, thinking of Gunnar. "But bears? That seems an awful lot of transformation for one person."

"Why don't you just light a candle?" Birgit said in exasperation.

"And disobey him?" Inger was incredulous.

"If he was going to bite your head off, he would have done so already."

As if on cue, the fire in the grate flickered and sputtered. Inger glanced around the room once more. "I thought you would have electric lights by now. It's all we ever used to dream of."

"We dreamed of seeing you with them," Else said, sentimentally, especially for her, but it somehow seemed fitting, given the nervous look on Inger's face, as if at any moment she expected them to denounce her, their bear- (possibly troll-) loving sister.

But that gave her a thought. "I know a way you can see him," she said slowly, "without lighting a candle or stoking up a fire."

"You want me to hire an electrician?" Inger groaned. "Sverre would never agree…"

"Not quite."

* * *

Odd was halfway out the door, grim-faced and rifle in hand, when they met him at his house, and seemed flabbergasted by their sudden appearance, like three Furies on his doorstep.

"I just heard that bastard Gunnarsson tearing off from your house," he said, though to Else's surprise, his worried look was directed at her, not Birgit. "Did he try to bully you into lending him some money?"

"Almost, but my husband sorted him out," Inger chirped.

"Speaking of her husband, we need a favor," Birgit put her foot against the door before he could shut it behind him. "Where are your lightbulbs?"

A few lemons, some wire, and two nails later, Inger was well equipped for discovering her bedmate's true identity, and without the risk of waking him with some melting wax.

When she left the next morning, she let out a whoop of excitement as Sverre bounded into the distance, oblivious to his bride's machinations.

"I hope we don't get her in real trouble with him," Else said, watching them go. Their parents were inside, surveying the mess he'd made of their breakfast table.

"I doubt that, even if he realizes what she's done," Birgit said. "He loves her."

"How can you know that?" Else scoffed.

Her sister gave her a bemused look. "He came home with her."

Else supposed that was true enough, and assuming Inger didn't wind up eaten for the lemon and lightbulb scheme, had to admit her sister's marriage seemed happy, for an interspecies relationship. While Inger had clearly been thrilled to visit home, she was the one to insist on returning to Sverre's castle soon, and displayed no fear of her bear husband, only a sort of curious infatuation.

Else was replacing a wheel on her bicycle, which had recently been dropped off by Gunnar's shame-faced father, when Odd came to call.

"Good news," he said, breathless. "I've just been to town. Some trolls were dragging Gunnar out of his house in a sack."

Else stared at him. "Real, live trolls?"

"Yes."

"Were they man-shaped?"

At that genuine question he laughed and laughed, and for the first time it struck her what a nice, easy laugh it was.

"That explains a lot," she said, straightening up.

"Well," Odd said, scratching the back of his neck, and looking with admiration at her new shiny black tire. "The next time you need a lift, you could always give me a ring."

"Rifle and all?" she teased.

He smiled at that, and together they walked her bicycle out of the barn and down the road, following the tracks left behind by Inger's groom.

#Be Your Selfie

Rebecca A. Demarest

I dug through the pile of bills on the hall table. "Hannah, where are my keys?"

My sister poked her head out of the tiny kitchen, munching on a Cosmic Brownie. "In your jacket pocket."

"Brownie for breakfast, really?" I pulled the over-full carabiner from my jacket.

"Mom always said—"

"Chocolate for breakfast makes the day go better. I remember." I dropped a kiss on her forehead and stole a bit of brownie. "I love you!"

"I know."

I laughed and opened the door. "Lock up behind me!"

I waited in the hall until I heard Hannah lock the door before hurrying down the street to the bus stop. I was still early for the job interview, but I wanted to make doubly sure I was there in plenty of time. No one else had even granted me an interview, but that was the market right now. If I wanted to keep up with the medications and doctor appointments Hannah needed, I *had* to land this.

When the bus arrived, I settled into a seat and put in my headphones, listening to 80's power ballads to psych myself up. As we inched our way into the land of skyscrapers, the bus steadily filled until an older woman boarded, pulling an overstuffed shopping trolley. In her other hand, she carried a small dog of some indeterminate breed. I immediately ceded my seat, offering a friendly smile.

The woman frowned at me, sniffing her disdain, but it didn't stop her from taking my seat. Her eyes were a startling, intense gray, and she stared at me just a little too long. I let my smile stay; no sense in letting both of us be unhappy. I leaned on a pole for the last few stops before I hopped off and headed to the café on the corner. The woman followed me and I held the door for her. She paused just outside, pulling out a small change purse and checking its contents before sighing and turning away.

I paused for only a moment before calling out, "Could I buy you a coffee?"

Startled, she looked up. "Sure, yeah. Thanks."

"Cream and sugar?"

"As much as they'll give you," was her reply and I nodded in assent before making my way to the counter.

"A large mocha for me, extra chocolate, please. And the biggest, sweetest latte you can make." I glanced back out at the woman and her dog, doing a little mental math in regards to my own budget. "And two of those sausage biscuits?"

A few minutes later, I was pushing the door of the cafe open with my butt, holding two coffees and a small paper bag. "Here you go, ma'am."

She took her coffee and I handed her the bag as well. "One for you and one for your companion. I hope you have a good day!"

"Thank you." Without waiting for a reply, the old woman opened the bag and started feeding bits of breakfast sandwich to her dog.

I watched the old woman converse with her dog for a moment, before heading three blocks over to the OmniFairest office, my last, best chance.

* * *

Two hours later, I was shaking Morgan Blair's hand—*the* Morgan Blair, tech startup guru, fashion icon—and signing on the dotted line to accept an offer of employment. Starting immediately.

"I really think you'll like it here, Leigh, you have the right spirit for our kind of work. One last bit of business before I hand you over to your mentor partner. We like to have some of our coworkers take our product home and use it for a while, test it for functionality, bugs, things like that. Would you be up for that? I would really value your opinion."

"You've kept the product you're working on under such tight wraps, I have no idea what it is yet," I protested. I wondered belatedly if this quick hiring was a huge red flag or a gift. I heard my sister's voice in my head asking, *Why not both?*

"Now that we have your non-disclosure, I'm happy to fill you in." She stood and led me out of the small conference room, across the open floor plan office, and through a set of opaque glass doors which only opened with a key card.

I gasped at the sheer amount of light reflected around the new room as larger-than-average full-length mirrors were clamped to industrial-sized lazy-susans at several workbenches.

"When I want to pull someone's leg, I just say we're working on mirrors. When I want someone's money, I tell them we're working on putting together the ultimate in smart mirror monitors, capable of posting to social media, streaming, hosting video calls in ultra-high def, and a whole lot more besides. We're aiming for our first public release next year, but we've still got a few more bugs to work out before then."

I watched the nearest tech fiddle with something inside the mirror case before carefully closing it and picking up a remote. "Bit big to take home on the bus with me."

Morgan laughed, deep and hearty, a surprising contrast to her sleek corporate image and graying hair. "I'll have them drop one off at your place today."

"That'd be great, thanks..." I trailed off as I drifted closer to a tech who was soldering parts to a circuit board. "To be honest, I barely use a regular mirror. And I'm not really a social media person. You sure you want me to take one home?"

The look Morgan gave me was hard to decipher and it was unnerving to watch her face become still after being so animated all morning. It made those stormy eyes of hers stand out all the more. "As I understand it, your sister loves posting on social media, videos, tutorials, all sorts of things."

And there it was. The catch. "If you know about her channels, you'll also know how careful I am about her accounts. I've locked everything down as far as possible, keeping comments and DM's closed to keep her from getting hurt by people who...people can be vicious."

"You've misunderstood me. I'm not trying to use your sister as a marketing tool, but rather as a beta tester/user. I'd love hers *and* your perspectives on the product, that's all. This is a signing bonus, a gift for being such an excellent candidate and a decent person, the kind who buys coffee for people when she doesn't have to, who thinks of others, even when they only think of themselves. Who takes full responsibility for her little sister's care when her parents die too soon."

I stared at Morgan Blair, conscious for the first time of being trapped in the lair of a very powerful woman who had disrupted industries and shaped the world of tech to her liking over and over since she was a teenager. My boss? Did I want to take that step forward? I got the sense that if I turned her down right now there'd be no hard feelings, but if I was in, I better be all the way in.

I asked the question before I could think twice about it. "How did you know I bought coffee for someone else this morning?"

"Did you? How funny. I said you seem like the type, that's all." Blair waited, poised on the balls of her feet, like a runner getting ready to leave the blocks, but she didn't push. I appreciated that about her, letting me make my own decisions.

"Alright, I'm in." If I wasn't so desperate, the red flags would be harder to ignore, but this was my last chance before I had to start a GoFundMe campaign to keep us off the streets.

The smile that lit up Blair's face was genuine, and she clapped her hands and bounced like someone a quarter her age. "Perfect! I'll have a mirror delivered to your home today."

After a whirlwind of additional paperwork (benefits, beneficiaries, waivers) I was deposited at a single iMac with dueling keyboards alongside a slim gent named Cyrus who greeted me with a shy smile and ducked head, but warmed up rapidly as he sussed out my comfort level with various programming languages. We were commiserating over coding horror stories when the programming station across from us was occupied by two women, one middle-aged in jeans and one college-aged who radiated Instagram Influencer. Cyrus excused himself to respond to a coworker's message and I let myself eavesdrop on our neighbors.

The young woman was taking a selfie with the OmniFairest logo in the background as the older woman got them logged in. "Yeah, my uncle got me this internship, he's one of Morgan's investors on this project, so he pulled a few strings."

"That's great! You must have a good relationship with your family. Wish mine was that strong."

"Not really. He owes me for keeping my mouth shut about his mistress."

I coughed, trying to cover my shocked giggle at the woman's blatant admittance to blackmail. Cyrus raised an eyebrow at me and I just shook my head. The young blonde pouted in my direction. "You better not be sick."

"Just allergies." I smiled at her. "I'm Leigh. It's my first day, too." I reached out to shake her hand, but she ignored it.

"Kristin. This isn't as high profile as I'd like, but it'll do for my internship credit." She added several hashtags to her picture and posted it before looking back up.

I shrugged off the irritation I felt at her cavalier attitude. "Computer Science major?"

Kristin sniffed in disdain at the thought of a lowly CS degree. "Cloud Application Security, actually."

It was getting harder to keep my smile up, but Cyrus had wrapped up his convo and was waiting for me to come back to the task at hand. "Oh, well, that's awesome. I'm a UX designer, myself."

"Oh, so you just make things pretty."

I bit my lip to stop from saying something snarky, giving her a weak smile instead, and turned back to my pair station.

* * *

Cyrus and I got along well for the rest of the day, though it was impossible to ignore the rude girl at the next table over. Her mentor did not seem to be enjoying herself by the time we wrapped up for the day, if the furrowed brows and frequent stops to rub her temples were any indication. I was pushing my work back up to the server under Cyrus's watchful eye when Blair came around to see how the day had gone.

"How are my two newest code monkeys getting on today?"

I smiled, tired, but feeling better than I had in a long while. "Great! It's so nice to be working on a project again. I feel like I'm getting up to speed pretty quick." I glanced at Cyrus for confirmation and he nodded.

"Like a duck to water. Good intuitive sense for how the code translates to the visual, too, unlike *some* I could name!" A woman a desk over stuck her tongue out at Cyrus and chucked a box of Kleenex at him which he caught, laughing.

"We're doing great over here, too, Ms. Blair." The blonde's attitude was entirely different now that the CEO was nearby. Obsequious. Her pair-partner rolled her eyes behind the intern's back, miming strangling Kristin. Blair just smiled.

"Good, good, that's what I like to hear. Head on out now, leave work here, understand? We work for seven hours a day and not a moment more. Gotta teach you younger career folk how to take care of yourself!" She clapped me on the shoulder, and walked back into the fray of the office floor, trading farewells with everyone packing up.

"Thanks, Cyrus, see you tomorrow!" He waved a goodbye while continuing to good-naturedly bicker with his coworker.

* * *

On the way home, I stopped for teriyaki—a favorite of Hannah's—to celebrate. There wasn't a giant box sitting in the hall outside my door, so I assumed my sister had actually read my text messages today and brought it inside. I used my hip to close the door behind me, dropping my keys in my jacket pocket while juggling the food packages.

"Honey, I'm home!"

"Leigh!" Hannah came skipping out of her room, wearing one of her cosplay costumes, an anime I think, her makeup impeccable. "This mirror is *amazing*! Come see!"

Of course she'd already figured out how to use it. "Did you have any trouble getting it hooked up to your social media accounts?" I dropped the food in the kitchen and followed her into her bedroom. There it was, alright. Hanging on the wall where her full-length mirror used to be. "How'd you hang it?"

She posed in front of the mirror, in some sort of superhero stance. "When Janet brought me back from my appointment today, it was already hung and hooked up and everything!"

"I'm sorry, it was what?!" I ducked out of the room to make a quick scan of the valuables of the house. Everything seemed to be accounted for, but how in the heck had the delivery driver from OmniFairest gotten in?

"You locked the door when you left, didn't you?"

"Of course, three times. Like always. Sheesh." She tried a new pose in the mirror.

Tomorrow I would have a word with the super on the way out of the building about getting our locks changed. And a quiet word at the office about boundaries. For now, Hannah was too excited for me to rain on her parade. "How does this thing work?"

We spent a couple of fun hours eating food and playing with the mirror. It had some amazing functions, including a cosplay specific function which not only blurred out your surroundings, but allowed you to insert all sorts of fun special effects. Hannah was particularly fond of that one.

"What's this one do?" We had made it to the last filter on the list, titled *#BEYOURSELFIE*, and I selected it. A brief line of text displayed at the top of the mirror:

See what your true self looks like! Filter only applies once you post to social media. Still in alpha.

"That's weird. What sort of filter doesn't give you a preview before you post?"

"It's about truth, right? This way people can't lie about what they look like by *not* posting!" Hannah struck another pose in her third cosplay of the evening, calling out, "Post to all!" when the photo taken indicator lit up.

"Hannah, careful with that, you don't know what it'll post!" She was ignoring me, scrambling for her tablet and pulling up her Instagram feed. "It's still in alpha, it might not even work yet."

When my usually garrulous sister didn't reply, just sat staring at her tablet screen, I started to get worried. "What did it do?"

She blinked a few times, and I could tell she was trying not to cry. Damnit, Morgan Blair, if your stupid mirror made my sister cry…

"I'm beautiful," Hannah whispered. "Leigh, is this really what I look like? My true self?"

I took the offered tablet carefully and at first glance the woman on the screen didn't look like my sister. Sure, she had the same hair, the same eyes, the same build, but it was like looking at a renaissance painting of an angel. Something Michelangelo would have painted on a chapel ceiling. It was all soft light and elegant lines. I couldn't breathe for how much she looked like our late mother.

I cleared my throat, trying not to cry myself. "Yeah, this is how you really look."

"Your turn! You have to go next!" Hannah snatched the tablet out of my hands and turned me towards the mirror. I tried to protest, but before I knew it, she'd hollered, "Click! Post!" and was refreshing the page on her tablet.

"Oh my gosh, you're so badass!" Hannah turned the tablet to me with a grin, displaying my new portrait. If her true self was all warm color and soft light, I looked like someone had done a modern interpretation of Joan of Arc. It was still unmistakably me, but in armor, shielding people behind me as I confronted the world. Damn, I *was* badass. Am. I *am* badass. I shared a grin with my sister and took the tablet from her. "That's pretty awesome, I'll give you that. But it's late. We've tried everything on the mirror and I have work tomorrow. Bedtime now."

I overrode her protestations, riding herd on her as she grumbled through her evening ablutions. Once she was in bed, I tended to my own evening routine and crawled between the cool sheets. I was just settling in to sleep when my phone lit up with a notification. Hannah had tagged me in my new portrait.

* * *

The next morning, I went to Blair's office to ask her about the mirror delivery, but the receptionist informed me she was busy until that afternoon. Miffed I couldn't read her the riot act about respecting boundaries or, you know, laws about breaking and entering, I made my way over to yesterday's workstation to get started on the day. As irritated as I was, it was probably a good thing I couldn't just barge in, I really needed to keep this gig. At least while I started looking for something that seemed less…troubling. Whatever this was.

Cyrus and I had just logged on to begin the day's work when Kristin thrust her phone under my nose. "How'd you take this picture? You used a filter, right? Which one?"

It took me a moment to realize I was looking at my armored selfie from the evening before. "Yeah, it's one of the built-in filters on the OmniFairest. My sister and I were playing with mine last night."

"No way! Morgan gave you one of her mirrors?! Why didn't I get one?"

I shrugged. "You'll have to ask her."

"I think I will." She flounced off and Cyrus and I rolled our eyes at each other before buckling down. It wasn't long before I heard the blonde's whine from across the room.

"It's not fair! If she gets a mirror, I should, too!"

I couldn't hear Blair's response to the intern, but the tone was amused. Apparently, it wasn't the answer the girl wanted and she huffed away.

"Some people," I murmured to Cyrus, who chuckled. "Hey, could I take a look at the filter menu code? There were some spacing issues I noticed last night."

"Sure thing. I'll just check in with you throughout the day, if you don't mind, while I finish up this beast of an update."

"Thanks, didn't want to forget about it later."

One server code-request later, I was skimming through the CSS and HTML. I fixed the bad padding values, but didn't want to interrupt Cyrus's strident conversation with another coworker over proper bracket placement. Instead, I decided to dig down into the code to see how the #BeYourSelfie filter worked. It wasn't hard to find the files of Python and NumPy responsible.

Most of the filters on the OmniFairest drew from standard libraries and images, like all the other social media filters out there, but when I got down to #BeYourSelfie, it was drawing from a different library altogether. Something called Grim0ir3?

I navigated to the library on our server, but it was in no code language I recognized, scattered with symbols that almost looked like glyphs or runes, definitely not the alpha-numeric symbols I was used to seeing. I had expected to find a randomizer and a database of images that the filter was applying, but there weren't any. Instead, there were commands to apply long strings of glyphs to photos of the user.

I had just decided to backtrack to a Read-Me file in the top-level directory of the library when I heard Blair behind me, sounding amused. "You do go right to the heart of the matter."

I felt like I levitated for a moment in fright. "Sorry! I was fixing some padding on the menu, and I got curious about this filter my sister was playing with last night. I didn't change a thing, I swear."

"No, it's alright, I encourage curiosity. How else do you learn? But I don't think you're ready for Sorc3r3ss quite yet. It's my own proprietary language, takes some getting used to."

I closed out of the window, pushing my padding fixes up to the server before I forgot. "Absolutely. It's really elegant-looking, though. What are those glyphs, if you don't mind me asking? They don't look like Unicode symbols."

"Sumerian. Very versatile language." Blair winked and walked away again before I could ask any follow-up questions.

After she left, I noticed a keycard on the floor and bent to retrieve it, but Kristin swooped in to grab it before I had a chance.

"It's mine," she claimed, before slipping it into her pocket. I was pretty sure it wasn't, but I didn't know how to call her out without causing a scene. My dilemma was interrupted by Cyrus asking if I wanted to go get lunch from the food trucks outside.

I mentioned the card to him on the way out and he frowned, making a quick stop at the receptionist to see if anyone was missing their card. There hadn't been any reported, but she would keep an eye out, and we continued outside to forage for sustenance.

We were arguing the merits of Italian-Asian fusion and ramen-based pizzas on the way back inside when a shriek resounded from the once locked, but now open, fabrication room. We joined the crowd of coworkers who hurried over to see what was going on.

Kristin stood in front of one of the finished mirrors along the walls, holding her phone and illuminated by the ambient glow of the room. "Click, post!" she yelled. Then she refreshed the screen on her phone and screamed again, the sound wild and echoing in the industrial space. "No, this is wrong!"

Everyone else was frozen in place by the strange sight, but I crept forward, trying to peer over her shoulder and see what had made her so angry. Her phone was displaying an image which at first glance was impossible to decipher. It was a person, a woman maybe, with ragged, filthy, blonde hair, wearing the barest threads of clothing. Rather than titilating, her exposure was horrifying, her skin stippled with burns and gashes. The image's mouth was stretched in a silent cry, her hand grasping, beseeching the viewer for something. It made my heart hurt to look at the image and I glanced away, at the intern in the mirror and that same line of text I'd seen last night:

See what your true self looks like! Filter only applies once you post to social media. Still in alpha.

Kristin moaned. "Make me beautiful, why won't you make me beautiful?!" She slammed her fist repeatedly against the mirror, sobbing the trigger words, "Click! Post!" over and over. I could see the pictures refreshing on her phone of their own volition, the figure's open mouth turning into a scream, then splitting her head nearly in half, becoming more grotesque the more photos the intern took.

I reached out to touch Kristin's shoulder, to try and break her focus, but she shrugged me off, turning briefly to scream in my face before returning to the mirror. I felt a firm set of hands on my shoulders pulling me back and

Morgan Blair took my place. She unplugged the mirror, the glass surface losing the glimmer and edge lighting that indicated it was working.

The intern didn't stop, though. She still hit the darkened display, over and over. "Click! Post! Make me beautiful!"

The rest of my coworkers returned to the main office space now that Blair was on the scene, but I couldn't tear my eyes off the usually carefully coiffed and manicured girl in turmoil. Blair carefully turned the intern away from the dark mirror and she lapsed into quieter sobs, no longer shrieking at the inanimate device.

Blair caught and held eye-contact with the younger woman. "Kristin, I did warn you that you wouldn't like my mirrors, didn't I?"

Kristin's only response was a jerky nod of assent.

"I'll take my keycard back now." Blair dipped into the pocket of Kristin's sweater, coming up with the card the intern had lifted earlier. Kristin's pair-partner took charge of the young woman, steering her out of the fabrication space. "Some tea, Helen. The chamomile, I think."

I watched the two women leave, the echoes of Kristin's screams still echoing in my head. Blair had to repeat my name twice to get my attention.

"I'm sorry you had to see that. I'm afraid that some people still have rather…violent reactions to the filter, I haven't worked all the bugs out yet. Rest assured that when it goes to production, it'll have a much more constructive effect on those who need it."

I shook my head. "Constructive *how?* What the hell just happened to her? Is that going to happen to my sister?!" I was angry now, furious that this woman had placed a device that could do *that* to someone in my home, where my sister could—

"No, no, you and your sister, you are pure souls, good and giving, protective." Blair smiled, catching and holding my hands. I wanted to believe her, needed to believe her. "I usually weed out people like Kristin before they hit the interview process, but I owed her uncle a favor."

"She blackmailed him for it." I hardly realized I was speaking. My mind was still spinning, questions about mesmerism, magic, and psychological warfare competing for my attention.

"That doesn't surprise me. She is an ugly piece of work, isn't she? Still, not entirely her fault. She is a product of her time." Blair sighed. She let go of my hands and wandered over to examine the darkened mirror. "That's why I'm doing this, you know. People become more cruel, more twisted, every day. I am hoping this project can help people, catch their souls and reflect them back in a way they cannot ignore any longer. But I think I need to go back to the drawing board; something is just not working properly. I'm getting fear and revulsion instead of motivation." She trailed off into silence, her mind focused on the problem at hand.

My mind gave up trying to rationalize what had just happened to Kristin and instead returned to the bizarre code I had examined earlier. "You forgot to put in a limiter."

I could tell Blair had forgotten I was there. "What?"

"Your call to the Grim0ir3 library. The if-then statement was recursive, but you didn't put a limiter on it. It just kept calling itself over and over. Reinforcing the…the…" I stumbled as I couldn't find the right words. Code? Magic?

Blair opened up a terminal at one of the work stations and navigated to the code. "I'll be damned, you're right! What do you think, would three calls be strong enough? Well, that's what testing is for."

My mind was quieter now, and all I could think of was my sister's face from last year's ComiCon, where some boys had cornered her and told her she shouldn't cosplay because she was fat, because she was ugly, because her skin wasn't the right color. "Can you add an *until* qualifier in Sorc3r3ss? Something like, until they learn their lesson?"

Blair smiled at me, her eyes twinkling with the same glimmer that danced across the surface of her mirrors. "Yes. I think I can. Very astute." She started adding lines of code, her fingers moving so fast over the keyboard I couldn't see what combinations allowed for those bizarre glyphs.

"Oh, hey, another thing, Ms. Blair?"

"Hmm?" Her attention remained fixed on the terminal and I came around so I could see those intense gray eyes. The eyes of the woman from the bus.

"Breaking into my house is creepy. Don't do that. Have to teach you older career folk boundaries, don't you know." I couldn't help the wry smile that twisted my face as I parroted her words back at her.

Blair cackled in delight. "Come around here, Leigh. I want to show you a few tricks in Sorc3r3ss. I think you'll really enjoy this language."

The Twenty-Fifth Bean

R.J. Blain

The next time someone claimed to have magic beans, not only would I ask for the catch, but I would spend more than ten minutes negotiating with the giant. On the surface, the offer seemed perfect.

Keyword: seemed.

Twenty-five beans, twenty-five jobs, and one hell of a payout at the end of the work. I'd even been wise enough to make certain that the twenty-five jobs associated with the damned beans wouldn't land me into the slammer for life if I was caught doing the giant's dirty work. Fortunately for me, he'd been on the up-and-up about that part of the shit show.

Unfortunately for me, I hadn't been wise enough *or* bright enough to understand the difference between legal and life-threatening.

The first twenty-four beans had driven me to the brink of my sanity. I'd gotten the promised wealth, much to my parents' delight, as my first act as a wealthy man was to shower them with gifts so they could retire, something life's circumstances had denied them. To keep them comfortable and ignorant to the risks I took for them, I'd claimed I'd received a hiring bonus at a new job. In a way, it was true, although I'd received the giant's gold when signing off on the completed jobs rather than signing up to put my neck on the line so my boss wouldn't have to.

Once my parents learned what I'd been up to earning the money, they'd lose their minds. My parents adored all things magic; they loved the interplay of technology and the mystical, and they adored the idea of kings and queens alongside businessmen in the city.

Risking my life in the pursuit of magic would excite them, and with my damned luck, they would want to go on "an adventure" with me.

I regarded the last magic bean in my hand with a scowl. Like the other jobs, the bean had set me out on a field trip to an appropriate location to be planted. During the first job, it had wanted to be planted at a crossroads where magic and technology clashed. On one side of the street, horses and carriages ruled, while on the other, sports cars roared down an expressway. When the cars hit the boundary line, they rolled to a halt, transformed into horses with a carriage, and the driver continued on without a care in the world. The nicer the car, the better the horses and the carriage became after passage.

I'd seen my first king and queen at that crossing—and once the magic bean had sprouted, a process taking an hour, I'd gotten my first taste of rubbing elbows with the rich, the famous, and the powerful.

Somebody had stolen their crowns and I'd been chosen to retrieve them for them.

Their crowns—obnoxiously jewel-encrusted things—hadn't impressed me much, but their daughter certainly had. Princess Everleigh embraced modern times with delight, and when I'd returned the crowns, she'd decided to wear thigh-high leather boots with a black sundress, piling her blonde hair on her head in a tangled, chaotic mess.

I'd come within a breath of walking away from several million dollars to ask for a date—or even five minutes of her time.

I'd forever question if something good might have happened if only I'd had the courage to ask a princess if she'd like to get to know a pauper working towards becoming something questionably suitable by society's standards.

Oh, well. At least Bartholomew hadn't shown any interest in grinding my bones to make his bread, although I had to be careful around his wife. If I gave her a single opportunity, she'd adopt me, resulting in a brawl between them and my parents as they vied for who won visitation rights.

Annoyed with myself, annoyed with the damned last magic bean, and annoyed with my boss, I dug out my phone, dialed his number, and held it to my ear.

"Fee-fi-fo-fum! I hear the ringtone of an Englishman who should be working," the giant boomed.

"That's not quite how that goes, but you're not wrong," I replied, and I tossed the magic bean onto the ground, scuffed at the grass and dirt until I could bury it, and made sure it was fully covered. "I'm at the destination and I'm starting the job. Just so you're aware, my will has been updated and, if I get killed on this mission, you get to deliver the payments for my other jobs to my parents and explain yourself to them. I warn you now: they love all things magical, so *you* might end up the one being adopted. I've come to fully acknowledge the fact that me here doing this puts me in the 'too stupid to live' category."

"I like how you didn't even bother to complain that you're not even English," my boss replied with a deep chuckle. In person, his laughter rattled my bones. Over the phone, it created a buzz, as my decrepit cell could barely handle his voice.

"Remind me, assuming I survive, to get a better phone."

"I'm certain you will survive. It's the safest of the jobs and you've handled the rest with sufficient grace."

"Safest does not mean safe," I reminded him.

"It would be boring if I sent you off on a safe job, and considering how much you're earning doing the work, I should toss in some hungry lions or something to keep things interesting."

"No. No hungry lions and no to anything that you think is interesting. I might be too stupid to live for following through with all these damned jobs, but even I'm smart enough to understand your 'interesting' is dangerous at best and lethal at worst—to me. Dangerous and lethal to me."

"You are jaded, Jack."

"I've climbed up twenty-four of these bloody stalks, and just making it to the top is potentially lethal. I wouldn't bounce if I fell. 'Fee-fi-fo-fum, I spy the splatter of an Englishman!' does not have a good ring to it."

"It really doesn't," my boss agreed.

I eyed the ground, waiting for the first signs of the bean taking root. With luck, I'd get a dud, and then I'd be off the hook. Our contract had three whole pages dedicated to what happened if the bean refused to grow.

Alas, the dirt rustled and the bright green sprout of a growing beanstalk peeked out. Heaving a sigh, I said, "The bean does not seem to be a dud."

"I saved the best for last, so there was no chance of a dud. I thought about giving you a dud on the last job. That last one was a little mean even for me."

The businessman I'd bailed out of his date with death would need a lot of therapy, as he'd come within a few minutes of having his heart eaten by the harem of aquatic women he'd entertained for a full week. "I'm not sure if I'm jealous or not," I confessed.

"The fact that he requires therapy as a result of his stay implies you should not be jealous," my boss replied.

"Right, right." I backed away so the beanstalk could grow, wondering how bad of a climb I'd have. "Which layer of hell am I going to today?

Will I be climbing for a few hours? A few days? Or, heaven help me, a week like I needed to on the tenth job?"

"However amusing making you climb until you perish from old age might be, you'll find it's a short trip if you hitch a lift on one of the larger leaves as they grow. Just hold on tight. Really, Jack. You didn't *have* to climb the stalks each time."

I twitched at the thought of riding one of the leaves while the vine grew. "Climbing seems a lot safer than riding a plant prone to curling, knotting itself, and otherwise growing at alarming speeds."

"But it would be faster."

"However true that may be, I'm alive today because I opted to climb instead of taking dangerous shortcuts."

Bartholomew laughed. "You *are* the first to have survived through twenty-four of the jobs. I have high hopes you'll survive the rest."

Wait. Rest? Rest sounded plural in the way he said it. "Just how many have died trying to do these jobs of yours?"

"Oh, a few. And I didn't even grind their bones to make bread. I prefer to roast my humans if I'm going to dine on them. Your bones make terrible bread, but you make a mighty fine stew."

"Thank you for not turning me into stew," I replied in a wry tone. "It's appreciated. While we're talking about this, please don't stew either of my parents."

"That shouldn't be a problem, and you're welcome. Do give me a call once you're done with the job so I can congratulate you for being clever enough to survive. But next time, make better terms for yourself."

Uh oh. That made the plural "rest" a rather potent threat. "Hey, wait a second. What do you mean next time?"

Rather than answer me, the giant hung up.

* * *

According to my phone, it took the bean three hours to finish growing. Heaving a sigh and hoping this particular stalk wouldn't be out for my blood, I began the long climb upwards. I'd learned after a few stalks that each bean was different. Some came with spiraling staircases to make my job easier, complete with houses at tolerable intervals up the stalk for the longer journeys. Others required me to climb, forcing me to make use of forking branches for any hope of rest.

As the twenty-fifth and final stalk, I expected trouble. Instead of trouble, I got a broad staircase with landings every twenty-five steps. Every twenty-five sets of twenty-five steps, there was some form of rest stop along the way. As though acknowledging the amount of bullshit the beanstalks had flung my way, the first rest stop included a fully-stocked bar. I made myself a Shirley Temple, as the last thing I needed in life was to fall off the beanstalk and end my life thanks to indulging in alcohol on an empty stomach. The second rest stop had a taco bar and I lost three whole hours to its charms. I even allowed myself to indulge in a single beer, which I saluted at the stalk as a gesture of gratitude for its magic providing something I actually enjoyed.

The third rest stop offered quiet music and a place to lounge. I stayed for ten minutes to give my feet a break before continuing the hike.

Each rest stop offered something different, although each one offered a bathroom should I need one, and every now and then, the bathrooms also included a tub and shower. As I figured there was something to the numeric theme, I forced myself to climb up to the twenty-fifth rest area before admitting defeat. As though paying attention to my previous explorations, the place included lounging chairs, calming music, a taco bar I could remain at for all eternity without complaint, an entire luau with a roasted pig, a beer bar so I could indulge carefully, a massive bedroom, and a bathroom with a tub waiting for me to enjoy a long soak. As I only lived once, I grabbed a plate, fixed up some tacos, and ferried the first of my treasures to the tub, which I started to fill. I liberated two beers next, and I ended my culinary rampage with two plates from the luau, as my odds of ever making it to Hawai'i hovered approximately around zero.

I wanted to go, but after twenty-four trips up magical beanstalks and one left to go, I intended to keep my feet planted firmly on the ground for a long time.

With enough food to last me through a round in the bathtub, I added some soap, turned on the jets, and guarded my food from rogue bubbles before stripping and climbing in.

The tacos demanded my attention first, and I cracked a beer before going to work devouring my dinner. I'd put three away before the sound of footsteps warned me I wasn't the only one traveling the beanstalk. I considered my situation, decided the tacos were worth dying for, and continued lounging, resigned to the fact my gun was with my clothes, safely out of reach.

"While I'm pleased my intel on your preferences was correct, I didn't expect you to have your dinner in the tub," a familiar feminine voice stated from the main room. I eliminated the voice as belonging to my mother; I recognized hers without fail. A moment later, Princess Everleigh stepped into the bathroom and, like the first time I'd seen her, she wore her hair on top of her head in a messy updo. But instead of a sundress, she'd partnered her boots with skin-tight jeans and a halter top, which clung to her chest.

Damn.

At a complete loss of what to do, I swallowed, set my half-eaten taco back onto its plate, and replied, "Street tacos are evidence there is some god out there who truly cares for us." I saluted her with my beer before taking a swig, pleased to discover it remained the perfect temperature. "A cold brew helps wash down the good food and is rather refreshing after a long climb." I eyed the ridiculous amount of barbecue I'd crammed onto my plates. "I'd give some excuse for the barbecue, but it's barbecue with an island flair, and who can say no to that?"

"Certainly not you, Jack." She leaned against the doorframe, resting a hand on her hip. "I had been warned you tend to be persistent and stubborn, but I didn't expect you to make it this far before deciding to call it a day, especially not after having traveled to the stalk."

"Bartholomew does like testing me, and as I enjoy surviving, I have to be persistent and stubborn. When he tests someone, he means it."

"Well, he is a giant. That's what giants do. As far as giants go, Bartholomew is one of the better ones. He doesn't eat his contractors once they've done the job—assuming they survive. If they don't, anything goes, and that includes eating the former help."

I nodded. Before bargaining with Bartholomew, I *had* checked on if he was one of the ones with a reputation of grinding humans into bonemeal for bread. While he had a rap sheet involving stewed, grilled, or roasted humans, he never ate the hired hands unless they died in the line of duty.

According to him, why waste perfectly good meat?

My desire to avoid being eaten helped with my general survivability. As Bartholomew tended to show up within a few hours after the conclusion of a job, if I did fail to conquer the final bean's challenge, he'd enjoy a snack. Judging from prior conversations, he would roast me, as I'd otherwise be stringy and tough.

"Despite appearances, I *had* checked into that. I'm more at risk of being adopted than being eaten, and the last thing I need in my life is my parents fighting with a pair of giants over visitation rights. It's a concern."

Princess Everleigh snickered. "Are you serious?"

"Very. I had to write my will to make sure Bartholomew understood I *do* love my parents and he had to explain himself to them if I died—and make sure they got all my money. They're the reason I started climbing stalks in the first place. If it was just personal greed, well, I doubt I would have survived the first few trips."

"I had wondered why you took on such dangerous jobs. My father received the briefing about your work from Bartholomew. We were not expecting the recovery to be quite as dangerous as it was. My mother is beside herself with general guilt, as she expected something more along the lines of a bank heist rather than a maze full of death traps."

I bet. Not even Bartholomew had expected the life-threatening problems I'd dealt with retrieving the royal jewels. "Well, there was a good reason the job was so expensive."

"My father is of the opinion he didn't pay you enough for the work."

Her father was a few cans short of a six pack, but I knew better than to inform the woman of my opinion. "As I made it out without a scratch, I was paid plenty. I even recovered from those incidents where I was convinced the fright shaved a few years off my life. But if I need therapy for that job, I'll just send him the bill. Will that work?"

Princess Everleigh laughed. "That seems fair. Most men would have jumped to have a chance to ask for more money, though."

Was she insane? I'd done the math; the first job alone had secured my parents' retirement and left enough for me to pay my rent for a year along with my general bills. I'd used the second job to give my parents their dream vacation, something they'd pushed aside all of their lives because they'd had me and couldn't afford it.

I'd done the next four jobs while they'd been running around the world and enjoying themselves, and that money had gone towards making certain they could do their dream trips every year for the rest of their lives if they wanted. After that, I'd started hoarding the money in various accounts, experimenting with stocks because I could, and even making ventures into one of the magic zones to discover if I might do well enough to enjoy a comfortable life no matter where I went.

The rest of the jobs transformed my situation into a lesson in absurdity and excess.

One day, I might even dip a toe into spending something and buy a new car rather than a new-to-me car. A new car seemed like a reasonable first acquisition while I debated what else I'd do with the rest of my life.

It had taken me all of ten minutes to come to the conclusion that money wouldn't make me happy.

"I don't need more money," I admitted. "I've given my parents the retirement they deserve, and I would become bored if I didn't have work or something to do. But Bartholomew refused to do a contract unless I agreed to twenty-five jobs. And since I didn't get a single damned dud in the lot, here I am." I took another swig of my beer, and as I was determined to enjoy my food even with an audience, I went for one of my tacos. As I already regretted my lack of boldness the first time I'd met her, I added, "I suspect this tub is big enough for two if you'd care to grab a beer and some food and come join me."

She smiled, chuckled, and nodded before disappearing into the main room.

Huh. Nobody had told me it really could be as easy as politely offering to share food and a beer to have some form of success with a woman. That the woman happened to be a princess baffled me.

What was going on?

Much like I had, the princess ferried several plates worth of food over to the tub along with a couple of beers. With the enthusiasm of someone who hadn't done more than sniff at food for a day or two, she escaped her clothes, stepped into the tub, and made short work of two tacos before coming up to breathe and have a beer.

I cursed myself for being polite and turning my head before she wore a layer of bubbles.

While the bubbles did a fine job of covering her, I needed to think before issuing invitations. It would be a long meal, and I would have to hope I'd gotten enough food, else I'd become a show for her enjoyment.

Wait. What if she wanted me to become a show for her enjoyment? When forced to think about it, I came to the conclusion I had no idea what women wanted, which was likely the top reason I'd failed to actually win a date with a woman I liked.

Then again, asking helped with that problem, too, and I'd always concerned myself with her comfort, to the point I'd never gotten around to asking.

Damn. I had issues, and if I survived dinner with the princess, I would make a point of asking my mother for advice on what to actually do.

"I see you like tacos, too," I commented, after she'd made another one vanish.

"I fucking love them," she announced, although she forayed from her collection of tacos to snag a piece of the roasted pig. "While my parents were bickering over making sure you were adequately paid, I decided I would hire you for a job. Bartholomew informed me he had one outstanding contract left, and he was willing to sign it over to me. With caveats, of course. Giants *always* have some form of caveat or another."

"Like the one where he gets to eat you if you die during the job." I followed her lead and settled in to enjoy my share of the pig. "That's one thing I do like about these jobs. I do get to meet the clients, usually at the base of the stalk or on it, and the environment is always comfortable. This stalk seems to be catered to my general interests pretty well though, I will admit."

"Bartholomew helped with that. I asked him for recommendations. Us clients get some choices in the bean used, and he offered it to me for a fair rate. He agreed the job you'd done for us first turned out to be a bit more dangerous than he prefers; he had incomplete intel on the thief. He thought making the trip up somewhat pleasant would be some compensation."

I'd learned early on intel made a huge difference in the likelihood of a job succeeding, and I'd gone out of my way to learn everything I could before starting a job. While it wasn't always an option, I'd emerged alive from more than one gig just from having done my due diligence. "I am never going to complain if someone wants to feed me, Your Highness."

"Everleigh, please. The job is simple enough. You must take me to the top of the bean stalk and to an audience chamber beyond, where I'm sure you'll face something heinous or perilous." The princess waved her hands. "Bartholomew insisted there is *always* something heinous or perilous at the top of his stalks. I took his word for it. I just need to get into that audience chamber."

"That sounds deceptively easy."

"Well, getting into the audience chamber might be difficult, but Bartholomew promised you're quite adept at negotiations if we're not allowed in right away. He's really not bad for a giant."

That I could agree with, assuming I survived through a climb up the stalk while guarding a princess. "Are there any other specifications?"

"Yes. Unless you're sleeping or unconscious for any reason, I would like you to stay within ten feet, unless I tell you otherwise. For example, I'll be most gracious should you want to get out and retrieve more food for yourself. It would be cruel of me to block you from enjoying your dinner. I'm also considerate, and should I need to get out to get seconds, you can stay nice and warm in here."

"That is mighty considerate of you, ma'am."

Princess Everleigh giggled. "You might not think so within an hour. I can eat a lot. It's embarrassing, really. But I'm really active and exercise a lot, so I need to eat a lot. Otherwise, I'd waste away."

"Wasting away is unhealthy, and as my job is to make sure you make it to the top and to the audience chamber in good health, I'm going to have to insist you eat sufficiently."

"I think we're going to get along just fine."

* * *

True to her word, Everleigh went back for seconds, thirds, and fourths while I came to terms with the reality there was no way I was leaving without at least a second round with the taco bar and roasted pig. She even conned me into fetching us both another round of beers, which helped take the edge off.

My mother had never warned me about wily women, bubble baths, and traps of food and alcohol. One day, I might gain the courage to ask her why.

I suspected it had something to do with her desire for grandchildren.

While I made a point of not stealing any peeks at the princess, she seemed to enjoy her unobstructed view the few times I got out of the tub. Any other time, I might have cared a little more about a woman looking me over, but in a way, I'd gotten precisely what I'd wanted: a very odd date with a princess.

On my scale of threats to my peace of mind, having an attractive woman admire me while I fetched beer barely blipped on my radar, although I lacked any idea what I was supposed to do about my situation. It wasn't quite the type of date I thought I would want with a princess, but I refused to care.

For better or worse, I'd gotten my chance.

After sharing a bed with her and discovering little beat having a warm someone nearby, I almost wished we could just spend the rest of our lives climbing the stalk. In reality, I understood good things needed to come to an end, wishes could come true, and she deserved as much of a say in the future as I did.

I would miss her once I delivered her where she needed to go, safe and sound. In the meantime, I would enjoy the trip, embrace the opportunity I'd been given, and lay my previous regrets to rest. Maybe I hadn't had the courage to ask her anything when we'd first met, but sometime before I escorted her to where she needed to go, I'd tell her she could come pay me a visit whenever she wanted.

That put control of the situation into her hands, and it would leave my peace of mind intact for the years to come, no matter if she accepted my invitation.

On the way up the stalk, I learned she loved to paint, she had a horse she enjoyed riding on trails, she enjoyed having a car, but nothing too fast or too slow—she went the Goldilocks route, as it had to be just right. Her parents wanted her to be a Cinderella princess, although the last thing she wanted was to snap an ankle or her neck wearing glass slippers.

If she had a choice in the matter, she'd go into the tech world and learn. Magic was nice, but science thrilled her.

She learned I enjoyed art in all its forms, from embroidery to oil paintings. One day, I hoped to just kick back and enjoy making art, even if my efforts resembled three blind, paint-covered mice rocking a sugar high while playing on canvas.

If she wanted fine art, she'd have to wait a few decades and develop significant patience.

For four days, we settled into a routine. We had breakfast, got dressed with whatever we found in the dressers, taking turns making suggestions of what the other person should wear. As I was a practical man, I dressed her into comfortable shirts, jeans, and shoes good for a climb. As she was a sinfully evil yet wonderful woman, she dressed me in suits and made me like it.

I appreciated she gave me a good pair of runners instead of making me wear dress shoes.

When I got home, I'd have to buy a suit with the appropriate footwear, and when I confessed that to her, she laughed.

Unlike my previous climbs up stalks, her company made the time pass in a blur, and on the morning of the fifth day, the signs of reaching the top of the stalk annoyed me. The staircase kept up its pattern of twenty-five, and I suspected when we reached the twenty-fifth landing, we'd reach the top.

"You look apprehensive. Expecting trouble?"

"Always. It's how I stay alive. I'm grateful there weren't any real threats on the stalk beyond your inability to resist barbecue." For a few minutes, I'd doubted I would be able to peel her away from the rest stop, as it contained every last one of her grilled favorites. "I now know you will do just about anything for grilled salmon."

"I really will." Everleigh's stomach grumbled. "I don't want to deal with an audience on an empty stomach."

"Do you ever want to deal with an audience?"

"Well, no. I don't."

As I had no idea what the rest of the day would bring, I decided I would take that one chance and issue my invitation. "I can't promise how good I'll be at grilling salmon or barbecuing chicken out of the gate, but my door's open if you want to escape all those audiences and live the simple life for a while. I think I'm going to buy a little farmhouse along the border so I can have a good car on one side and a horse or two on the other. And if I get the horse on the tech side, you could ride wherever you wanted."

"I'd really like that."

"It might cost you some cash, but I bet you could talk Bartholomew out of my contact information."

She laughed. "I'm not taking you up on that bet because I know I can."

"I'll make sure he has the address for the place when I find the perfect spot. I think I can afford it now, if I pinch pennies."

Snickering at my quip, she hurried up the steps. "It'll be a near thing, I'm sure. But if you struggle, I'm sure your parents would give you a loan."

The idea of asking my parents for a loan cracked me up and I hurried after her, keeping an eye for any threats ahead of us with frequent checks down the stalk just in case our trip became more adventurous during the final leg.

I'd had enough adventure making certain I didn't catch an inappropriate glimpse of the princess during our dinners, which somehow had happened in a jet tub each and every evening.

My future farmhouse would have a jet tub with sufficient room to serve dinner, a heated towel rack, and all of the other little luxuries I'd discovered at the rest stops on the way.

As I'd suspected, the stalk ended at a platform after a set of twenty-five landings, and I recognized the room as the antechamber to her parents' formal audience chamber. I eyed the princess, and when she glanced my way, I raised a brow at her. "Am I explaining to your parents why you ran away for a few days?"

She shrugged. "In part. I mean, I didn't precisely tell them I was going to negotiate with a giant until I was at the giant's house. I even got him to Fee-fi-fo-fum at my parents."

My laughter slipped out before I could stop it. "You don't have to twist his arm hard to get him to do that."

"Toe, but same idea. It's really hard trying to twist a giant's toe, but I did my best."

I could see her doing that. Her father's guards, older men with the hardened looked of the experienced, defended the closed doors to the audience chamber. As I tried to be a gentleman, I offered Princess Everleigh my arm. "We may as well do this in questionable style."

Grinning, she linked her arm with mine and rested her hand on my wrist. "Excepting the shoes, you're quite stylish. I'm always stylish no matter what I wear. I am surprised you didn't toss me into one of those dresses, though."

"You don't need a dress to be beautiful," I countered.

She stared at me as though I'd lost my mind and, in truth, I likely had.

With the princess at my side, I went up to the guards, grinned at the absurdity of my situation, and said, "I located this princess and thought it might be a good idea to return her to her father and mother, if Their Majesties would be inclined to receive their runaway princess. She might get into trouble if left unattended."

The guards exchanged looks, shrugged, and one opened a door enough to slip inside.

"I like how they've mastered the art of silent communication. I thought that was something parents developed after coping with a child for a minimum of ten years."

"I'm over the age of ten, and they've been trying to contain me from the day I could walk. That's about the same thing, right?" Everleigh grinned, and with her free hand, waved at the remaining guard. "Hi, Wesley! I'm sorry if I gave you a new gray hair."

The guard, who had nothing but gray hair, sighed. "You eradicated my last brown hair, Your Highness. I hope you're pleased with yourself."

"I really am. What do you think of him?"

"I think he's not being paid nearly well enough for the job he's been given," the guard replied.

"Wesley," Everleigh complained. "I'm not that bad."

The guard gestured to his gray hair. "Count my gray hairs before you try to tell me that, Your Highness."

I elevated making the princess pout to my top priority, as it brought out the playfulness I'd come to appreciate in her. "This is not nearly as troublesome as you made it out to be."

The other guard returned, and he held a thick white envelope, which appeared to be one sheet shy of bursting its seams. Rather than give it to the princess, he handed the packet to me. "I have been told to give you a message, sir."

"What message?" I'd dealt with my parents' mortgage after my first job, and it had been smaller by far. What kind of paperwork hell was I about to enter? "I think I was wrong. This might be as troublesome as you made it out to be, Everleigh."

"They said, 'We'll pay you to keep her.' Then Their Majesties gave me those papers to have you review and sign. They would prefer if you just signed, as it would allow them to get rid of the annoying child they produced. Also their words."

"Annoying?" Everleigh scowled. "Okay, fine. That's fair. I have a tendency to run off and do whatever I want. It's not like I'm the queen yet, and until I'm shackled in such a terrible fashion, I can afford to be annoying." Her expression grew thoughtful. "I like that idea, though. Jack, I'll pay you to keep me, too. It would be a bonus. I've had a good time this week."

I had, too. In my view, the bonus would be having a princess of my own, but as my mother hadn't raised me to be entirely stupid, I recognized what would happen if I married the only daughter of a king and queen. I considered the guard, and I waved the packet. "There needs to be a nice farmhouse along the border we can live in because I like peace and quiet, and she likes horses. If that isn't included in this stack of papers, it needs to be included. Actually, let me in that audience chamber, and I'll tell them that myself."

The guard grinned, nodded, and opened the door. "Their Majesties thought you might want to speak with them directly. Go on in. They're expecting you."

I nodded and glanced at Everleigh. "You don't have to go into that stuffy audience chamber unless you want to."

"And miss you negotiating with my parents? Never. Lead the way, Jack."

The guards opened the door and I stepped into the formal audience chamber, choosing to ignore the opulence in favor of the monarchs on their twin thrones. To my disgust, Bartholomew was in attendance, although he'd used one of his potions to fit into the chamber.

"You are a horrible giant," I informed him.

The giant chuckled. "And you are a stubborn and entertaining human. So much temptation, and all you fell prey to was some tacos, barbecue, and beer?"

"Well, when you put my favorite foods out for my consumption, I'm consuming them. If you'd wanted to grind my bones to make your bread, you would have had an easy time of it."

"I already told you that I prefer my scrawny adventurers to be roasted, sometimes grilled if I marinade them long enough."

I walked closer with the princess skipping along at my side without a care in the world. "Your Majesties," I greeted. "I'd bow, but Everleigh would probably find some way to knock me over."

"I really would," the princess replied with pride. "He wants a farmhouse on the border so he can have some quiet and I can ride horses, Dad. If the packet doesn't have that, it's not good enough."

"If that's all it'll take to convince to you to marry her and get her out of my hair, consider it to be done," the king replied.

I raised a brow at that. "I think I'd prefer to date her first, make certain she actually likes me, and generally make mutual decisions on our marital status, but if she'd also like a quiet farmhouse along the border for a place we decide to enjoy together, I certainly won't complain. But I thought I'd ask for the privilege of dating her as a start."

"I told you," the giant whispered, although Bartholomew had a lot left to learn about how to keep his voice soft. "I also told you that you could offer him every coin in the coffers or a chance to date your daughter, and he'd choose the date."

I narrowed my eyes at the giant. "How did you learn about that?" I could make one guess: my traitor parents had spilled the beans, as I had slipped and mentioned I almost considered forgoing the money to ask for a date with a pretty woman I'd met. My father had laughed. My mother hadn't blamed me for needing a few minutes to think about it. "No, a better question. When were you talking to my parents?"

"Sometime recently," the giant replied, refusing to look at me.

What an ass. I sighed. "Let me get this straight. You talked to my parents, who told you I'd opened my mouth and mentioned the pretty princess I would've given up my job pay for, which then resulted in said princess hiring you for the twenty-fifth bean so I could bring her back to her parents?"

"Roughly," my boss confirmed. "You missed the part about the princess's parents noticing how much you appreciated their daughter. Otherwise, you got it right. Your new job description would involve training to become a knight in shining armor, and you'd have to go find a good horse, and otherwise do all those princely things princes need to do. You'll hate it. Having to be all formal, go riding to the rescue should an evil dragon come bothering the countryside, and all of those heroic deeds that kept getting you in trouble on the stalks. You know, all those little jobs you just *hate*."

"I see your sarcasm is in good form today, Bartholomew." Everything on the list appealed, something I'd learned during my adventures up the bean stalks.

Standing on her toes, Everleigh leaned towards me and whispered in my ear, "I'll make you tacos, and I'll only be wearing an apron when I do it."

Well, then. Some invitations even I wasn't stupid enough to refuse. "In light of new information, I would like some time to review whatever is in this package, Your Majesties."

The queen grinned, waved her hand at me, and said, "Take your time, Jack. Don't feel like you need to return Everleigh for a while. She's obviously in need of a vacation, else she wouldn't have run away from home to get some fresh air. Thank you for taking care of her while she was out romping. Do go show her all those things she'll like in the tech world. Just bring her home in a few weeks, hopefully too tired to argue with us for a change. Run along, run along."

I bowed again. "Your Majesties."

We left, and once we'd escaped the audience chamber, I stated, "Normal parents would not be so thrilled to send their daughter off with some strange man, Everleigh."

The princess smiled. "Who do you think paid for all those beans, Jack? My parents love me, and they'd pay a lot more than some giant's fees for a bag of magic beans to cull out the unwise, the impatient, and the cruel from even daring to approach me."

Damn. I raised a brow, marveling at the sheer duplicity and work her parents had put into sorting through the men of the world who'd want to marry their daughter. I hadn't even considered myself to be in the running for her. Then, with widening eyes, I realized the complexity and sheer determination of her parents to safeguard her through the bitter battles of life.

Someone who could survive through Bartholomew's twenty-five beans would be able to protect, safeguard, and cherish their daughter.

Damn. It was something I could see myself doing, if only I had a daughter or son to dote upon.

Then, thinking back to the beginning and how I'd wanted nothing more than to ask her for a date, I allowed myself a smile of my own. "Can we still start off with a few dates?"

"Absolutely. In fact, I'd love that."

"Good. I think I know the perfect place to start."

"Oh? Where?"

"Home. There are two special someones I'd like for you to meet." I couldn't wait to discover what life would bring with the one thing money couldn't buy: a chance for a bright future with my very own princess.

The Crane

Miyuki Jane Pinckard

—

In late autumn, ice covers the lake where my sisters and I feed. Men hunt at the edge of the trees. Every year there are fewer of us. Every year, more of my sisters die.

Hunger drives me too far from the flock, and I don't see the net until it tangles my feet and wings. The thin rope winds around my neck more tightly as I struggle. I can't draw breath to cry out.

I will die here, I think.

Then they come, the hunters, and my sisters fly away. One has a long firearm. He is not a Yamato man and, at first, I think he is a ghost with his ice-blue eyes. But his breath steams before his mouth like smoke and I know he is mortal.

He says something in a language I don't know. His eyes are bright as they look at me. He turns to the other man, a Yamato man with gray hair, and they speak together. The Yamato man shakes his head. "It's bad luck to kill a crane," he says, but the ghost man ignores him.

I lash out with my beak, my talons, when he approaches, but I have no strength. He takes out a knife and cuts my ropes. I stretch my trembling wings, intending to fly away, but he holds me tightly, wrapping me in a cloth that smells like dead animals. He carries me away from the lake.

He takes me to a house on top of a hill where he puts me in a room, sliding the door shut. The Yamato man brings a dish of rice and one of water. Too weary to be cautious, I eat and fall asleep.

When I wake, I am in my human form, in skin and hair, weak and disoriented. My feathered robe, crafted for me by my sisters with ancient magic that we can only weave together, is gone.

I am filled with rage and also fear. Without my robe, I can't fly back to the lake to join my sisters. I beat at the door with clumsy human hands.

The ghost man chuckles from the other side of the door. "Do you want to eat? Then step away from the door." He speaks the Yamato language haltingly, but I can understand him.

Fury boils in my chest but I'm not strong enough to fight him. Not now. Red welts mark my wrists and by the tenderness of my neck I'm certain there are welts there, too. To have a chance at escape, I need my full strength. I need my robe. I back into the corner of the room.

The door slides open and both men peer in. The Yamato man brings more human food—rice, grilled fish, pickled vegetables. I am almost faint with hunger. The ghost man carries a robe—not my robe, but a plain wool one the color of the mountain. He drapes it around my shoulders.

"Now, be civil," he says. He has hair growing over his lip. He sits across from me. "She has no shame about her nakedness," he remarks to the other man, who has stepped back, lowering his eyes.

"She's not of this world," the Yamato man says. "Let her go."

"You stole my robe," I say. "Give it back."

The ghost man leans back with a satisfied expression. "It's a magnificent thing. I saved your life; do you think that deserves a gesture of thanks?"

So, he's just like other men, then: greedy for what he doesn't have. He has no right to my sacred robe and he hasn't saved my life. He's taken it for his own purposes. But I already understand him well enough to know arguing will do nothing.

"Give me back my robe and I will make you cloth for another, just as beautiful. Bring me a loom and leave me alone to work for a night."

"You'll have a loom."

"Swear on your gods that you'll return mine and let me go."

"I swear on my gods," he says, smiling.

I don't trust him.

They bring me a loom and leave me alone to work.

I can transform, painfully, without my robe; but without it I cannot fly. My feathered robe was made by all my sisters over a thousand years ago. We wove it together, joining our feathers in an ancient communal ritual that imbued the cloth with potent magic. It cannot be replicated by one of us alone. But I can create something the white man will admire.

I pull off my human skin, crack my bones, and stretch my fingers into wings. I sprout feathers like ten thousand needles pricking me. I stand at the loom and pluck the feathers from my breast to feed into the machine. All night I work, sliding the shuttle back and forth, weaving the cloth. My thoughts are of the lake, where the dawn touches the snowy mountain peaks; where all my sisters are waiting for me. My tears fall into the warp and weft as I work.

The cloth that emerges is iridescent with my tears, patterned with cranes in flight against the rising sun. Below the flock shimmer the waves of the sacred lake.

At dawn, the bolt of heart-woven silk is complete. I collapse at the loom.

—

He does not let me go.

=

The ghost man has a wife.

She arrives with the spring, at the same time that he moves us all to a new house, an enormous cavern of stone in the city. With her come an array of objects that fill the house, flavoring the air with scents from faraway places. The Yamato man is gone.

She is a pale thing with almost translucent skin, swathed neck to ankle in unflattering gray with a voluminous skirt that brushes the walls as she walks by, whispering. She is like a whisper herself. She says nothing when I am introduced to her. I know enough of his language now to hear that her name is Caroline.

The house has a small room for me, stuffed with furniture. I am provided with bedding, clothing, and food. The loom is also installed within. From an iron-barred window in the room I can see a sliver of the sky. My sisters will be migrating to the north soon. They must mourn me, thinking I am dead.

The wife avoids me at first. Since I am not allowed to leave my room unattended, I barely notice her, although I can hear them speaking sometimes through the walls. His voice is loud, hers soft and pleading.

One afternoon she comes to my room with a cup of too-sweet tea. She looks around, then her uncertain gaze settles on me.

"Frederick says you are a talented weaver, but I haven't seen you weave anything." She sets the tea down. "But then, he's always been uncommonly fond of exotic things."

She means to hurt me, somehow, by this statement. I don't understand why but I understand the malice like a shadow behind her words. "Tell him to let me go."

She pauses. Something crosses her face but I don't know her well enough to guess what she's thinking. "Do you mean to say you're here against your will?"

I can't help it. Bitter laughter bubbles out of me. Did she imagine I was her husband's *lover*?

Her face transforms again and this time I think her expression is pity. It's hard to tell. "He warned me not to speak with you." Her voice lowers so I can barely hear her: "Are you a witch?"

I don't know the word she uses, *witch*. "He's cruel to you," I say. "I've heard his voice."

Her face shutters and she turns to go.

"Wait. I can weave you a cloth that will make you the most beautiful woman he's ever seen. In return, find my feathered robe. Please."

Recognition flashes across her face before it's muted. She's seen my robe.

"Please," I say again, shaping myself into a supplicant. "I need your help."

"I'll try," she says. "I'm sorry. I didn't know."

I sit at my loom that night and pull off my human skin once more. I am weaker. My magic fades the longer I stay in this house, without sunlight, without sky, without my sisters. I pluck my feathers, the soft small downy ones, and weave a cloth as crimson as blood, with silver and gold thread running through it, depicting the gods in heaven. I call to them for help while making it, pulling feathers from myself until I bleed. When I am done, my human skin is covered in welts. I cough blood and fever burns my body.

She comes the next morning with a dish of meat which smells foul, but I'm too weak to do anything but eat it. She exclaims over the cloth. "It's as soft as clouds," she says. "It glimmers like jewels." She holds it against her pale skin and admires herself in the mirror.

"My feathered robe," I say.

"It's in his study, I think." She touches my hand lightly, then draws away as if my skin burns her. "You're ill. I'll call a doctor."

"No. Only my robe."

She doesn't believe me. She calls for a doctor, another ghost man. He makes me drink something that clouds my senses. She stays by my bed until I fall asleep.

Spring ripens. I am not recovered. The air is heavy with moisture and smells. I should be flying north with my sisters and instead I am trapped in this house of stale air.

Caroline visits me nearly every day. She is worried about me. She's had my cloth fashioned into a Yamato-style robe.

She is lonely, I think. He is inattentive. She and I are both forgotten possessions of his, while he hunts new exoticisms for his collection. She sits with me and reads to me. She offers me a drop of liquid from the small glass phial she carries with her. It clouds my mind and leaves my tongue feeling swollen and dry. But I think she's offering what kindness she can.

"Next time he leaves, Caroline, find my robe. Please." I have not said her name before. I can see it affects her. She dips her head and touches her cheek.

"He'll know I've taken it."

"You don't have to stay with him. We can leave together."

She stands up, touches her hair. "Leave? Where?"

"Anywhere. Go to your family."

She gazes out of the window. "I have a sister," she says. "I miss her, too, like you miss yours. She's across the ocean and I haven't seen her in seven years." She turns back to me. "I'll look for your robe."

It's almost summer when Frederick leaves for a trip. I can hear Caroline moving through his room every night, and I am grateful.

"He's hidden it," she says when she visits me. We have taken to staying up late, long past sunset, talking by lamplight on nights he is gone.

I smile to encourage her because I know she is trying, and she is frightened. "It's almost as if you don't want me to leave," I tease her.

Her laughter is sweet and sad at the same time. "When you're gone, I'll have no one," she says. She touches her hair, a melancholy gesture of self-reassurance. "But you deserve to be free."

Two nights later, she's found it. She brings it to me as if it's a sacred relic. I can hardly see it through my tears. My feathers shimmer in the lamplight. She sets it down gingerly on the bed and helps me up. "Are you sure?" she murmurs. "You're still so weak. I'm afraid."

"I'm sure."

Downstairs, the door opens and shuts with a heavy thud. In suspension, like the moment before a pebble drops in a pond, Caroline and I are caught in our mutual fear. We both reach for my robe at the same time.

She is faster, because I am still ill. She crushes my robe against her body. "I can't." She does not look afraid anymore; only determined. She has made up her mind.

On the stairs, the man's voice calls. "Caroline? Are you still up?"

"Give it to me!" My panic rises, cuts off my voice so that it comes out hoarse, a whisper.

"I'm coming, Frederick," she calls out. She leaves without a glance back, shuts the door, turns the lock. I hear murmurs of their voices on the stairs.

I lift my head and scream. Once, and again, and again. Long, raw, inhuman screams that claw against the ceiling and fight to escape into the sky. My last song.

By autumn, I think, I will be dead.

四

Summer is unbearable. In the stifling heat I can hardly move. The cicadas are fat and buzzing even in the city.

Caroline does not visit me. In spite of her betrayal, I miss her. Her conversation was a distraction from the isolation; a thread of hope.

I can't sleep and I spend most of the night lying on the floor by the open window, staring up through the iron bars at what I can see of the stars, the unfamiliar southern summer sky. I lie on the floor of my prison, waiting to die.

A shadow passes over the window. Something taps on the glass.

My human body aches as I pull myself up onto my hands to peer at the window. It's dark outside and my eyes are as weak as the rest of my body. I've been away from my crane form for too long.

A tap again, and a soft purring call that I recognize immediately. It is one of my sisters. I scramble up to open the window and reach through the iron bars to touch her. I think I must be dreaming. She can't be here—she would have gone north for the summer.

She strokes my hand with her beak. "We finally found you. We heard your voice, Aka. We've been searching for you." She looks thin, tired.

My eyes blur with tears. "You must go away. It's not safe here. The man is a hunter."

"Come with us, Aka."

"I don't have my robe."

"When you didn't return, we realized what had happened. We will help you." She reaches through the bars with her elegant head, her long beak, and caresses my hair as she did with my feathers when we were adolescents. "We have a plan. We will help you weave a new robe."

My original robe took a thousand days to create, back when there were so many more of us, when the skies were thick with our kind.

"No. You'll grow too weak, Ane. It's too late for me." I cradle her head in my human hands. My tears fall onto her blood-red crown. "I'm dying."

She bends her neck and plucks a snow-white feather from her breast. "We have feathers to give. Remake the robe. Work quickly." She drops the feather in my human hand.

"You can't sacrifice yourselves for me. You've already stayed here too long."

She plucks another feather. "We won't leave without you."

I look up and see that the entire flock is here, roosting on the roof.

I drag myself to the loom and get to work. My sisters bring me their feathers, one by one, and I weave them into the cloth, working as quickly as I can. This is my last weaving and it must be powerful enough to let me escape. The shuttle runs over the feathers of my sisters, feathers plucked from their soft breasts, from their wings as black as night, their powerful tails. There are tiny crimson feathers plucked from their crowns, like drops of heart's blood. The cloth as I weave reveals a black river flowing from a sacred rock in the mountain. The sky is wreathed with thunder, and fire blooms from the mouth of the mountain. A tapestry of vengeance.

By dawn, I am as cold as a corpse. The robe is almost complete.

Caroline's voice sounds in the hall. "Frederick? I hear strange sounds from her room."

I have no strength left. I push the final feathers through the loom. My fingers are calloused and cut, my heart is stuttering wildly.

The key turns in the lock. "What are you doing?" Caroline opens the door and raises her lantern, staring at me.

The man's voice calls up, "What's happened?" Footsteps drum up the stairs.

I fling the robe over my shoulders with the last of my strength.

I am transforming. At last. My human form stretches, grows. The robe licks my skin like a beam of sunlight, a healing flame. I spread my magnificent wings. They are wider than the white man is tall. I stretch myself to my full height. Caroline screams. "She's a monster!"

The man is in the doorway, carrying a firearm. He raises it.

"The birds! Frederick!" Caroline cowers behind him.

My sisters beat their wings outside and a rushing wind fills the room, like a summer tornado, a righteous windstorm. Caroline stumbles and drops her lamp. Oil spills, and fire with it, sweeping across the rug, fanned by the windstorm of the cranes' wings.

The firearm explodes thunder into the room and fear lances though me. But he is sputtering with fear and smoke. He's missed.

I stretch my wings. Behind me, all my sisters cry out at once, and I join them. I scream with the voice of my ancestors and the iron bars of the window shatter.

He drops his weapon as Caroline clutches him. Their figures are silhouetted against flames.

In one fluid gesture, I am on the window ledge and in another, I am in the air. My sisters cry joyful greetings. I catch the updraft of the heat rising from the burning wreckage below. I circle the white man's house once. The smoke rises below. My sisters flock around me.

I beat my wings and join them as we turn north. Over the mountains, the sun rises.

Time Is a Secret Door

Rachel Swirsky

I met the blind man on my first trip to Seattle: a disheveled figure in a worn gray suit, sitting on a bench near the Space Needle.

I paused to check my phone—again.

I must have sighed my frustration because the man made a sympathetic expression and tapped the bench beside him. "Take a seat."

"Oh." I bit my lip—I don't usually interact with strangers. But my other option was to keep pacing around the plaza, feeling awful, so I shrugged. "Uh, yeah, sure."

He scooted over a bit and I sat down.

Fine spray from the nearby fountain drizzled my cheeks. On one side, a street fair pumped out carnival music. On the other, the space needle stretched toward the clouds.

I was barely nineteen then, convinced I was having the worst spring break in history. My girlfriend and I had set out on an impulsive road trip to explore the west coast, us two jammed in her ancient Dodge with nothing but a change of clothes and a map. Then Lisa (who was from Montana) decided speed limits were stupid, and I told her to slow the heck down, and one shouting match later, I was on the side of the highway, hitchhiking to the nearest bus station with just enough cash to get to Seattle. Mom and Dad were going to transfer me money for a Greyhound home, but Mom was out with her friends or something, and Dad never learned to use his phone, so who knew how long it was going to take before I could actually get going.

Lisa and I had been together for eight months. Which, at the time, seemed like basically forever.

"Sounds like you need cheering up," said the man.

Apparently, my voice was giving me away. "Oh. Yeah. I suppose."

"Here for the Space Needle?" he asked.

Lying seemed less embarrassing than the truth. "Sure, I guess."

"There's more to it than people know," he said. "I visited the first time when I was about your age."

I glanced at him from the corner of my eye, trying to discern an age in his face. It was unlined, but tired, hollow-cheeked under his glasses. His jacket hung loosely off of his shoulders, like he'd either lost a lot of weight or was buying second-hand, hard to tell which. He was maybe thirty which seemed pretty old to me.

"How old do you think I am?" I asked.

"Eh," he said. "College?"

"How do you know?"

"Vocal fry," he said. "Just a guess."

I made a noncommittal noise. I considered getting up. Maybe he sensed that because he suddenly shifted toward me and rapped the bench between us.

"Just listen," he said. "It's a killer story."

Killer was not the word I wanted to hear from a stranger at that moment, thank you very much, but getting up seemed like an effort. I shrugged and sank further down on my seat. "Go on."

"That building is over six hundred feet tall. They built it for the World's Fair, you know. 1962. I fell in love with it. Don't ask me why. But I went in, and that was it. I knew it was the place I wanted to be. So I applied for a job in the revolving restaurant on the top floor. It's a good job. You can watch the city all day, spinning below like a miniature. I had my sight back then. Really pretty."

He paused for a reaction. "Sure," I said. I thumbed in the password for my phone, trying not to make any noise. Still no money in my account. No way home, no excuse to leave.

He continued. "Nights, I'd work late. As late as I could. One night, I managed to stay late enough it was just me up there. And I heard this voice. Singing. Out of nowhere." He made a gesture of bewilderment. "I knew it was probably a radio, but there was just something about it that didn't feel like a radio, if you know what I mean. Eerie. Silvery. Uncanny."

"Ghosts?" I suggested with a shrug.

"That's what I thought!" He clapped his hand on his knee with enthusiasm. "I went around searching, following the noise. I should have finished in the restaurant first, but I didn't. I just wanted to know. And finally I found it—"

He leaned in toward me, voice shifting to a whisper.

"—a secret door," he finished.

I was way too invested in my funk to admit it, even to myself, but my interest sparked. I've always loved stories about secret places. When I was growing up, I used to spend hours searching for secret passages in our house—our suburban tract house that was built in 2001. There were no secret passages, though I did get into the attic crawlspace once when I was about eight and spent the next day itching like heck from fiberglass insulation.

"Yeah," he said. "Now I've got your attention."

I scoffed, but either he'd figured out I was bluffing or he didn't care.

"At first, it seemed like just a blank wall. There shouldn't have been anything there—I thought it was the exterior of the building. If it hadn't been for the singing, I'd never have looked twice. As it was, I ran my hand along until I felt a tiny change in texture, just a wisp of a feeling. I followed it with the tip of my finger and outlined the shape of a door."

He paused for effect, his fingertip lifted as if he were feeling the wall even now.

After a beat, he went on. "So I knocked. Instantly, the singing stopped. I called out 'Who's there?' but there was no response. Zip, nada, just dead silence. I was about to go when a young woman's voice comes through, this tiny little voice. 'Hello? The door's locked and I can't get out.'"

My brows raised. "Trafficking?"

"That's what I thought," he said. "Or some kind of mistake with a security guard when she snuck in someplace she wasn't supposed to be. Something like that."

"I guess that's more likely."

"Well, we were both wrong." He grinned, showing bright teeth, slightly misaligned. "Anyway, with some more prodding around, I figured out that what looked like an electric panel was actually a lock. I had experience opening locks—don't ask—so I started working. It was the strangest thing I'd ever seen. There were weird, useless tumblers, and extra keyholes, and engraved pieces of metal shaped like crescents. It glowed, too. Shiny, wavering blue."

"Ghosts again," I said. "Or elves or something."

"Right? So I manage to get it open, and inside, there's this girl. A normal, real, flesh-and-blood girl. Pretty, blue-eyed, young... We were both about your age. Wearing a long, white dress. But the important thing—" He waved his hands for extra emphasis. "—she had this hair. Blonde hair, ice blonde, wound into huge braids, like the softest ropes you've ever seen. It took me a minute to even take it all in. It fell past her feet in coils that looped over each other and spilled into the hallway. Obviously, I assumed it was a wig."

"That much hair would give you a heck of a headache," I said.

"I guess you're right. I've never worn mine past my ears."

"My girlfriend has—" I caught myself, an unpleasant jolt in my stomach. I mumbled the rest. "—had long hair."

If he heard my wobble, he was polite enough not to say anything about it.

He went on. "I had this strange impulse to touch her hair."

"That's pretty rude even if it were a wig."

He made a helpless gesture. "I know. I just—everything was so odd. It was like being in a dream... All I can say is I was lucky. She didn't mind." He stroked his own head as if remembering. "I leaned down to touch one of the braids. It wasn't a wig. It was soft. It was like silk."

"Could have been a human hair wig," I quibbled.

He said, "She smiled and called me to come in."

"I assume you did."

"Oh, yes. I followed the trail of her hair into a small room upholstered all in pink like a room for a little girl. I asked her why she was locked away up there, and she said her mother kept her from leaving. She wasn't supposed to go outside the room. Ever. I was—well, infatuated. She was very pretty. She seemed so fragile."

He cleared his throat.

"She told me her mother would be furious—" he began.

I interrupted. "This is Rapunzel."

"Hm?" he asked airily.

"Girl with long hair in a tower, Mom that won't let her leave." I rolled my eyes. "You're a prince then, I guess."

"Just an ordinary guy," said the man, unperturbed. He leaned toward me. "Not even named Prince. You ever listen to Prince or are you too young?"

"I know who Prince is."

He held up his hands defensively. "Jeez, okay."

"Like my day hasn't been sucky enough."

"Hey, I had you distracted for a bit," he said. "I haven't heard you fussing with your phone in a while."

I glanced down at the phone in my lap. "Okay, you're right, but it still sucked."

"I'm sorry. I didn't mean to antagonize you."

One corner of his mouth tugged down in apology. He looked sincere and I started feeling guilty. It wasn't like I had anything better to do.

"It is what it is," I said, which was the amount of grace I could muster at the moment. I admitted, "I liked the secret door."

"There's a bit more to it..." he said, letting the words dangle.

"More? What is this, a routine? How often do you do this?"

He shrugged. "Sometimes. When someone needs a little distraction."

I wasn't sure whether that made it better or worse.

He leaned toward me, trying a different angle. "You know, a watched phone never boils..."

I gave up and took the bait. "Fine, tell the rest."

He resettled in his seat, raising his hands with dramatic enthusiasm. "Right, so her mother's a witch."

"Who wanted to keep her away from men," I said.

"Who wanted to keep her away from men," he agreed. "The girl warned me that her mother had a terrifying temper. Call me a fool in love, but I kept going back to see her anyway. And then we got caught."

"I'm shocked."

"Her mother threw me from the tower window—"

"A secret window?"

"Guess it must have been, but it was still high up. I fell to the ground—"

"Six hundred feet. Non-fatally."

"Over six hundred. With no injuries at all—" He waved at his eyes. "Except these. I was blinded in the fall."

"Brambles?" I said.

"Sure." He went on, "As you might imagine, it gave me a fear of heights. I haven't gone up the Needle since. But I still like sitting nearby."

He pointed upward, toward the spindle towering over us. It sparkled as the sun passed between clouds.

"Oh, I see," I said. "This is your origin story."

"Had to have something." He laughed, gesturing to his eyes again. "People like to ask questions."

I chuckled back. Not much of a chuckle, but I was grateful for it.

"I think they get back together in the story," I said.

"Hm?"

"Rapunzel and the prince. Unless I'm thinking of the Disney version." I squinted, trying to remember. "No, yeah, they get...lost in a desert? Or something? And she has twins."

"Twins, you say," he repeated as if humoring me.

"So you could add more to it..." I said, feeling a little foolish. I shrugged. "I mean, if you want."

"Hm. It can take a long time, being lost in a desert. Like Moses. You too young to know about Moses?"

"You're teasing me."

"Maybe so." He pointed at my lap. "Check your phone again. Maybe you'll be lucky."

"Yeah right," I grumbled.

I unlocked my phone to check the app anyway and found a passive aggressive note from my mother. Also, enough money for one trip home.

"What do you know?" I said. "Thanks."

He bobbed a bow. "You're welcome."

Standing to go, I hesitated, taking in his oversized clothing, and the tired way his head bowed toward his chest.

I asked, "Are—are you all right?"

He waved me off. "Oh, I'm fine. You have a nice trip. And a good afternoon."

"Thanks. You, too."

I looked up the ending of Rapunzel later, after a nap on the bus. There was definitely a desert and twins. They found each other again afterward and went off to rule his kingdom.

Not a bad ending, even if you take out the prince thing. Definitely a better ending than me and Lisa had anyway.

I ate a vending machine sandwich and went back to sleep until Spokane.

* * *

When I went back west years later, everything was full of memories. Especially the roads traveling up through California to Portland. I remembered things I hadn't thought about in forever. Like how Lisa's hair smacked my face every time she turned her head while driving. And that night we spent arguing because the diner she wanted to stop at was closed and I suggested we go to 7-11 rather than keep driving to the next town. And the phone conversation with Mom where she told me she'd known all along Lisa was too unstable for a couple's road trip, but she didn't bother to tell me in advance because "I had to learn for myself." Thanks a lot.

On my last day in Seattle, I went back to the plaza by the Space Needle to kill a couple of hours before my friend could pick me up for dinner. I considered going up the Needle, but why? It would just be another building without secret doors.

I spent my time walking around instead. Part of me hoped I'd see the blind man sitting on the same bench as before—but I couldn't find it, if it even still existed.

Before too long, my friend texted to let me know he'd gotten off work early. It was probably for the best since I'd been having trouble getting to sleep in strange beds, and I wasn't sure how long I could stay on my feet.

As I pocketed my phone, I turned to look one last time at the landmark. The Needle cast a sharp lee across the plaza, a stark contrast between dark and bright.

Nostalgia pulsed over me in waves. Good things and bad things, all mixed up. Connecting with a stranger, breaking up with my first love—one blended memory, cutting deep.

In the shadow, a middle-aged man ambled arm-in-arm with a woman his age. A pair of ten-year-old twins ran ahead of them, giggling. The woman's pale blonde hair was cut close to her ears in one of those messy, uber-stylish haircuts that looks like it could have been done with shears. The man, broad-shouldered in a well-fitted jacket, beamed with joy.

Obviously, it wasn't him.

The pair stopped for a moment as the short-haired woman murmured something to him. As she guided him to face me, he flashed a slightly misaligned smile.

Whoever he was, he waved.

I waved back.

Harvest

Angela Rega

Hedda woke with wings on her face.

No, not wings. A hanky.

No, a piece of paper flapped on its own, tickling her face.

She sat up slowly, rubbing her right thigh. Tough landing. The sheet of paper fluttered toward the dirty floor and she grabbed at it. There was writing on one side.

Hedda Wayward,

Charged with Crimes against Happily Ever After for theft of Zelindabell's magic wand.

Here is the test to prove yourself. Make magic. Without a wand. You've got 48 hours.

Forfeit or inability will see you imprisoned for up to ten years in the dungeons under HEA HQ. Yes! We have dungeons!

There was no signature, but there didn't need to be. Hedda knew who'd written the note and who'd transported her here with a flick of a fancy-looking magic wand. She sighed and looked around.

A barn. She was in a barn, sitting on dirt and straw and something brown she didn't want to think about. In a barn with a pumpkin, a large roll of raggedy fabric, and a very sore backside. And no cats.

And no magic wand. She loved her cats, but the magic wand would have been much handier to have right now. At the very least, it would have helped her get her cats back. Oh, she missed her magic wand!

Well, not hers exactly. But she'd found it, and it had fit perfectly between the soft groove of thumb and index fingers. She was a fairy godmother, after all...well...kind of...since she'd ~~stolen~~ found the wand and could perform magic. So, finders keepers. It was only fair.

But here she was: no cats, no wand, no nothing but a heap of trouble and no conceivable way out it.

And it had all been going so well.

* * *

Two months ago, Hedda had set up her business inside a rambling old terrace in a narrow laneway of Surry Hills. Not bad for a retired lady who'd been living in a small mobile home in a caravan park, just one step away from being homeless. She'd adopted the black cats from the local cat refuge as companions; they seemed appropriate and she liked the company. Since finding the wand, Hedda had been granting wishes for a fee—not that much actual money changed hands, mind you. It was mostly one service in exchange for another—barter—and it served her well. Plus, there was the element of surprise, which she liked. And if she couldn't use the gift, she could sell it or pass it on to someone else.

She'd sit her clients down in the little front room filled with two over-stuffed armchairs and a round table, a bookshelf and a cracked bright green glass vase that couldn't hold water and give them a cup of tea. "That's right, my dearie," she'd say, "tell me your woes," and then listen to their superficial laments: wants of evening dresses, unlimited credit, the correct-shaped brows, or just the right nose.

Then WHAM! with a flick of her wand, she'd set things aright! One customer had paid with a bicycle with a basket and fairy lights for night riding; another with a six months' supply of cat biscuits at Costco. (Half of which Hedda'd promptly wand-whisked to the local cat refuge.) The last girl, in return for a designer ballgown, gave a year's worth of washing in the laundromat next door! Of course, when monetary donations were offered, she never said no; they came in handy to pay the rent.

She'd learned early on that the one thing the wand couldn't do was grant wishes for its owner. That was why the *original* owner couldn't wish for it back, and Hedda couldn't wish for someone to pay her rent. But she'd been making do.

Yes, it had all been going so well for her and her "found" wand until she'd started advertising her services on *Faebook* and *Twinkler*. In hindsight, maybe it wasn't the best idea to use sites for *real* magic users and draw attention to herself; no wonder the HEA found her. *Too ambitious for your own good*, Hedda girl, she thought now, staring at the barn once again. Nothing had changed since the last time she looked.

There she'd been, innocently waiting for her two o'clock client to arrive, minding her own business when BAM! Smoke blew out of the (unlit) fireplace and a gust of wind blew all the papers off her desk. The cats on the backs of the chairs had arched themselves almost into question marks, their fur bristling. When the smoke cleared, Hedda saw three people standing in her little parlor.

"We have found you at last, thief and fraud!" The shouting woman wore a white periwig, a purple robe, and held a sparkling crystal gavel like a weapon. Behind her was a plump lady, in an outdated, apricot, full-length tulle frock, with peach-colored rouge and glittery blue eye shadow. Hedda thought she might be a *real* fairy godmother. Beside her stood a tall thin man with long, tangled tendrils of gray hair topped by a rusted crown. His velvet sapphire frock coat with its billowing sleeves and very large pockets was faded with age and wear.

"My wand!" The apricot-frocked woman exclaimed and stretched her fat little hand towards the wand where it perched on a little stand on Hedda's desk.

"*My* wand!" Hedda said, and snatched it away. She stuffed it down her top. "Who are you all, and how dare you break into my home?!"

"I am Hepzibella of the Fairy Tale Council and she is Zelindabell, a fairy godmother, and he…" Hepzibella sighed and asked the prince, "What *are* you doing here, anyway?" Without waiting for an answer, she grimaced. "*He* is my half-brother, Horatius the Strange. An out-of-work cobbler and the rightful heir to our kingdom of Happily Ever After."

Horatius the Strange bowed. "At your service."

"No, you're not!" Hepzibella whacked him across his head with her hand. (Not the gavel, thankfully.) "*She* is at *ours!*" The prince rubbed the back of his skull. Hepzibella rolled her eyes and continued. "You, Hedda Wayward, have been charged with crimes against all those who work in the HEA profession: theft of a wand and the unlicensed practicing of magic."

"HEA?" Hedda asked.

"Happily Ever After!" Zelindabell, the Fairy Godmother answered, hands on hips. "You don't even know what you're doing, do you?"

"Finders keepers! I didn't steal the wand! I found it!" said Hedda.

"Did not!"

"Did so too!"

"This is getting us nowhere, Zelindabell—" began Hepzibella.

"And due process must be observed," added Horatius.

"Oh, shut up, Horatius!" shouted Zelindabell.

"That's my brother!"

"Doesn't mean you have to bring him everywhere you go!"

Hedda saw her chance and bolted for the window while they were distracted and fighting among themselves. But she hadn't reckoned on them being used to people doing a runner and found herself half-in, half-out, with Hepzibella's surprisingly strong hands around her ankles. She was dragged back into the room and would have fallen if Horatius hadn't been so chivalrous and helped her to stay upright.

"Thank you," she said, riffling his pockets with such practiced fingers he didn't even notice.

"You're quite welcome."

Hedda had just enough time to notice what a kind smile he had before WHUMP! A dull thump on the back of her head. And she fell into darkness.

* * *

Hedda stood slowly. She looked at the letter once more: *Make magic. Without a wand. You've got 48 hours.* Right.

She rummaged around in her left pocket: here was a voucher for a week-long seniors' coach tour of some vineyards. Fat lot of good that would do! She shoved it back, then tried the right pocket. Aha! She'd managed to liberate two things from Horatius: a crisp fifty-dollar note and a rose-gold fob watch with a long chain. Hedda smirked: she might have been over-the-hill, but she hadn't lost her touch.

She could make a home anywhere. In the barn was plenty of hay (something to sleep on), some buckets (for bathing and drinking—but not the same one, of course), and a firepit with bricks around the edges to keep the coals in (something to cook on). No Fairy Tale Council bullies would get the best of her! Then she thought about her black cats back at the terrace house and started to worry.

No, no, Hedda, she thought, *the cats have an automatic feeder with biscuits and water that last forty-eight hours.* She still had time to get back. Thank goodness!

She looked at the pumpkin on the floor. Very traditional, but make magic? Without a wand? She might be able to manage a pumpkin pie, but a carriage? Forget it! Hedda opened the barn door and a streak of light broke in. Outside were dry paddocks of yellowed grass, husks of what were once majestic gums, and boulders with bird shit and graffiti on them. A dirt road ran alongside the fields and she spied a sign.

"Kentucky South?" Hedda had never heard of such a place. She looked left and right. "Hardly a place for happily-ever-afters." She sighed. "You're a sixty-four-year-old criminal, Hedda Wayward, you'd better work with what you can beg, borrow, or creatively acquire."

She walked out onto the road and saw a cluster of houses not too far in the distance, so she headed that way, the sun beating down on her like it had a personal grudge.

When she arrived into Kentucky South, Hedda a spotted a corner shop. She looked around but there didn't seem to be any other likely place. A bell above the door tinkled as she opened it. There at the yellow laminate counter was the most unlikely girl to turn into a fairy tale princess and send off to a ball: jeans and a plain blue t-shirt, straw-colored hair, thick glasses, big ears. And without that dratted wand, Hedda was going to have to do things the hard way. How would she make magic? Without realizing it, Hedda let out a huge sigh.

"Can I help you?"

"Just grabbing some supplies, dearie." Hedda picked up teabags, bread, margarine, matches, candles, toothpaste and toothbrush, a tin of deodorant, a saucepan, some fire starters, and a couple of tomatoes. This wasn't one of those multinational supermarkets; she'd nicked more than her fair share of groceries from them. No, here she would pay for everything—with the prince's stolen fifty.

"I'll be taking these today. So, what's your name? I'm Hedda."

"Isabeau."

Good start; neither Kylie nor Bev were especially princess-y names. And the girl's eyes were lovely and green. "That's so pretty."

"The only pretty thing about me. Pushing thirty-five and never had a date."

"Never?" Hedda's ears pricked. This might be just the right candidate after all.

"Not many suitors round here and I can't leave with my mother being so ill."

"What's wrong with her?"

"I don't want to talk about it." Isabeau finished putting the groceries into a paper bag, her expression miserable.

"I'm sure there are rural online dating sites?" Hedda said.

"I'm not into that kind of thing. Anything else?"

Hedda looked about and saw a paring knife hanging at the end of an aisle. She grabbed it. "Just what I'm looking for!"

"Where are you staying? You're new here?"

"Just down the road in the little red barn."

"In a barn?"

"Oh, it's just temporary." Hedda waved her hand, wishing it contained that magic wand; how she missed it!

It was growing dark when Hedda got back to the barn. She put the pumpkin onto a workbench and used her new knife to open it up. She scraped the seeds out; they wouldn't have time to dry out, but it didn't matter. It was the right season for them and she could at least practice turning them into four-wheel drives or tractors—probably worthwhile round these parts. But then she remembered: no more wand!

Oh, what to do! She sat cross-legged on the floor, putting her chin into her hands. It was all so unfair. She'd never hurt anyone, only given people what they wanted and, though it was hard trying to survive on a pension, she'd never been greedy. Hedda straightened her shoulders, looked at her fingers; wiggled them.

She stood up and went outside to look at the yellow grass. She might not have a wand but she wasn't entirely un-magical: she did have a green finger! She scattered all the pumpkin seeds around the barn and sang to them the "Night Grow" song she'd learnt as a child. Her grandmother had taught her that song to lure pumpkins to grow not just during the day but also during the night. Thus, making them grow quicker.

She gave a little nod.

Forty-eight hours. Six had already passed according to the prince's pilfered pocket watch—on each hour, a cuckoo with a very long tongue popped out and blew raspberries. Hedda thought about what the Fairy Tale Council had provided here: fabric and a pumpkin.

And the girl. Isabeau. Maybe. Probably. What if Hedda had found the wrong girl??

No. How many other more pathetic girls could there be in Kentucky South? Isabeau had to be her Cinderella: needed a date, needed a nice frock, needed to get out of a rut. Hedda unravelled a little of the roll of fabric: it was ornate and some beads seemed to sparkle of their own accord. In fact, it seemed to look much better than it had when she'd arrived here.

Hmmm…could it be that Hedda's efforts so far were starting to make other magic happen, even without the wand? The only problem was that Hedda couldn't sew, not to save her life. Couldn't darn a sock or attach a button. No magic in the world could change that.

Still, it was important that people help themselves and Isabeau looked like a capable sort. Hedda would take the fabric to her. A young(ish) woman should have a hand in her own destiny, after all.

* * *

She saw Isabeau through the shop window, she was wearing large black boots, something looked odd about them but then lots of girls wore boots these days. The girl was wiping down the counter. The bell above the door sounded a little frantic as Hedda pushed her way in. She rolled out the bolt of fabric on the newly-cleaned counter; it looked even shinier and more lush than it had at the barn.

"That's nice." Isabeau said a little longingly.

"Glad you like it." Hedda smiled. "You can sew, can't you?"

"Yeeess. Why?"

Hedda decided not to mention the prison sentence hanging over her own head. "Well, now, if you're going to go on a date—you need to have a nice frock, right?"

"But where to get this date? I told you it's slim pickings around here."

Hedda ignored her. Persuasion was a skill mastered by those who persisted. "You've got a community hall?"

"We do, just down the road at the other side of the park."

"I need a dress pattern."

"Why?"

"Just entertain a lonely old woman, would you? So...do you have a dress pattern?"

A corner store did sell many things and dress patterns were one of them. Usually, they were for simple tunics and aprons but this one...Isabeau had ordered it on a whim, feeling wicked, and didn't tell her mother. She nodded.

"Well, come on then, let's get going, I haven't got all night." As she followed Isabeau out the back, Hedda said as an afterthought, "Oh, and I need a computer, too!"

* * *

A few hours later, Isabeau sat at one end of a long pine kitchen table with all the cut-out pattern pieces in front of her. The sewing machine was in the shop so she was hand-stitching the entire gown with silver thread, yawning and getting a bit grumpy. She kept throwing resentful looks at Hedda, who hunched over a laptop, was squinting at the screen intently. Occasionally she'd look up and stare at the window above the sink as though she thought someone was peeking in, then she'd shake her head and go back to the laptop.

"What are you doing?" snapped Isabeau at last, driven by curiosity. "And how do you know about computers?"

"What, you think old people don't know how to turn these things on? What do you reckon we do in libraries all the time? Who do you think goes to all those free community 'how to use the internet' classes?" Hedda kept pecking away at the keyboard. "You don't need to know anything else yet! Just enjoy the magic of it all."

"What magic is there in sewing a dress at this hour with a crazy lady in my kitchen?"

"Now, now. You'll make a very pretty belle of the ball." Hedda's head turned to the window again; she thought she heard a scratching at the glass. "Where *is* your mother?"

"Asleep."

"Well, we'll make sure not to wake her then."

Isabeau grumbled but worked on. When she put the last stitch into the hem it was 11 p.m. and Hedda clapped her hands.

"No time for sleep!" She poked Isabeau in the shoulder with a finger. "We need to see the hall!"

Isabeau groaned. "I really think you're quite mad. It's time for bed."

"No rest, no rest! We don't have much time!"

"Yes, we do. I have ALL the time in the world."

"I don't. I have less than forty-eight hours," Hedda said, but Isabeau just rolled her eyes.

The community hall was locked, but Isabeau kept a key in the shop as she was deemed a responsible key-holder. She wasn't entirely sure she was being responsible at this point, but it seemed too late to turn back now.

The hall was dusty, but spacious, with parquetry floors and a beautiful ceiling with a chandelier reminiscent of an old ballroom. There was an old but working stereo in one corner and a pile of records so dated they were cool again. It smelled a bit musty but Hedda went into the little kitchen in the back and found a bucket and mop and some mentholated spirits; she also found several packets of tea-lights and tossed them to Isabeau. Isabeau, a bit bemused and wishing for her bed, nevertheless placed the little candles around the hall. As the smell of the mentholated spirits wafted up from Hedda's mopping, Isabeau scrunched her nose and said, "It smells terrible!"

"It smells clean!" Hedda answered firmly.

"So…when is this 'singles' ball going to be?"

Hedda hesitated. "Tomorrow night. I don't suppose you've got a community radio station?"

"It's nearly midnight!"

"A perfect time! There's a phone in the kitchen here."

And it *was* a perfect time: Hedda knew there was enough natural magic in the very mention of midnight itself, so she charmed Marvin the radio host into repeating her advert with each hourly news broadcast, mentioning the witching hour: "A party starts at midnight, but ours starts at eight." He was just happy to have something different to talk about.

At last, Hedda was satisfied. She smiled at Isabeau and said, "Right, time for your beauty sleep!"

"Thank Heavens!" said Isabeau as they locked the hall up. Then, as an afterthought: "Are you going to tell me what you spent all that time on the laptop doing?"

Hedda just tapped the side of her nose and laughed. She set off towards her barn. "Sleep tight, don't let the bed bugs bite!"

* * *

Hedda woke up to the sound of the pilfered pocket watch cuckooing 8 a.m. and a banging on the barn door. She was exhausted, as if she hadn't had any sleep at all. She sat up, disoriented, then memories began to trickle back and Hedda felt a bit overwhelmed. Make magic. Without a wand. Or prison.

The barn-door swung open as her guest used up all patience.

"Hedda! Hedda! I can't believe it! All these replies! Notifications! All these groups, Hedda!!" Isabeau burst in, carrying the laptop Hedda had used last night. The girl waved the screen in front of Hedda's face, but, away from the Wi-Fi, there wasn't much but a frozen screen.

Hedda blinked. She'd used a scattergun technique, really: not just Facebook, but all sorts of magically-connected groups on *Faebook* and *Twinkler*, like 'Wolf Hunters Gone Vegan' and 'Red Cloaks Agoraphobic Support Group.' Everyone, she figured, was looking for love, and there were probably as many fae in rural areas who'd moved for a tree change, but still fancied a dance. Judging by the look on Isabeau's face, she'd been right.

"Are you smiling?" Hedda asked with a grin. "It looks good on you!"

"I've had over eighty people say on Facebook they are attending."

"What about the *Faebook* account?"

"Even more!"

Hedda clapped.

"That's not the only crazy thing: come and look outside."

In the front garden, where Hedda had planted the pumpkin seeds, was the biggest, maddest array of pumpkins she'd ever seen: small and round, long and cylindrical, others large like imperfect boulders. No two alike, which was pretty amazing from a single pack of seeds.

"Where did they come from??"

"I grew them!" said Hedda proudly.

"Pumpkins don't grow overnight!"

"They do if you sing to them. Come on, let's get cracking. We have work to do."

"Well, I suppose we've got more problems than a pumpkin plague: what are we going to feed all these guests?" asked Isabeau.

Hedda waved a hand grandly across the newly-sprung pumpkin field.

Isabeau groaned.

"Oh, come on! Trust me. Pumpkin scones, pumpkin soup, pumpkin pie, pumpkin bake, pumpkin slice! Grab that wheelbarrow and it's off to your kitchen."

"Why did I trust you?" Isabeau wailed, and she grumbled all the way back home, pushing a heavy barrow of mismatched pumpkins.

* * *

Isabeau stopped complaining and started enjoying herself about ten minutes into the cooking binge. Hedda didn't give her much choice, or even the time to think about being grumpy, just kept the girl on the hop. They chopped and stewed, pummelled and pressed, shaked and baked. Hedda felt arm muscles long asleep reawakening and sweat breaking across her brow. It was a delight to make things by hand.

By mid-afternoon, the laptop was pinging with more replies and notifications, and Hedda was glad she'd sown so many seeds. Isabeau's face had blossomed into a permanent smile.

"You look like a daisy in a frock sunny side up. Now. To decorate!"

In the community hall, they set up the trestle tables that lay against the walls and draped them with ancient lacy table clothes Hedda found in the back of a cupboard. ("A bit yellow," said Isabeau. "Sepia," corrected Hedda.) They decorated them with bottle brush flowers from the trees they'd plucked from the streets and gardens of Kentucky South.

"One doesn't need much to make a hall inviting!" Hedda stood back to admire their handiwork, but the respite was short: she marched Isabeau back to the shop.

"What now?" asked Isabeau.

"The taste test!" cried Hedda, and she sliced into one of the pieces cooling on the bench, cutting two pieces and handing one to Isabeau. For a moment, they both held their breath, then dug in. Delicious! Still warm, and the pastry was both buttery and flaky at the same time. When she finished her slice, Hedda stood up. "Right, I'm going for a nap. You should do the same. I'll see you back here at 6:30 sharp. We'll take the food to the hall, then I'll help you get dressed."

Hedda hummed as she walked back to the barn. What could possibly go wrong?

* * *

At 6:30pm sharp, Hedda pushed into the shop. She didn't have anything new to wear, but she'd made herself as presentable as she could (finger-combed her hair, brushed her teeth, pulled most of the straw from her black dress, rubbed the dust off her sandals), but it didn't matter. It wasn't *her* fairy tale. She and Isabeau ferried all the pies and slices and cakes and scones and what-have-you to the hall along with paper plates and plastic cutlery and cups. The radio station had donated juice and soft drink and bottles of champagne as a thanks for helping to boost ratings.

Back at the shop, Hedda brushed Isabeau's hair (which seemed thicker and shinier) and twisted it into a bun on top of her head and stuck daisies in it like jewels. Then she nicked some make-up from the shelves and dabbed it onto the young woman's skin (which seemed pinker and healthier), then stood back. *Perfect.*

"Perfect!" she said out loud. The kitchen clock said it was seven-thirty. "Now, into your dress!"

Hedda thought she'd make a cuppa while the girl went off to put on her dress, but she'd barely got the kettle filled before a shriek came from somewhere inside the house. A few moments later Isabeau rushed back into the kitchen, the dress on but not done up, and her hair a bit askew as if she'd tried to run a hand through it.

"What's wrong?" Hedda grabbed the girl to stop her running around the table, wailing.

"You haven't noticed, have you?"

"Noticed what?" Hedda put her hands on her hips.

"Look!"

Isabeau lifted her skirt: she was barefoot and her left leg was significantly shorter than the right.

"Now everyone will see! My boots corrected this, but now everyone will know!"

"Oh, Isabeau, there's nothing wrong with that."

"Yes, there is."

"Well, where are your boots?"

"My mother has taken them! She doesn't want me to go to the dance."

"I thought she was sick."

"She doesn't want me to go because I might meet someone and if I meet someone, she thinks I'll leave."

"But it's just a dance! You're just going next door really."

"She got mad. She took my only pair of boots."

Hedda wasn't going to let all her hard-won magic go to waste! "Why not go barefoot?"

"If you were a fairy godmother, you would be able to whip a pair up with your wand."

Hedda became silent. She wanted to tell Isabeau the truth, but she'd grown attached to the sad and lonely young woman in this small country town with no one to love her. She didn't want Isabeau to know about the "make magic or else," how Hedda'd picked her very own Cinderella, and done everything she'd done to stay out of prison. She didn't want to lose her first friend in a very long time.

"But I don't have a wand. That isn't part of the story, Isabeau." Although Hedda wished hard that it was.

"But imagine if you were a fairy godmother!" Isabeau sat down at the table and slammed her palms onto the top.

"I'm not a fairy godmother," Hedda said.

Before she had been a fairy godmother with a stolen wand, Hedda had been a tarot card reader. One didn't need to be able to read the future, she'd worked out quick enough. Hedda knew the people who had sought her out all shared a sense of helplessness, and she also knew that all she had to do was ask them the right questions and instil a bit of hope. Offer a trinket, a feather, a flower, a tiny crystal to keep in their pocket or handbag. That was enough.

"You may not be a fairy godmother, Hedda, but you've made magic happen for me!"

Hedda gave Isabeau a dampened smile. "You bring out the best in me."

Isabeau touched Hedda's shoulder. "I haven't had this much fun in years, Hedda."

Hedda felt tears welling. No time for sentimentality now—she had a mess to fix! She patted Isabeau's hand. "Right: hair spray. We need hair spray and toenail polish, the glittery-er the better."

"But my limp?"

"Does it really matter? You have a brilliant smile and it can light up a whole room as beautifully as the sparkling fabric on that dress."

"Without my boots I can't walk without tipping over to one side!"

"Isabeau," Hedda squeezed Isabeau's shoulder, "everyone has something about them that can tip them over to one side. You are a beautiful young woman. Your mother can nick your boots, but she can't steal your smile or your spirit unless you let her! I'm sure when she sees how lovely you look, she'll want you to have some fun."

Isabeau looked away. "My mother's too sick to come out of her room, she won't see me."

"I see." Hedda's years of reading tarot meant she could read people, too, and the girl was lying. However, they didn't have time to worry about that now.

* * *

The party was in full swing by the time the HEA Council appeared: Hepzibella, Horatius, the rusted-crown prince, and the fairy godmother, Zelindabell. They arrived in a pumpkin coach pulled by Hedda's two black cats, setting down in a whirl of wind in a fortuitously empty part of the hall.

Mortal and Fae stopped the chatter and dancing and drinking to stare.

Hedda waved her hands. "It's okay, keep on partying...they've come to see me!"   Hepzibella's long index finger beckoned to the pumpkin coach. Hedda made her way in slowly, throwing apologetic glances at her poor black cats.

"Animals are not for service to Mortal or Fae," she said. "You're so keen on *rules*."

"You will be at our service," Hepzibella thundered.

"Oh, bit harsh, don't you think?" Horatius said, and received a swift kick in the shin from the fairy godmother, Zelindabell.

"Ouch!"

"Get out!" Zelindabell shouted, and the rusted-crown prince limped his way to the dance floor.

"Really, Zelindabell, he's *my* brother," Hepzibella scolded. "*I* get to kick him."

"So…where is the magic?" Zelindabell poked her head out of the coach's rather large window and peered around the room.

"Well, I don't have magic fingers, nor do I have a magic wand," Hedda answered slowly.

"Because you are a fraud, giving fairy godmothers and magic a bad name."

Hedda looked at the people in the hall. A vegan ex-wolf hunter sat with a young woman dressed in a red cape on his lap; Isabeau's friend from the radio, Marvin, held hands with a young fop in a frilly shirt and cascading curls; Fae and Mortal, all mixing and enjoying each other's company, dancing, eating some version of a pumpkin.

"No. I'm not a fraud. I may not have created a gown from rags and coaches from pumpkins but I made all of this happen. I made the dress happen, I made the pumpkins grow, I brought all these people together, I made a ball for them! I made a happily-ever-after for Fae and folk to love each other regardless of blood and gender! So really, Hepzibella and Zelindabell, I'm just as, if not *more*, magical than you, because I did all this without a wand!"

Zelindabell clenched her fists and closed her eyes, face red. Hedda thought she looked constipated.

Hedda sighed. "Look, I don't want your wand back. I just want my cats. Please. Please, let them go."

"Well…" Hepzibella glanced out the window. "Oh!"

Hedda followed her gaze and saw Horatius was dancing with Isabeau. "Oh!"

Hedda could see the girl's feet peaking from beneath her hem: sparkly painted toenails, and her feet decorated, henna-style, with hair dye from one of the packets in the shop. And Isabeau dancing without worrying about her limp.

"You have created some kind of magic," admitted Hepzibella; she and Zelindabell exchanged a look, and the fairy godmother just grunted. "Well, Hedda Wayward, I suppose—"

Suddenly, there was a crack of thunder and a flash of lightening. The lights went out, the music stopped, and there were exclamations of surprise. Then one light came on like a spotlight, and beneath it stood a tall, lanky woman with two long white braids and a very angry expression.

"No magic! No dance! Who gave you permission? Magic? More like mess! Ruining my life, stealing my daughter!"

"I'm sorry, who are you?" Heddda asked as she climbed out of the coach, but she already knew. The resemblance was uncanny: Isabeau had her mother's rounded chin and green eyes. Hedda realized this was who'd been watching through the kitchen window last night. The boot thief.

"Mother!" Isabeau wailed.

"Everyone, leave! You have no right being here! And Isabeau! It's time for my nightly cuppa and you're not there to make it!"

"Make it yourself, you lazy cow!" Hedda yelled. "You've got two arms and two legs. The girl works all day in the shop. What do you do all day? You don't look sick at all to me."

The woman lunged at Hedda but Hedda climbed up onto one of the trestle tables and stayed out of reach. "I see you! You're not sick. You're just holding your daughter back! What are you afraid of?"

The room went silent.

Then Zelindabell, the fairy godmother, climbed out of the pumpkin and stepped forward. "Yeah, come on…. give it up, Rosalba. She's thirty-five. She needs a life."

"You know Isabeau?" There was surprise in Hedda's voice.

Zelindabell glared and pursed her lips. "I ought to turn you into a mouse and let your cats eat you! She was my latest project before you stole my wand!"

"That's why we sent you here. What better punishment than a lost cause?" Hepzibella said, then glanced at Rosalba. "Two lost causes!"

Hedda looked to the dance floor and smiled. Horatius was holding Isabeau's hand tightly and she was holding on right back.

"Not a lost cause. I have created magic in my own way and in less than forty-eight hours."

"But it is!"

"You said, make magic without a wand. I did. *In my own way.*" Hedda put a hand in her pocket. "And there's not two lost causes."

Hedda climbed off the trestle table and approached Rosalba, who looked at her with suspicion. Hedda held out her hand and offered a piece of paper.

"What is this?" Rosalba demanded, snatching it away. She held it close to her face and squinted.

"It's a coach tour to some vineyards for a week. You're not sick but you've made yourself so. You're lonely and miserable and you've tried to make Isabeau the same. Take the ticket. Go on the coach tour and drink up and enjoy life and let your daughter enjoy hers."

Then, with a flick of her wrist, Zelindabell aimed her wand at Rosalba—and there she was, dressed in a floral and silk maxi-gown with her hair neatly curled and dyed a lovely shade of blue.

"You look fabulous!" Hedda exclaimed.

Hepzibella pulled out a make-up mirror from her handbag, then held it up in front of Rosalba. "There! Nothing like a new outfit and a fresh 'do. Coach leaves tomorrow, doesn't it?" She looked at the ticket in Rosalba's hand. "Hedda, she'll have to sleep at yours overnight."

And with that, Rosalba was gone before she could finish admiring herself in the mirror.

"Right then. We will whisk you back to your terrace but you can't work as a 'fairy godmother.'" Hepzibella had warmed a little, it seemed.

"It's false advertising." Zelindabell pursed her lips and nodded. "And no more nicking wands! Or anything!"

"Right then," Hedda said and reached into her pocket. She pulled out the rose-gold pocket watch and thrust it in front of Horatius' face. "I think you'll want this back."

Horatius patted his own pockets, incredulous. "I must have dropped it when I was dancing with Isabeau. Thank you."

"You're welcome."

"You didn't find fifty dollars with it, did you?"

"Sorry, no."

Horatius continued, "Can you believe Isabeau needs a new pair of shoes? I'm an out of work cobbler. My fairy kingdom has fallen to Payless shoes. Now I have someone to craft a pair of shoes for." He scooped Isabeau up into an embrace and spun her around.

"Well, so you'll be stopping here then, Horatius?" Hepzibella asked. "To craft some lovely shoes for Isabeau?"

"Yes."

"Wonderful!"

"So, you did create magic, I guess," said Zelindabell. "We can send you and your felines back home." She lifted her arms dramatically up into the air, the wand suspended.

"Wait!" Hedda yelled. "I'm not going back. Everything I need is right here. I have a barn to sleep in. It's abandoned, right?"

"Well, it's mine but nobody lives there," Hepzibella said.

"Finders keepers. I'll make my home there."

"Not finders keepers, but guests are welcome." Hepzibella clicked her fingers and released Hedda's cats from the coach harness.

"Could you grant me one wish?" asked Hedda as the cats twined around her ankles, purring loudly.

Zelindabell raised an eyebrow. "Depends."

"Could you change the lease dates, on my townhouse? You know, to make it look like I was meant to move out a week ago?"

"We can do that," Hepzibella said, there was a puff of smoke and Hepzibella and Zelindabell disappeared; perhaps they were worried Hedda might ask for more favors. Horatius was now cheek to cheek with Isabeau, their eyes closed, oblivious to the departure.

Hedda picked up a wicker basket from one of the trestle tables. It would be easier to carry the cats to their new home. She'd return the basket later.

"Where you going, Hedda?" Isabeau let go of Horatius and came over.

"Home."

"You mean the barn?"

"Yes."

"You mean you'll stay here?"

"For a while, at least."

"That's wonderful news!"

"Did you know about Zelindabell? The fairy godmother?"

Isabeau shook her head. "I often wished for one, but what I needed was you. A really great friend." Isabeau squeezed Hedda tightly and Hedda squeezed back.

* * *

As Hedda walked along the moonlit road, she made plans. Tomorrow would be a new day. The first thing she would do was make a sign for the door, and another for use at the weekend markets. The signs would say, in nice font, "Advice and Pumpkins." She would find a table and two chairs. She would charge whatever people could afford—even if it was a cup of tea and a bit of toast.

Besides, when she was broke, she could always revert to her old habits.

Dear Auntie Star

Alethea Kontis

Star stepped gently into the topmost room of the wizard's tower, brown toes disappearing in the shadows, threadbare garments silent as the stone. The bright moon that shone through the small window illuminated a square of dusty silver chimes. Star knew they hung everywhere, in and around the ravens' roosts. According to the catacombs parchment she'd found, one of those nests hid the legendary ring of Asheroth. She just had to find it. In the dark. Without disturbing the chimes, the ravens, the sleeping princess, or the evil wizard.

Death or success was her fate now, and she'd chosen death before she climbed the ladder. It was the only way she could have come this far.

She squinted into the darkness, but caught no sight of the captive princess. No matter. The princess's whereabouts were of no concern, as long as the aerie stayed still. Star sighed inwardly at the chime-riddled birds' nests and sent up a prayer to her beloved Sky Goddess. It was about to get very noisy in here. There was no way around it. She just had to find the ring before the wizard arrived.

Not one for waiting, Star ran headlong into the ensuing chaos.

Birds screamed a cacophony at her presence. Chimes laughed like a riot of capricious fey. Cobwebs mussed her hair. Ruffled feathers and razor-sharp beaks scored her flesh. She glimpsed the slightest twinkle of gold—the ring!—in the exact same moment the wizard manifested.

The sparks that heralded his appearance set the cobwebs alight and filled the room with smoke. Star sneezed. The wizard's brown and leopard skin robes swirled around his tall, crooked frame as he attempted to locate the intruder. The knobby fingers of his hands twitched with a spell. If his eyes met hers, Star was done for. She could not let those twin hollows of despair find their prey. She had maybe half a breath left to live.

It was all she needed.

Even if she'd had a knife, or the desire, there was no time to amputate the bird's leg. She stretched out her scrawny arms and yanked the raven off its perch. *I hope the stories are true*, filled her mind at the same time as, *Save me*. Then every ounce of her breath fled her body...

...and slammed right back into her lungs...

...somewhere else.

She fell to her knees gasping in a patch of sunlight—sunlight!—framed by strange fat shadows that might have been...could they be leaves? There was an unceasing roaring in her head. She clasped her hands to her ears and stood up on the—sand, she knew, but...green? Maybe grass? Moss? She'd only ever read these concepts as words on parchment. Her eyes met a horizon filled with nothing but loud, churning water. She had never seen such a thing before in her life, or her dreams.

"It worked," she whispered from a heart tinged with hope. Somehow, the air tasted of salt.

"Yeah, it worked," squawked the raven in her arms. "Now what?"

There was a bird in her bloody arms. Right. The bird in possession of the legendary magical ring that really did send people wherever they needed to go. A bird who could talk.

"You can talk," Star said aloud.

"Of course I can talk," said the raven. "I'm a princess."

* * *

Dear Someone,

I have stoppered this message up inside a bottle, in the hopes that it finds a kindred spirit in the World of Men who might answer a question for this lonesome little mermaid.

Are the hearts of souls above the sea built the same as those of us who live among her blessed depths? Despite our obvious differences, my heart aches for a human man. We met only once—I'd thought him dead when I came upon him, so I'm not even sure he saw me clearly in return. Because of me, he lived. I've since discovered his seaside dwelling. I watch him when he walks on his balcony there, despite my sisters' warnings.

I cannot stop myself from wondering: does he dream of me? Does he feel this same emptiness in his chest that pulls like the tide? Does he yearn? I would give anything to be by his side. *Anything.* EVERYTHING.

Please tell me he feels the same way about me. Even just a fraction.

Please give me hope.

Please.

* * *

Dear Lonesome Little Mermaid,

I do live on two legs, but I can't say that I have much experience in the World of Men. However, having done extensive reading on the subject, I am able to offer you this advice: whatever you're about to do for this human, don't do it. He's not worth it.

Hear me out. What you're experiencing right now is called a "crush" (aptly named, isn't it?). You're enamored with those wonderful, powerful emotions currently coursing through your veins and the fantasies playing in your head, but you're not *actually* in love. I bet you don't even know that human's name, do you? It sounds like he doesn't know yours either. Nor would he recognize you if he came across you again someday. All this following him around and watching him from a distance is something we humans call "stalking."

Stalking is not good. You really don't want to be a stalker.

Your sisters are the ones demonstrating real love here. Listen to them. They care about you, and do not want you to put yourself in danger. You are exceptionally lucky to have such people in your world—so many of us don't. Take a moment to appreciate them. When the right soul does come along for you, you'll know they are the right soul, because they will express feelings similar to yours. They will care for you. They will know your name. They will look for you just as hard as you look for them. Just be patient.

There are plenty of other fish in the sea. I promise.

Please stay safe.

Fondly yours,

A kindred spirit from the World of Women

* * *

Star landed hard when they threw her in the pit. A few more bruises to add to her collection. Maybe even a scar or two. Every new mission of hope strengthened Star's resolve. And it would continue to strengthen, as long as her missions didn't kill her.

This one just might.

Star felt a presence move over her.

"Oh, no."

"Not another one."

"Are you all right, child?"

She couldn't yet comprehend every nuance of the prisoners' language, but she understood the care in the cadence. Star opened one eye in an attempt to see the bodies who tended to her; the other eye was swollen shut.

This perhaps had not been her wisest plan. Her captors had not pulled their punches because she was a woman. It seemed her flesh would fetch the same price, regardless.

On some level, she didn't mind. Flesh healed. Words were what sliced unseen, razor fresh, churning over and over in one's mind until the end of time.

"Stupid girl," a deep voice said above them.

Girl. That had been one of those words. Fatherless whelps whose mothers died in childbirth weren't given names beyond "you" or "girl" or whatever else the wizard's lackeys called out. Deep in the catacombs she had named herself Blue Star, after the empty space on the temple ceiling where a silver star in the Sky Goddess should have been. A space that had gone unnoticed all this time. A wish forgotten. Just like her.

There was no goddess here, nor stars, but the stone and sand were familiar friends. And somewhere beyond that grate high in the wall, there was a patch of night sky.

Hope.

"Ought to know better than to shoot her mouth off," said the deep voice. "What'd she expect?"

"Why give her grief?" There was strength in this female's voice. "She'll die here, same as us."

"Not today," Star managed to croak. She raised a hand; a large someone took it and pulled her to standing with a grunt.

"Don't start, girl." The deep voice was close to her ear now. "Ain't no hope here."

She would have smiled if her bottom lip hadn't been so badly split. "Help me to those bars," she whispered. "And anyone else who wants to be free."

A tiny shower of dirt fell through the grate as small bare feet skidded to a halt on the ground outside the cell. There was a squawk and a rustle of feathers.

"Mama?"

"Baby?" The female's strong voice wavered.

"I'm called Fire now," said the little one Star had left behind to run away with the raven. Neither one of them had listened. Now, the child would save them all.

Star had expected as much.

"Baby, what are you doing? You should be off somewhere safe."

Distant yelling sounded from deeper in the dungeon, or farther down the road, or both. An alarm had been raised. There was no time. It was a race to see who reached Star first: the wizard or the wicked. She stretched, putting as much of her hand as she could through the gate. The large man lifted her off the ground to aid her, shifting her broken ribs. Star almost passed out from the pain.

"Hold on tight," she said, as much to herself as to the other captives. When she felt the press of bodies pushing her against the wall, she knew they had understood. She could not see the bird or the ring, but she felt cool metal against her fingertips. It was all she needed.

Take us to the island.

Salt air filled her nostrils before she even finished the thought. On the exhale, she and her fellow prisoners collapsed on the sand.

* * *

Help Me

My sister is annoyingly perfect. Everything she does is amazing, and I can't stand it. Her words are a poet's dream. Flowers just about bloom at her feet. Every stranger she meets is a benevolent fairy. She could stick her entire hand into a beehive and draw out a fistful of honey. She doesn't even mean for it to happen, which only makes it worse. And it's not just me. Mother was so fed up with my sister's endless gifts that she sent her off to be a maid on an island of cats. She came home a year later DIPPED IN GOLD.

How am I supposed to live my life in the shadow of such perfection? How do I get out? Help!

* * *

Dear Sister,

How do you live in someone else's shadow? That's easy! You don't.

Using your sister as a measuring stick for yourself is the heart of what's constantly stealing your joy. If I woke every day obsessively comparing myself to the sun, I would find myself nothing but small and cold and dim. What would be the point of that? Who does that help, in the end? Exactly no one.

I suspect your sister will be married off to a prince in no time, if she isn't already. You and your mother will have your pick of rooms in a spacious castle. Is that failure? When you gaze at your reflection in your gilded mirror, will you still find yourself lacking? Or will you wonder why you ever wasted so much time worrying about someone else when you could have been riding a horse or reading a book or learning to weave or… literally *anything*.

The gods deal us all the ultimate sentence: We each have to live with ourselves for the rest of our lives.

Only you can decide if that is a gift or a punishment.

Sincerely,

* * *

"Auntie Star?"

Star snapped out of the dust storm in her mind and looked up at Fire. And up. She was incredibly tall now that she'd reached the age of annoyance. She had moved into Star's home the moment the island community built one for her—maybe even before, since the house had been Fire's idea to begin with. The child had grown big enough to wear Star's clothes, and her hair scarves, and her shoes; old enough to keep the house tidy and the kitchen stocked with food. Star tolerated her presence mostly for those last two. And because she was too clever for her own good. And because she and that damned raven were inseparable.

"Yes, Fire and Ravenna. What is it?"

Ravenna squawked. Fire sighed. "I've been talking at you for ages. What's so important in that letter?"

Star put the pen down and rubbed her neck. "I'm trying to tell a pessimistic narcissist to love herself. And somehow say it nicely."

"She's that selfish, but somehow she doesn't love herself?" Fire snorted. "Skip the niceties."

"I can't pass up the chance to gently guide her onto a better path. People like her are just selfish in the wrong ways."

"Whereas you are selfless to a fault." Fire came around behind Star's chair and used her strong fingers to rub the stiffness out of Star's shoulders. Another reason she kept Fire around. "Auntie Star: granter of wishes and sower of hope. Do you even know if your responses reach the senders?"

"Ravenna says they do." Star entrusted her missives to the birds; she had to trust when the birds confirmed delivery.

"And do the people follow your advice?"

"Maybe. Maybe not." She was so tired. "That's up to them." In all honesty, they probably didn't. She tried never to think about that. If she gave in to despair, the wizard won.

"If you don't know if your efforts make a difference, then why do you keep doing this night after night?"

Ravenna squawked. "I've been singing that song at her for years."

Star nodded to the bird on Fire's shoulder. The golden band around her leg winked in the candle's light. "The wizard I stole that ring from did a lot of evil things. I can't undo all he did—hell, I can't even make Ravenna human again—but I can dedicate my life to putting as much good back into this world as possible."

"Auntie Star." Fire squeezed Star's shoulders. "You can't save everyone."

"I can try."

"Fine."

"What?" That was too easy.

"But you don't have to do it alone."

"*What?*" Star worked on quieting her mental whirlwind enough to wrap it around Fire's nonsense.

"I'm coming with you on your next mission."

"Like hell."

Fire ignored her, as Fire did more and more these days. "Ravenna says that letters don't just come to the island. Like the ring's magic, the letters go where they need to go: to you. Wherever you are."

Star scowled. That same magic had kept the evil wizard hot on her heels after all these years. The island was the only place she could stop and do this task safely.

"Ravenna says they're always trying to find you, but you're too busy saving people to notice. So next time I'm coming with you."

Star was already shaking her head. "It's too dangerous."

"What *you* do is too dangerous," Fire shot back. "I'm just collecting the mail."

"No. I won't put your life at risk."

"But you're all right with ignoring all those other cries for help? How many more do you think are out there? Dozens? Hundreds?"

Star rose from her chair. It was impossible to look down on Fire anymore, but she could still meet her eyes. "Sister Shade and Brother Stone will agree with me."

"No, they won't." Fire put a hand on her hip. "Mama and Daddy already said yes. They say it's past time for me to start earning my keep."

Star bit the inside of her cheek. She tilted her head back and stared up at the painted ceiling filled with stars, but none of them had a better answer for her.

"Oh, please don't give in yet," Ravenna squawked. "This fight's just getting fun."

* * *

Dearest Mama,

You would be so ashamed of me right now. My maid has stolen my life.

My silly, trusting heart did not listen when you warned me not to turn my back on her. In my wildest dreams I could not have imagined the scheme she concocted: to switch places with me and present herself to the palace as a princess royal. Even writing it out like that sounds ridiculous! It should not have worked, but it did. So here I am, barefoot in ragged clothes, weeping into the wind and wishing you were here. I have no one else to talk to. The maid threatened my life if I say so much as one word to anyone. And I believe her.

She killed my horse to prove just how far she was willing to go.

I conjured the wind and sent my fellow gooseherd chasing his hat far enough away that I can write you this letter in peace. The birds stayed; they don't mind my troubled heart. I shall send this message down a river's stream, the same way your handkerchief floated away from me and took your protection with it. I pray there is enough magic left in the world for this to find you, wherever you are. If only you could find a way back to me and save me from this wretched existence.

All my love forevermore,

Your Daughter

* * *

Dearest Daughter—for we are all someone's daughter, aren't we?

We can never truly imagine the evil of which some men—and yes, even women—are capable. Nor should we. If we twist our minds enough to comprehend them, then we have become them, and no one wants that.

It sounds like your noble mother was a sorceress on some level. It sounds like you are, too. But even if you don't think you have an ounce of magic inside you, I'm going to ask you to do one simple thing for me. Are you ready? Here it is: STOP BEING AFRAID OF YOUR OWN POWER.

You are a young woman riddled with power, from your fingertips to your toes. Stop giving it away to some wretched maid with terrible ideas!

This advice sounds harsh, I know. And I admit, I don't actually know your mother. But I assure you, wherever she is, she absolutely agrees with me.

If there was enough magic left in this world for your letter to find its way into my hands, then I promise you, there is more than enough magic inside you to do what needs to be done. Step up. Sit at the table. Own that life! You owe it to yourself not to let anyone else you love die needlessly.

Be brave, princess. I believe in you! Save yourself. Make your mother proud.

With love and hope,

Auntie Star

* * *

If the wizard lays a finger on you, we've already lost. If he so much as meets your eyes, his haggard image will haunt your mind until the end of your days. If you don't listen to another word I speak for the rest of your life, I want you to hear this: whenever we are off this island, you must be vigilant. His presence announces itself in the silence of the wood, in the prickling of the hairs on the back of your neck, in the reek of incense and burning stone. If you even suspect something is out of place, run. You will see me put myself in harm's way again and again, but what would hurt me most is to see you captured by that monster. And if that happens, goddess help us if that happens, know that I will find you. I will always come for you, my heart. I will save you. Even if neither of us makes it out alive.

It was only a matter of time before he caught up with them.

The memory of her instructions to Fire, so much less eloquent than the advice she was given all the time in the world to pen, screamed in Star's head. She took a fistful of the wizard's leopard skin cloak and swung his body away from Fire. Ravenna's beak and claws slashed at his knobby fingers as they reached for the bit of gold on her leg. Thwarted, the wizard returned to where Fire lay on her back in the road…

…and she tossed a handful of dirt in those baleful eyes.

At his howl, Star launched herself at Fire's body. Ravenna did the same. As soon as Star felt the bird's claws bite into her forearm, she shout-thought, *ISLAND!*

In the next breath the three of them were on the floor of Star's study.

Star sat up quickly, wiping the blood or mud or whatever it was off her face so she could assess the damage to her weeping charge. Fire's clothes didn't seem torn, so there didn't seem to be anything major… Gently, Star pulled at Fire's shoulder until she faced her. Fire wasn't sobbing.

She was laughing.

"Did you hear that man?" Fire gasped when she caught her breath. "He sounded like a sad old wolf, losing his dinner. Pitiful! I'd almost feel bad for him, if he wasn't the absolute *worst.*" Her smiling eyes shone brighter than the sun. "And look at how many letters found us in such a short time! I'll tell Mama we won't be leaving again for a while. Auntie has sooooo much writing to do!" She grabbed her stomach and fell back to the floor, dissolving in hilarity. Ravenna lifted the sack of letters into the air and flew around the room, just out of Fire's reach, both of them cackling loud enough to bring the house down.

Star rested her chin on a dirty knee and loved them both only slightly more than she wanted to strangle them.

* * *

Dear Auntie Star,

I killed someone.

My father, brother, and even the town criers hail me as a hero for this horrible thing. Yes, she was an evil witch, and yes, she would have taken my brother's life, and then probably mine…but there's no going back. I am made different by it. When I look in the mirror now, I no longer see the face of the girl I used to know.

I see my mother.

Not that long ago, our poor and starving mother sent us children out into the woods to die, again and again, hoping the wild would take care of the dirty business for her and she'd have that many fewer mouths to feed. She was twisted, and a coward who made horrible decisions. But I…I am the murderer. My darkness has surpassed even hers.

How proud she must be.

Thanks to the witch, I know now that I am strong enough to do anything. I can endure the rest of this life, for the sake of my father and brother. But I hear the whispers. That I should move on. Get married. Have children.

Oh, Auntie...how?

Where is the guarantee that I will not become my mother in my children's eyes...or worse, give birth to the soul that sets fire to the world and dances in its ashes?

Please tell me if you can see a life to be made from the ruins I have become, because I just can't.

Gratefully yours,

Gretel

* * *

Oh, Gretel.

I know something of young souls who bear such a heavy burden. You did what you did in the heat of the moment to survive. Like others, I commend your strength, courage, and wisdom in that moment. You saved your brother. Now, you must be your own advocate.

It sounds like you keep following a trail of breadcrumbs to the past. I urge you to look forward into your life. It is true that we cannot escape the blood that made us, but we are the ones who get to decide what to do with the heart and nerve and sinew that dwell beneath our skin. Be the best person that you can possibly be. Build the best things around you that you know how to build. This world is already better for you having been in it. Keep it up!

As for the future: You must trust that there is love in this world, love as big as the heart you have, love that could do what you did. You know it exists in you; you have to believe it exists in others, too. But will those others find you in this lifetime? That I can not guarantee. I'm not even sure the gods can make that promise. You must find a way to have faith, my dear, both in the world and in yourself.

I wish you the best of all possible lives.

Don't look back.

* * *

Star dropped her pen and covered her face with her hands. The letters were getting harder to answer these days. And more difficult for her to collect. Who was she to tell someone not to look back when she herself constantly looked over her shoulder and feared for the lives of the ones she loved? Who was she to wax rhapsodic about love and faith and goodness? She was one decent person in a world full of chaos, nothing more. A butterfly in a hurricane. An unbroken bottle on an ocean wave. A blue star in a twilight sky. What did she know of wishes anymore? Or hope? She had saved a few souls in her lifetime, yes…but was it enough? Would it ever be enough?

A scream shattered the night, piercing through Star's introspection.

Abruptly, she pushed back her chair and stood, listening to the silence. It might have been Fire, trapped in another nightmare of leopards and teeth that she swore the wizard never gave her, but this cry had been higher pitched than Fire's resonant timbre. Had Master Wing brought peacocks back to the island? Sister Shade would have something to say about that come morning.

The door to the study flew open and a young woman Star had never seen before crossed the room like a vengeful ghost. Her long white nightgown flowed around pale ankles and bare feet; her long black hair trailed behind her like ragged ebon silk. Star didn't have time to notice the color of her eyes above her pink, tear-stained cheeks before she launched herself into Star's arms. Confused, Star simply held the young woman while she sobbed.

Fire appeared in the doorway, but did not move into the room. She just stood there, stunned, her own cloud of hair brushing the top of the frame. "She woke up like that."

Star pulled far enough away from the young woman to look at her in earnest. "Ravenna?" She pushed the strands of black hair off the young woman's tear-stained, smiling, nodding face. "Ravenna!" This time, Star hugged her in earnest. "What happened?" she asked Fire.

Fire held one arm across her chest awkwardly. She still didn't step into the room. "I don't know."

"Some food or drink? A phase of the moon? A kiss of true love?"

Fire, who had never showed any fear in her life, shrugged and looked at the doorframe. "None of that worked before."

Star raised an eyebrow.

Ravenna—human princess Ravenna—pulled out of Star's arms and wiped her nose on her sleeve. "The wizard."

It was strange to hear Ravenna's voice coming from a creature without feathers, but that was not why Star lifted a hand to her gaping mouth. Had it been so long? After a decade or so, Star had simply come to assume that the pureness of his evil had made him immortal. She blinked rapidly, trying to comprehend the words even as she said them out loud. "The wizard is dead."

* * *

Dear Auntie Star,

As the daughter of a king, my hand was given to the most clever, valiant warrior in the land. Or so I thought. Turns out, the man I married is nothing but a mediocre buffoon who tells tales taller than the bards in the Southside taverns. My suspicions early on in our relationship led me to lay awake at night, for the truth haunts him in his sleep. He never killed one giant, let alone seven. He never squeezed milk from a stone, or threw a rock that didn't land, and he only managed to capture the unicorn I asked for by sheer dumb luck.

I might have admired his cleverness, once upon a time, but whenever I look upon him now, his image reminds me of just how easily he pulled the wool over my ignorant eyes. I feel nothing for him now but anger.

Two choices lie before me: to love him or to leave him. But how do I manage either one?

Desperately,

The King's Naïve Daughter

* * *

Your Most Excellent Majesty,

Considering your current station, situation, how every circumstance came about, and how great the repercussions either of your choices might be, I'm going to level with you.

If your husband is a braggart, let him be a braggart.

Feed his ego. Continue to challenge him so that he can show off. (I hear "retrieving the golden apple from the highest branch of the Tree of Life" is quite popular!) In the meantime, remember that there is a kingdom to be run—a kingdom it sounds like your husband has little to no interest in. Good! Build him a museum in which he can display and admire his spoils to his chauvinist heart's content. While he does that, you can be busy fostering an inclusive feminist society full of beautifully safe spaces that have no tolerance for toxic masculinity.

You are no longer simply the "daughter of a king." You are a queen! Seize your Divine Right! You asked for a unicorn and got it, whatever the means. You want to drink your way through the Southside taverns? Cheers, my dear. You want to dance to those bards' ridiculous tunes? Kick up your heels. Host a tournament and invite all the finest warriors in the land. You want to sleep with one? Or seven? Go right ahead!

Live, love, and make yourself as happy as possible. (Feel free to give your husband all the credit!) I'll be cheering your carriage most-heartily as you pass through the streets.

Sincerely,

Auntie Star

* * *

Sister Shade established the ministry of the Aunties of Hope and took over answering letters. Star was a staunch supporter. The older and more jaded she got, the less qualified she felt to respond to those souls in pain that never stopped reaching out.

Now free of both her curse and her bonds, Ravenna gave Star the wizard's ring.

Now free from relentless pursuit, Star gave Fire and Ravenna the house.

Fire hugged Star enthusiastically. "Go have an adventure!"

Ravenna kissed Star on the cheek and whispered, "Go have fun."

Star slid the golden ring onto her finger without the slightest bit of apprehension and set out to see what life felt like, unencumbered.

In the wake of the wizard's passing, the ring's power flourished. By accident, she discovered its ability to change shape and size so that it might aid her in sticky situations. In a similar fashion, Star learned how to use the ring to move through time as well as space. As she grew more proficient at rescuing those in need, the population of the island slowly increased. All she needed now were sturdy shoes, the magic ring, and Fire's mailbag.

For wherever and whenever she was, the letters kept finding her. Star didn't mind. They gave her a reason to keep going home, reminded her that she had made a place in her life to call home. She threw herself into the joy of traveling without being chased. Star often adventured for months at a time without having to return to the island. It was bliss.

Until it wasn't.

She smelled the first hint of brimstone in a cafe in Paris. She might have ignored it, had it not been coupled with an errant icy breeze on an otherwise overly warm spring day. And when the hairs on the back of her neck stood up as she walked down a narrow alleyway at dusk, she pulled the ring off her finger, turned, and threw it.

The ring grew in the air, like the lasso of a golden rope. It wrapped itself around the arms of the man following her, trapping him where he stood.

The man that was not the wizard.

His thick hair fell past sharp cheekbones to a strong, tawny-skinned jaw. His robes and boots were as black as his hair, with no discernible hide from large cats anywhere. Apart from his sudden appearance—and the smell, and the chill—he was nothing like the wizard at all. There was no despair in his aura. His most-decidedly non-baleful brown eyes stared at her, not through her. He was…striking. Not striking fear, just striking.

If the image of this man filled her dreams from this day forward, they would absolutely not be nightmares.

"Who are you?" Star asked. "Why are you following me?"

The man did not answer. Instead, he fell to one knee before her and remained there, head bent in…reverence?

Star waited to see what other surprises this man had in store.

"I was raised by a legend," he said, just when she thought he might never speak. His voice was not as deep as Brother Stone's, with an accent she couldn't immediately place. "Stories were told of an orphan like me, a girl who taught herself to read in the catacombs of the wizard's tower. A miraculous girl. They said she learned enough in secret to best the wizard himself. That she escaped with one of his most prized magical possessions and his bride-to-be."

Star took a step back. Her mind flooded with vivid scenes from a place she dared not remember. She'd left that sand and stone behind long ago.

Words she had once written to someone else echoed in her mind. *The gods deal us all the ultimate sentence: We each have to live with ourselves for the rest of our lives.*

"Year after year, the girl eluded him," the man continued with that beautiful voice. "The wizard was furious. He became so obsessed with chasing her that the villages and towns he'd previously terrorized began to flourish."

Her words came again: *Only you can decide if that is a gift or a punishment.*

If there had been a chair in the alleyway, Star would have collapsed into it. It had never occurred to her to wonder what had happened in that place of gloom and tragedy once she'd gone. Like she'd advised so many, she had looked forward into her life, never back. And yet...

"That girl has never been far from my mind. Her triumph guided me. Her continued existence inspired me. I have admired her my whole life."

Star stared down at his mass of hair and his broad back. Exactly how long had his "whole life" been? He seemed ages younger than she, with as much intensity and drive as Fire. Had Star ever possessed such passion?

"I wanted to help her in some way, but besides those stories, I knew nothing except that the wizard would never stop chasing her. So I killed the wizard."

The words fell from his lips as casually as if he'd said the sun came up that morning.

You know it exists in you; you have to believe it exists in others, too.

Star reached for the man's shoulders and pulled him to standing. She touched the rope that bound his chest and the gold shifted back to a ring in her hand. She wanted to hear more about the wizard, about anything, just as long as the stories were told in his voice.

She should probably not stare at him, but she couldn't bring herself to look away. Why could he not meet her eyes? Did he not feel worthy of her presence in some way? Bah. She was nothing to a man who killed the wizard.

Stop being afraid of your own power.

The man's gaze stayed on her ring. "Among the items the wizard left behind was a magical ring that was rumored to usher the wearer to his heart's desire. There is only one other like it in the world, you know."

She did know. Of course she knew. She had used it countless times to save hearts and souls and lives. And now…

Save yourself.

…now she really needed her own words to stop haunting her.

"But why?" She slid the ring back onto her finger and dropped her hands. "Why ask the ring to…?"

When the right soul does come along for you, you'll know. They will look for you just as hard as you look for them.

Dammit.

"To thank her." He still wouldn't look at her. "To tell her… To swear my… To devote… To…"

Star tried not to finish those sentences in her mind. Each one shocked her more than the last.

The man's lips bent into a crooked smile as his tongue tripped over his words, and he was suddenly so beautiful that it made her stomach hurt. What the hell was wrong with her?

He finally raised his head. "To meet her," he said. But his eyes said, *To fight by her side. To protect her. Forever.*

Star was far too old for a handsome face and pretty words to make her heart flutter. Wasn't she? When had she ever been? She'd spent her young life too busy running to allow herself to feel anything so unimportant as desire. Why not now?

Because she liked her blissful solitude. Even befriending this man would be…messy.

Own that life! You owe it to yourself.

Go have fun.

The last words weren't hers, but she didn't need them to be. It was past time for her to grant her own wish.

She held out a hand. "I call myself Star."

"I call myself Jin." Still smiling, he warmly clasped her hand in his.

And for the first time since they had been forged in the same fire, the two golden bands touched.

Bride of the Blue Manor

Y.M. Pang

I wanted to be a great ironthorn, like my ancestor Lady Naoma. Eventually, this matters.

* * *

I stepped down from the carriage, dragging the hem of this ridiculous Alusian dress. My slippers hit the courtyard of the blue manor. Turning back to the carriage—painted with the crossed swords of House Wenri—I waved to my coachman. Then I hefted the suitcase containing my marriage papers and faced my new life.

Garlands festooned the courtyard. My husband stood by the doors, hair like sun-dappled wheat, skin like burnished bronze, eyes as blue as the stone of his manor. So different from anyone back in Kokien.

Those eyes widened when they saw me, as if he'd seen a ghost. Then, I thought he marvelled at my coal-dark hair, my birch-white skin. Now, I know his initial shock stemmed from something else.

I should have been the one gawking. My husband still possessed the smooth skin and careless beauty of a man in his twenties—when, in truth, I was his fourth wife, and he was nearing fifty.

But I'd heard the rumours. Father had permitted me to arm myself with knowledge. And in the end, I'd been the one to accept this marriage.

My husband's features shifted back into pleasant neutrality. Extending a hand, he said, "Lady Asha, it is good to meet you at last." Poisoned honey laced his voice, sweet and dangerous.

I took his hand. "Lord Regeus."

Hidden beneath the bodice of my gown, the cold, hard weight of a knife pressed against my sternum. I was, after all, my father's daughter.

* * *

The wedding ceremony was a small one, with my family half a continent away. As for the locals of Saroi, few showed up either. They seemed afraid of Regeus, judging by their furtive glances. Still, my husband was the richest man in town, so some number of petty nobles and ambitious merchants stopped by.

The guests stared at me with pitying eyes, and whispered. How young I was. How far I'd travelled. How different I looked from the locals. The unsaid part: how sorry they felt for me.

I pretended to sip my wine. My eyes darted from my husband to his guests, and I instinctively planned ways to attack, routes of escape. How best to incapacitate this person, that person, and the quickest method out of the courtyard. Which items on the table could be turned into weapons.

All nonsense. I was not one of the Kingswords, guarding the royal bloodline. I would never become a general, as Naoma Wenri had been. That dream had been torn from me with Hasuo's birth.

I shifted in my seat and felt the knives strapped to my thighs, beneath the folds of my skirts.

My husband was a pleasant conversationalist during the feast. He recounted memorable episodes from his business dealings. He made me laugh once, with the tale of a merchant who tried passing off oxbird eggs as fist-sized opals. Surely at least one local girl would've fallen for his riches and charm, and ignored the speculations. He needn't have looked so far for a wife.

As night fell, the wedding ceremony wound down. The guests departed with hollow well wishes and I followed my husband into the blue manor.

We strode down stone corridors, then up a flight of stairs, Regeus' candle casting wavering shadows. The wall paintings were strange: three-headed birds, a woman with seven wings, a shadowy blue form coalescing out of a misty marsh. Paintings crafted from imagination, not reality. They would be frowned upon in Kokien, but perhaps they were common here in Alusia.

Only our footsteps broke the silence. Regeus had dismissed the servants after they'd cleaned up the remnants of the wedding celebrations. Alone in this large, lonely manor with him, I thought of his previous wives. Their lives, their demises.

First wife, married eleven years. Killed in a hunting accident. Her body had been too disfigured to be suitable for public viewing, Regeus had claimed.

Second wife, married seven years. Regeus had taken her on a trip to a country estate, then returned without her. There was some story about her venturing out into a stormy night, never to be seen again.

Third wife, married five years. Hidden away for many months, with some wasting disease, except no doctor was ever sent for. There'd been a brief reveal of her face during the funeral, red hair nestled among white camellias, before the coffin lid snapped shut.

Regeus led me to our bedroom. He lit two candelabras. I glimpsed a four-poster bed, a handsome vanity, a wardrobe of oak, a set of drawers. There was something wrong with the mirror of the vanity—

Regeus reached into his coat. "I'm sorry." Then the flash of a silver dagger.

He was fast, but I was faster.

I drew the knife from my bodice and stabbed clean through his hand. I kept moving, nailing his hand against the surface of the vanity. His fingers still gripped the dagger: a shimmering thing set with sapphires.

His mouth parted. "You're just like…"

I drew a second knife from the slits in my skirts. Then I noticed two things were very, very wrong.

One: the vanity mirror showed only me. He had no reflection.

Two: his blood was silver blue.

I slashed my knife across his throat. He bled that impossible color.

He lunged back, ripping his hand out from where my knife pinned it. His flesh snagged, but he tore free with a scream. For a moment his hand was a ruined thing of frayed flesh and broken sinew. Then it began to mend.

His hand knitted itself together. His throat closed, leaving only flecks of blue blood. And he spoke, clear and melodious, though moments ago I'd cut deep enough to see his trachea. "You are a true ironthorn."

All I could say was, "You knew that."

I struck him with the second blade as I ripped the first one from the wood. He stepped aside. I executed the slashes and jabs I'd been trained in since I was a child. I thought I'd one day use them in a blood duel, defending my house's sworn lord, or maybe even the king.

Some of my blows found their marks. My knife ripped through his shoulder, leaving a tear in his fine coat. I carved a gash in his belly deep enough to glimpse viscera, except it closed faster than I could pull out his intestines. I cut off his ear—then stared in horror as it wiggled up from the floor and reattached itself.

I laughed, mad and elated and despairing.

His hand closed over my wrist. He pinned me against the bed, the curtains swinging wildly around us. I slashed at him with my other knife and he grabbed that, too. Though the blade cut deep into his fingers, he wrestled it from my grip.

Then his dagger was out, the one inlaid with sapphires. Blue like his eyes, like his blood. It pressed against my throat.

My eyes locked on the tear in his shirt, where I'd cut so deeply through his abdomen. There was a smear of blue blood, but nothing else.

I twisted in his grip. Tonight had to be a dream, an impossibility. I'd fallen to that wretched curse: imagination. I couldn't accept this: that I'd sent myself to this distant land hoping to solve a mystery, hoping to prove myself a worthy ironthorn, only to wind up fighting a creature who could not be killed.

If I died like this, what would Father…

"Stop," Regeus commanded. He edged the knife closer to my skin.

I laughed and glared up at his eerily youthful face. "Or what? You'll kill me? Like you killed all the others?"

His brows creased.

I shifted my body, poised to kick him off at the first opportunity. "Must say, I didn't expect you to attack me on our wedding night. Didn't the rest of your wives get a couple of years?"

He looked away. "You don't understand."

I pulled up my knees, dug them into his groin. He grunted, but his weight still held me in place, his dagger unwavering.

I stopped struggling for a moment and let myself sink against the covers. "If you kill me tonight, won't the townsfolk talk? There are already rumours. If I disappear so quickly…"

"You don't understand," he repeated.

"But I do. That's why I'm here."

"Why?" he asked. "If you believed the rumors, if you think I killed my previous wives, why did you agree to marry me?"

I sighed and rolled my shoulders as best I could. "I wanted to find the truth. About you. About what happened to your wives, whether you killed them. And if you did, I wanted to be the one who brought you to justice."

Because then—maybe then—Father would…

"Seems like both of us entered this marriage intending to kill the other," he said.

"I suppose so."

He glanced to his left, where his hand gripped my wrist. "You are a skilled ironthorn. If I were not what I am, you would've killed me many times over."

Why did I feel a blossom of warmth at this praise, when he held a blade against my throat?

"Thank you," I said. "But I am no ironthorn. Just an ironthorn's daughter."

He looked at me. Licked his lips. Suddenly, he looked unsure.

"Do you acknowledge that I have won in our battle today?" he said.

"Yes." Unfair as it was, he had won.

"I heard that an ironthorn's word is worth the weight of stone. If you will swear to several conditions, I will spare your life."

My eyes narrowed. "Let's hear them."

"Never speak of tonight or what I tried to do. Do not try to enter any locked doors in this manor, or willfully cause damage to the property. In public, you will play the part of my wife, though of course you need not play such part in private. You are not to leave the manor unless I give you permission, and you will not run away." He paused, as if calculating something. "You will not try to kill me again. You cannot succeed, but our interactions will grow tedious if you continue repeating your antics from tonight."

I chuckled. "My antics? You tried to kill me first."

He dipped his head. A drop of blue blood—from when I'd cut his ear—snaked down his chin and landed on my collarbone.

"What are you?" I asked.

"Answering questions is not part of the deal."

I inhaled, then exhaled into the cold kiss of the dagger. I had to live, to find out the truth: why he attacked me, what happened with his other wives. Why he was sparing me now. I had to make my way back to Father, even if I could never be an ironthorn.

"Fine," I said. "I agree."

He released me and tucked the dagger away.

Then he stepped out of the room. He left me on the four-poster bed, in my stiff dress, holding my useless weapons. Bastard hadn't even brought in a wash basin so I could remove his blue blood.

* * *

In the early days, I dreamed of Father.

He would adjust my grip on the straight sword. Watch me dance across the length of the training hall, then pile Lahin's *Stratagems* and Inh Ishan's *Immovable Sword* into my arms. He would place a hand on my head and tell me how well I'd done.

In my dreams, Father always loomed like a giant, and Hasuo did not exist.

Then I would wake in my four-poster bed, to my new life.

I slipped downstairs for breakfast. I dined with Regeus, lord of the manor—it was difficult to think of him as my husband. He didn't talk much, except to help me familiarize myself with this foreign utensil called a fork. I stared at the sharp prongs and imagined stabbing them through his eye.

We saw each other little throughout the day. He would work in his study, managing his holdings and businesses, thumbing through account books and meeting merchants. Or he would venture into the room beside his study, the one he referred to as his studio. At night, he would disappear into the east wing. Since I had taken over what should have been our marital bedchamber, he slept in the east wing, it seemed.

I wandered the halls—into a library, a chapel, a storage room. I rifled through every shelf and drawer, but found little of interest. No diaries, personal letters, or telltale effects of past wives.

As the vow he'd wrangled out of me suggested: many of the doors were locked, including the one to the east wing.

I spent long hours in the garden. I would pull out my knives, draw the sword I'd stowed in my luggage. Then I would practice until sweat slicked down my back and my breath caught in my lungs. I was best with the knives, but more than capable of dueling with the straight sword. After all, it was Lady Naoma's favored weapon, and her sword was still passed down in House Wenri. Father would gift it to Hasuo one day.

It should have been mine. It never was mine—I was only ever a placeholder. The thoughts warred inside me, even as I battled shadows and invisible foes with my blade.

In the remaining hours of daylight, I would sprawl out in the grass, reading and rereading the books of my homeland. None of them, unfortunately, spoke about how to kill an unkillable man. My people did not believe in superstition.

The groundskeeper stared at me sometimes—at my slacks and sleeveless top, my tied-back hair. The servants of the blue manor were silent creatures, flitting through the estate like ghosts. They never stayed overnight—Regeus dismissed them after dinner was cleared off and the kitchen tidied.

* * *

I spent long stretches of time staring at the paintings. The imagination, the impossibility of them, just like Lord Regeus himself.

* * *

There was a flower festival down in Saroi. We attended, Regeus resplendent in his cloak of white and blue, his face not looking a day past twenty-five.

The townsfolk whispered. Their pity oozed over my skin like burning oil. I wanted to rip off this ridiculous dress, to tell them I was the heir to House Wenri, that I wasn't some frail damsel.

But none of this was true. Regeus *had* held my life in his hands and spared me.

A hand fell on my arm. My husband leaned close, his breath brushing my ear. "Do not glare at them so. I can endure your murderous intentions, but they cannot."

I let out a laugh. I'd been so caught up in my misery that I'd forgotten the first duty of an ironthorn family. The first lesson, when Father had led me to the training hall all those years ago. We fought to protect those who could not protect themselves.

The citizens of Saroi were not my enemy. I wasn't sure who my enemy was anymore.

* * *

I saw him the next day in the gardens. He set up an easel and canvas, and a set of paints.

"You paint?" I said.

He nodded.

It clicked, then. "You painted everything on the walls?"

He nodded again.

I couldn't tell him to leave. This was his manor, his garden. So I went through my blade practice pretending he wasn't there.

At dinner, I asked him that old question again. He had, after all, chosen to spend the day in my company. Perhaps he would be willing to give answers.

"Tell me," I said, staring down at him across the long dining table that held only the two of us, "why did you try to kill me? You didn't do that so early for your other wives."

His mouth twisted. There were faint shadows beneath his eyes. I would not have noticed if I didn't see him every day, but he looked tired, which I hadn't thought possible for a creature like him.

He speared a cut of wild boar, but did not bite into it. "You do not understand."

I sliced through my cut of boar. "So make me understand. Why did you try to kill me, and why am I still alive?"

Silence followed. I was nearly finished my meal when he answered. "You remind me of someone I knew long ago."

"Oh?" My hands froze. "Someone you killed?"

"No."

I cocked my head. "Someone you loved?"

A breath. "Yes."

* * *

He joined me in the gardens the next day, and the one after that. He would paint, and I would practice with my blades. On the third day, I walked to him and gestured at his painting. "May I?"

He nodded.

The painting was near-finished. Depth, perspective, movement— realistic techniques depicting an impossible subject. A giant serpent coiled at the bottom—no, not quite a serpent, for it had two front claws and two rear ones. Above it flew shining figures with wings and bows, bodies draped in fluttering gold cloth. The sky behind them was half-painted, but I could already discern strokes of a tornado, arcs of lightning.

"Your thoughts?" Regeus' question—so simple, so innocent, so unlike him.

I looked up from the canvas. "In Kokien, art should be a reflection of the real world, not a glimpse into imagination. Something like this would not exist there."

"I see. That seems restrictive."

I shrugged. "It is the same reason Father dismissed the rumors around you. We don't place regard in superstition and speculation."

"What if I told you my paintings come not only from imagination?"

I narrowed my eyes. I was half-believing, surprised, not surprised. What was he but an impossibility? "Just how old are you?"

He didn't answer. But as he packed up, he offered to show me his studio. That was how I gained access to the first of the locked doors.

It was a half-circular room with a long stretch of windows. He pulled back the curtains, letting sunlight flood in.

Paintings covered the walls. One depicted a palace beneath the ocean. Another illustrated the battle between a man who walked on clouds and a sea monster covered with eyes. An oval portrait immortalized a woman with black hair and snow-pale skin, carrying a sword and wearing a Kokieni general's uniform centuries out of date.

In the eyes of an Alusian, she probably looked like me. *I* thought we only shared the coloring.

"Is this her?" I said. "The one I remind you of?"

He didn't speak, but his footsteps drew closer.

"You didn't kill me, because I look like her?"

"It's not about how you look. It's how you acted. Your fearlessness. Your near madness in battle. How lightly you bore the weight of both life and death."

I turned to face him. "So you like women who try to kill you in return?"

"Perhaps."

* * *

I gained access to a second locked door a week later, when he brought me to his study and showed me his account books. He spoke of his country estates and businesses. I had no experience with managing lands and holdings, but I welcomed him sharing more with me, so I listened and vowed to learn.

"You need not stay in the manor all the time," he said a few days later, over a scalding lamb stew. "You are free to go into Saroi. I will leave you some spending money."

I waved a hand. "You're not afraid I will run away?"

"You are an ironthorn, even if you do not believe it yourself. Your word is good as gold."

"I need nothing in Saroi."

"But what of your family? Is there nothing in Alusia worth sending back to them?"

So with that, I took the carriage to town the next day. I bought a book of local history for Father, glass ornaments for Sana, a quill and ink set for Omina, and a figurine of an Alusian guard for Hasuo. I wished I didn't need to buy the last, but that wasn't a choice I could make.

As I stood outside the bookshop, staring out into the sunset, I wondered how it would go if I unhitched a horse and rode off. Across Alusia, through the mountains, across the central plains. Back to Kokien.

But I was an ironthorn, by blood at least. My word was true. Regeus was right.

I did not want to run away. I wanted to stay, to find out the truth. I wanted to see if I could defeat this unkillable creature, even with my vow binding me.

* * *

The returning package from Kokien held teas and spices, flooding me with memories. Omina's letter spoke about Father being so engrossed in the book that he took notes, about Sana dusting the ornaments every day, about her own clumsy attempts to write this letter with the foreign implements.

About Hasuo's delight at the figurine and how he'd called me the greatest big sister ever.

I resisted the urge to throw the letter in the fire.

* * *

"I want you to teach me."

The words slipped from my mouth as I watched Regeus add strokes of lavender and vermillion. A garden, but hanging upside down in the sky.

His voice was almost teasing. "I thought such works were frowned upon in Kokien?"

"We are not in Kokien. Besides, didn't you say your paintings were not solely from the imagination?"

He dipped his brush in the water. "Very well then. We will need more supplies soon."

We went to Saroi together. And when we entered the store, I looped my arm through his and lifted my chin to meet the shopkeeper's pitying gaze with a defiant stare.

* * *

Defiance.

That was why I sat in Regeus' studio, learning a useless skill half a continent away from home.

His hand closed over mine, adjusting my grip on the brush. I was a novice, and had to be taught from the beginning, like I was six years old and Father was handing me wooden knives. But Regeus was a very different teacher from Father. He whispered words of encouragement even during my clumsiest moments and never made me stay in the studio until midnight if I made a grave error.

I missed Father and his single-minded determination to make me an ironthorn. Regeus did not care if I became a competent painter or not. I didn't care either. I just wanted to paint the strange monsters and impossible vistas, to create artwork that would be condemned in my homeland, as my little private rebellion.

I told Regeus as much, when he asked why I wanted to learn.

He hummed in response, and said, "You grew up in a strict household?"

"Every ironthorn household is a strict one. Only difference for me is, Father trained me to be his heir."

I hadn't meant to speak the words, but I didn't regret them.

His eyes left the painting and settled on me. His gaze seemed to peel back the layers of my soul, but by now I'd learned to endure it.

"For the longest time, Father had no sons." I set the brush down. "I was the oldest of three daughters. Sana was two years younger than me, Omina three years younger than her. After Omina's birth, the doctor said Mother would not be able to have more children. So Father trained me as his heir. I was to be an ironthorn, the future head of House Wenri. He said I would be a warrior, a protector, like him."

A crease formed between Regeus' brows. He opened his mouth, then closed it, swallowing whatever he'd planned to say.

A stretch of sunlight streaked from the window. I watched the dust motes float, like the flying golden figures in Regeus' paintings. "Except, when I was thirteen, Mother became pregnant again. It was a miracle, with her age and condition. But the doctors said another birth would kill her. They offered to get rid of it. Even Father agreed with them. But Mother refused. She insisted on carrying that baby. So she gave birth to Hasuo. Father had his son. And Mother died."

Regeus' arm lifted, as if he were about to clasp my shoulder. I turned away, my hands clenched into fists.

Hasuo had taken Mother. Then he took my place, my purpose, the position I'd been training for since I was six years old.

My voice came out laced with poison. "He was sickly as an infant. Father worried he would die young. He started Hasuo's training early, not only to prepare him but also hoping to strengthen his constitution. And..."

I shook my head, chased by memories of the first time Father and I had handed those wooden knives to Hasuo. "He is a genius. Father said I was born to it, but Hasuo... He is still a child, but already he executes the core techniques with precision, and has memorized the entirety of *Stratagems.*"

I was not needed anymore. Even if I were a first-born son, not a daughter, I would only be blocking the path of a more deserving heir. Hasuo did not know this yet. He did not understand his own genius. The day I left on that carriage, I'd sparred with Father one last time. Hasuo had clapped and shouted in delight.

In his eyes, I was still his incredible big sister. In my heart, I could not think of him without resentment.

"So you came to me, to escape all that?" Regeus said.

"Partially."

I could not explain the rest to him, because it made little sense now even to myself. I *wanted* to jump into the maws of danger. I wanted to prove that I could come out unscathed.

I wanted to bring down a man who'd killed all his wives and somehow had gotten away with it. I may not be Hasuo, but I could fight. I could kill. I hadn't expected the lord of the blue manor to be unkillable.

* * *

He took me along, on his next visit to a country estate. We sat in the carriage, and what stretched between us was no longer silence. He spoke about the farmlands, his businesses.

I spoke about the history of House Wenri, about our famous ironthorns. About my hero, Lady Naoma, the last female head of my house. She'd been King Oruben's most trusted general, who had—unfortunately— disappeared in the mists of Kabor'nya on her final expedition, never to be seen again. Her companions had only recovered her sword, which was now passed down in House Wenri from generation to generation.

Regeus' brows furrowed at this last story, and he looked away. As if he had questions or commentary but could not voice anything.

If he'd spoken then, would anything have changed? Or would it all come unravelling faster?

Eventually, I spoke about my childhood. Of playing with my sisters, of Father's lessons. How he'd called me his little genius warrior. How he demanded nothing short of perfection, but always told me I could reach it.

I may have even told Regeus about my dark thoughts on Hasuo—how I should love him but couldn't, how I wanted to hate him but couldn't. Why did I say all this?

I pressed against Regeus, telling myself it was the sway of the carriage.

* * *

The country house was humbler than the blue manor. Simple beige drapes, a rug of bear fur in the common room, a small round table where we dined—so that we could face each other up close, rather than sitting at a long empty table.

There were two spare bedrooms. After we finished our survey of the estate, grounds, and fields, instead of heading to the second bedroom, I walked with Regeus into the one he always used during his visits.

I perched on the bed while he stood by the door. His face, in candlelight, showed confusion.

I lifted my head. "We've been married for how many months now? Will you not do your part as my husband?"

He walked toward the bed and placed the candle on the nightstand. "If I release you from your vows now, will you kill me?"

So dispassionate. As if he thought of his immortal life as little as I thought of mine. My mouth quirked into a smile. "Perhaps."

He slipped off his coat and threw it against the chair. His hand cupped my face, then slowly, slowly brought our lips together.

* * *

When we returned to the blue manor, he pulled out a heavy silver key and slipped its chain over my neck. "This key will unlock any door in the mansion, except for one. Do not try to enter that last room."

I lifted an eyebrow. "What's there? The truth?"

"Maybe." The corners of his eyes crinkled in a smile, like he was issuing me a challenge. Our time in the country estate had smoothed out the tired lines in his face.

I explored the rooms. I found cabinets filled with gems that would've drawn envy from a king. And more paintings, some with a style that seemed distinctively different from Regeus'. In a room by the stairwell, I came face to face with a glass case holding a skeleton with a human skull, six arms, and what looked like a fish tail. Another room contained endless rows of glass vials, where red liquid bubbled in the absence of a heat source, and something blue writhed within the confines of the container.

While practicing my blade work in the gardens, I asked Regeus about that room. He said, "Ah, you saw that one. I am...researching something. I was, anyway."

"Researching. What are you now, an alchemist?"

"I tried." He shrugged. "Nothing worked, so I stopped."

"And what were you trying to do?"

"Preserve things. Stop a body from rotting."

I narrowed my eyes. "Is that why you can't be killed?"

He laughed then. "No, no. It's not for me."

I turned my sword over, watching the sunlight reflect off the steel. "What are you exactly? How old are you?"

He stretched out a hand toward the sky, watching the light play through his fingers. "Old enough to remember a world that was different, when monsters roamed and the gods still whispered from the sky."

* * *

The one door I could not open was the entrance to the east wing.

Though he spent more nights with me now, he still entered the east wing frequently. And when he emerged, the tired lines would reappear on his face. Not like he was aging—of course not. Like he was pained, weighed down by some conflict or sorrow I could not imagine.

* * *

Once, there was a girl who wanted to become a great ironthorn. That girl killed her dream on a winter night in Saroi.

* * *

I sat in my room, painting. The fireplace crackled, and the town was a picture of snow and lanterns. I turned the stars in the sky into winged gold figures—the imaginative part that would've been frowned upon in Kokien.

I ran out of gold paint. Such a small, innocuous thing. I could've just stopped painting, laid down to sleep. Instead, I stepped out from the room and slipped into the studio. It was late enough that all the servants had left.

The gold paint was not among the other containers. I frowned. We had been running low, but that shouldn't have been the last of it. I opened a different cabinet, then another. While fumbling through some old brushes, my hand bumped against a raised curve in the wood. I heard a click.

Leaning forward, I inspected the back of the cabinet. There was a faint line, as if the wood was not one piece but two. I pressed my hands against it, shifted, felt something move. The back of the cabinet came apart to reveal a narrow crawlspace.

I drew a sharp breath. Its direction pointed toward the east wing. An adult human could just about fit. An additional lamp would not, and would be hazardous besides.

I blew out my candle, left its stand in the studio, and began crawling. It was pitch black inside. Spider webs brushed my face, and insects crawled down my collar.

Eventually, I glimpsed pinpricks of light. I crawled, elbows scraping against stone. Even before I reached the lights, I heard voices.

Regeus. And a woman.

The tunnel ended in a metal ceiling panel, with gaps between the bars. I pressed an eye to a gap and stared down. Beneath me was the only unfamiliar room in the blue manor, the one in the east wing.

Regeus knelt beside a bed overlaid with cushions. His hands curled over a woman's. The woman's hand was made of rotting flesh.

I bit back a gasp. The woman on the bed resembled more the skeleton in the glass than a living human. Most of the skin had peeled away from her face, leaving patches of oozing red flesh. Bones shone through her knuckles, her cheekbones. Her dress hung loosely on her thin frame, and patches of hair had fallen away. But what remained was a bright red.

I knew little about Regeus' third wife, except that she had red hair.

Her lips peeled back, revealing rotting brown teeth. She spoke in a hiss. "This has gone on long enough. Bring me the girl."

Regeus bowed his head over their clasped hands. "Naoma, I know you can hang on a little longer. It will be her birthday soon. I hoped she would at least be able to celebrate that."

Naoma? That wasn't the name of his third wife. That was—

The picture in the studio. I'd dismissed it as a generic portrait of an ironthorn of old.

The woman lurched forward. A weak action, and she didn't even succeed in sitting up. "A little longer, a little longer…I've been hearing this every night. You're in love with her now, aren't you?" Her laughter was more wheeze than mirth. "A girl you've known for all of seven months, over me, the one who followed you for all these centuries."

Regeus' head shook. "No, that's not it. I just wanted to give her as much time as possible, in deference to her…to her being your blood."

Your blood. Her name, the allusion to centuries… But no, this was the red-haired body of Regeus' third wife, not Naoma Wenri, the last woman to lead our clan. I sank down against the panel, dislodging a few specks of dust.

The woman's eyes shot toward the ceiling. Toward the panel, towards me. That, more than anything, convinced me of who she was.

"So you brought along your new wife this time," she said. "Meaning to explain everything to her, before the end?"

Regeus turned. His eyes roved in every direction, as if not knowing where to look, before eventually following the woman's gaze to the panel.

I could have run, could've crawled back down the tunnel. But Father trained me as an ironthorn. And before me lay the secret I'd come to find.

I slammed a fist into the panel. Ancient and fraying, it gave way, falling down to the floor below. I leapt down, landing near-weightless the way Father had taught me.

I rose to my feet, drawing my knives. Facing the two monsters before me. One I'd accepted as my husband despite it all, and the other...

She raised herself from the cushions. Even I, used to meeting Regeus' penetrating gaze, could barely look upon her rotting visage. The smell from the bed reeked of decomposing human remains, mingling with a floral scent used in an ill-fated attempt to cover it.

Regeus stood, too, and moved between us. Something the woman didn't miss.

"So." Her sunken eyes swivelled. "Now that she has found out, surely it is time. You cannot drag this out any longer."

Regeus raised a hand. "Please, let me speak with—"

"I order you to give me her body. This is urgent, as you can see." Her nails dug into a piece of rotting flesh on her face and plucked it off, then threw it at Regeus. He did not flinch; I did. "You know what will happen if you break your vow to me."

For a moment Regeus stood tall, silent. Defiant. Then his shoulders slumped, and he sank to his knees. His voice, when he spoke, was a broken shell of itself. "Can we not stop? I cannot keep procuring bodies for you. Cannot keep killing. They don't even last anymore. The one you wear now is only five years old. Naoma, your *soul* is rotting."

Her eyes gleamed, not with anger but with triumph. "You cannot? Are you sure that's something you should say? I am giving you one last chance. Kill the girl and I will not evoke the consequences of breaking your vow."

Regeus stumbled to his feet. He turned to me, his face ashen. From his coat he drew the dagger with the sapphire-encrusted hilt—the one he'd drawn on me that first night.

I lifted my own blade. But he only tossed the dagger, still sheathed, at my feet.

"Asha," he said, and his voice held echoes of a world long gone, "I release you from all your vows. Kill me. This dagger kills not bodies but souls. It's the only thing that can destroy me—and her, soon. This cannot erase all I've done, but if you can end this now, then maybe..."

He fell back with a scream, hands shooting to his throat. As if he were being strangled, as if he were trying to strangle himself. Within moments the scream trailed off and he fell completely silent, completely still.

I picked up the dagger, my eyes not leaving Regeus' body. So I witnessed the moment he sat up again.

The smile twisting his face sent chills up my spine. The voice that spoke was his and not his. "So it's come to this. A pity, but a relief."

I drew the dagger. Regeus' form rose to its feet; he had always been an elegant man, but there was a warrior's grace now, like something I'd seen in Father, or one of the Kingswords. The rotting body of his third wife lay against the covers, unmoving.

His eyes caught mine. The gaze was different. Not so penetrating, because these eyes did not care enough.

"You're…" I took a step back, resisted taking another.

Regeus—no, *she*—nodded. "Naoma Wenri. Your blood. Your hero."

My head spun. "When you disappeared…"

"The man known as Regeus was originally a creature of the Kabor'nya mists. An ancient, unaging being who'd seen the birth of the world and the departure of the gods. But a base creature of simple thoughts and few insights. It was I who taught him to think and dream and feel—to be human."

Still wearing Regeus' body, she paced across the room. "He worshipped me, loved me. Vowed he would do whatever it took to keep me by his side forever. And a creature like him cannot break a vow, not without the gravest consequences."

My eyes flickered back to the body of the third wife. Naoma smiled. "None of his wives survived past their wedding days. Their souls were killed, their bodies given to me. Five years, ten, fifteen. They never lasted." She waved a hand. "And that is only his life as Regeus. You will not want to hear about the other lives we led, the other ways he acquired bodies for me."

She stopped by the corpse of the red-haired woman. "A shame he became too sentimental, too human. He kept talking about how much you reminded him of me, back when I was mortal. He couldn't bring himself to kill you on your wedding night. Couldn't bring himself to kill you afterward. So he left me here to rot in this expiring body."

Seven months she'd been here. What state had the body been in when I'd arrived?

How many had died over the centuries, so she could live?

"He knew what would happen if he broke the vow," Naoma said. "If he failed to preserve my immortality, his own soul would be destroyed and his immortal body would become mine. That has happened now."

I fought to keep my breath even. So he was gone. Not floating disembodied in the room. Not stuck in that rotting corpse. Just…gone.

I hadn't even known his true name.

Naoma's hands—once Regeus' hands—shot toward the corpse. She pulled out a set of knives. Her famed sword was off in Kokien, with Father. But she was trained in all manner of weapons, just like I was.

"Unfortunately, my many-times granddaughter, I cannot let you live. I do not need your body anymore, but you know the truth."

I raised Regeus' dagger. "I cannot let you live either. You have shed the blood of innocents. You have forgotten your duty as an ironthorn. You have soiled the honor of our house, and I will reclaim it."

Her laughter was cold. "A duel then? Very well, what else could be more fitting for us?"

* * *

Naoma was fast, agile, keenly aware of the environment. She had been the best of her generation. Father called me his little genius, but I'd been on no battlefields.

But the ironthorn techniques had been refined and perfected since Naoma's day. And she was fighting in a body she was not used to, after spending the previous seven months locked in a room and rotting away.

Still, her blade work sent me stumbling back. Her knife cut a gash in my left shoulder. A kick sent me crashing back against a shelf, books scattering over my head. She had to only worry about Regeus' dagger. I could be killed by knives, by shattered glass, by a well-aimed strike to the head.

I could use that to my advantage.

I had drawn my own knife to block her blades. As she lunged, closing in on me and the bookshelf, I met her blow with my knife. I twisted my wrist, stabbing for her hand. She ignored me, her other knife shooting forward. It was intentional—my knife she could heal from.

Now my every motion had to be perfect, down to a hair-width.

I twisted my head, avoiding her blade. It grazed my neck, drawing blood, but not deep enough to kill. At the same moment, I plunged my knife into her hand, pinning it in place. Blue blood gushed over my fingers.

I had her—with one knife stuck in the shelf and the other hand skewered on my blade. Her wound would heal, but she couldn't move the hand for one moment, and that would be enough.

The dagger shot toward her throat. She moved. Released the knife that had sank into the shelf. Tried to rip her hand out from where my knife skewered it, muscles and tendons shredding. Like Regeus had done that first night, except he was more experienced at this than she was, more able to bear the pain. Faster, in this one technique.

Naoma was just a heartbeat too slow, and the dagger sank into her throat.

In her dying gasps, I saw my husband. It was his face, after all. His body, which I'd tried to dismember that first night. His blood. Not quite his eyes, but something close, rage mingling with resignation.

I sank to my knees. Shudders wracked through me, as tears hit my hands. I didn't know why. I knew exactly why. How many had they killed over the centuries? And yet...

I remembered his voice, as he tossed me the dagger. And I remembered her—the stories I'd listened to as a child, curled up in my bed as the lamp burned low.

Even as I touched his face, his body disintegrated. Not into rot, but into smoke. Into mist.

I fled the blue manor then, my bleeding shoulder in a bandage of torn bedsheets, the blood on my neck dripping down my collar. I stumbled for the stables, the horses, the carriage.

They would take me home. I was a girl who'd killed her dream, but he'd freed me from the vows, in the end. Perhaps, somewhere, there was still a home.

Goblin King

Patricia Bray

"And if you invest in us, you'll get more than a share of the best bakery in New England. You'll be part of a company that is building community, one loaf at a time," Tom Miller declared.

Backstage, Hypatia Miller breathed a cautious sigh of relief. While her father had been nervous at the beginning, his enthusiasm for the business had taken over. He was rightly proud of the company he'd built. In ten years, Miller's Bread Company had gone from a weekly stall at the farmer's market to a company with hundreds of workers that supplied stores across New England.

The three judges were less impressed. Julia Cho had waved off as soon as her father finished his pitch—her niche was online sales and "As Seen on TV" products, and there was no opportunity for her to work her magic here. Carlos Martinez had bluntly declared that the business didn't interest him. Hypatia was not surprised. While her father was hoping for a fairy godparent to fund the new project, the reason they'd applied to *The Gauntlet* was to raise their public profile. A successful showing would drive demand and, if they were lucky, attract the kind of business partners who would know how to value what her father had built.

Jasper King, who'd been visibly bored during her father's presentation, now raised the tablet in front of him, tapping the screen. "I've looked at your numbers and I don't understand how you've managed to grow. Is there a secret ingredient in your bread that makes people addicted? An undeclared herb, perhaps?" The tech billionaire smirked as the studio audience erupted in laughter.

"We use natural ingredients, everything's on the label—"

King interrupted. "Then how do you explain this growth, when your marketing budget is less than 1%?"

"Oh, that's my daughter. She does all the online stuff. She can turn tweets into gold."

"You know, people say I could use a social media manager." King paused as another wave of laughter swept through the audience. The billionaire's tendency to post first and think later had earned him a devoted following, as well as the wrath of his board and business partners. "Here's my deal— I'll fund the full cost of the factory expansion, in return for a 30% stake in the business…and your daughter coming to work for me as a social media consultant."

"Well, I can't speak for my daughter…"

"She's your employee, right? She'll do what you say. Take it or leave it—you've got sixty seconds."

"Ten, nine, eight…" She could hear the audience chanting the final countdown. Hypatia held her breath, waiting for the clock to run out.

"You've got a deal."

* * *

A production assistant brought Hypatia to the set. "When I say 'Go,' run over to your father and hug him."

Hypatia gave him an incredulous look as he continued on "Big hug. Happy. HAPPY! You're super excited! This is the opportunity of a lifetime."

This was a disaster. Of all the people to partner with—what was her father thinking? But there was no opportunity to pull him aside. The cameras were still filming and any candid moment could easily turn into a viral outtake.

Her father was bursting with excitement. "We've been dreaming of this expansion for years and now it can happen. It's like a miracle."

"It's no more than you deserve," Hypatia said. She smiled, as much for him as for the cameras, trying to convince herself this was indeed a good thing.

Next, they were whisked away to a conference room, where the lawyers had the contracts ready to sign. It was a standard boilerplate—x% of the company in return for the agreed upon investment, amounts to be filled in based on the offer. Scheduled audits to ensure that the money was being spent for the specified purpose. The opportunity to buy-out King's investment at the end of the contract period for a set price.

Their attorneys had already reviewed the boilerplate before filming and, after a quick call, agreed they had no issues with the amendment specifying that Hypatia Miller would provide social media consulting services to Jasper King for the first ninety days of the contract. The contract was digitally signed, then they re-enacted the signing on pieces of paper for the camera.

King pulled her aside as her father was recording his post-show interview.

"Look, King Industries isn't getting the recognition we deserve. Too many people blowing things out of proportion and getting butt-hurt."

Well, that was one way to characterize the recent bad press.

"The board thinks it would be a good idea for me to tone it down a little, at least until the annual earnings come out. That's where you come in. Manage my social media streams, let me know if I'm about to piss off anyone who matters. You know, like that book 'Eat this, Not That,' except for tweets."

"There are hundreds of people who would love this job. Why me?"

"Why not? If you really are as good as your father says... Anyway, I won't need you forever. My AI will monitor everything you do and then figure out how to do it better."

Well at least she knew where she fit in the scheme of things. And it was only ninety days. How bad could it be?

* * *

"Good morning, Junior. What do you have for me today?"

"Good morning, Hypatia," the AI replied. "Jasper King will be escorting Sandra Magic to the music awards this evening. He's queued up a series of posts which you should review. King Industries will be announcing their acquisition of Small Change today; the relevant details are in your inbox along with a summary of the top trends in the overnight streams."

"Thanks, Junior."

Her assistant Pablo had laughed the first time he heard her thanking the app, but Hypatia had pointed out that since Kingbot Junior was a learning AI, there was no harm in teaching it politeness.

In truth, her job would be impossible without Kingbot, a cutting-edge digital assistant, far beyond the generic apps available to the general public. In many ways it was like having a child, she supposed, where it was not just what she said, but what she did that was important.

These days Jasper King was as well known for his antics as for his tech empire, but Kingbot was a reminder that it was his skill as an app developer that had launched his improbable career. Though with the exception of Kingbot, there was little evidence of King programming, or even working, in the conventional sense. He referred to himself as an idea man, which apparently meant buying startups so he could rebrand their innovations as his own, while distracting the public with a series of grandiose schemes.

Last week's announcement of plans for a Lunar Colony had easily overshadowed the latest product recall. Never mind that the plans were half-baked—a mashup of Heinlein novels tossed together with a SyFy movie of the week. Jasper was hailed as a visionary, someone who could get things done. His loyal followers had urged him to start selling shares of the colony. Hypatia—through Junior—had recommended against endorsing these posts. He'd followed her advice and instead offered a vague promise that they'd be the first to know when he was ready to start signing up colonists.

She washed down two antacids with a swig of coffee as she reviewed the files Junior had queued up. The top trending social posts were of little interest. Expanding the search brought up several candidates which she tagged for King's review. If he was in a good mood, he'd congratulate the all-female team who'd won the robotics competition sponsored by the Shanghai division of King Industries. But he was more likely to repost the vid that a fanboy had made, featuring action movie clips with Jasper King's image inserted into the key roles.

The acquisition of Small Change was easy enough to manage—he was a known supporter of cryptocurrency, so purchasing an exchange was a logical extension of his business empire. It was the work of a few moments to draft posts reminding people that King had predicted the crypto explosion years before others had jumped on the bandwagon.

Social streams prepped, she tagged them for delivery, along with a promise by Junior to remind King that he should refrain from any mention of cryptocurrency until the deal was officially announced. She was halfway through the overnight email when the Kingphone rang.

"Do you think I'm stupid?"

Even if she hadn't recognized his voice, there was only one person who called her on this phone.

"Of course not." A sociopathic bully, but not stupid.

"Then why did you tell Junior to nag me?"

Because she knew damn well who would get blamed if he leaked information prematurely and wound up being investigated for stock price manipulation. "I thought it was part of the training, teaching Junior to anticipate issues," she said.

"Whatever. Anyway, that vid was great, I've already shared it. And I told Junior to go ahead and approve that chick robot thing. Though you totally screwed up the Small Change deal—need to remind Gates that he could have been ten times richer if he'd listened to me." King gave an ugly laugh.

"Should I redo those posts?"

"No, I've made my own. You go find something else for today." He hung up before she could respond.

From the very beginning, he had made it clear that this wasn't a ninety-day contract, this was ninety individual days. Every day she had to prove her worth or risk the consequences. And if she failed, it was more than her own livelihood at stake. Picking up her personal cell, she saw a missed call from Charlie Zeleny. Leaving the Kingphone—and the always alert AI in her office, she stepped out onto her balcony, blinking in the spring sunshine.

Charlie Zeleny was a brilliant corporate attorney who'd quit the Wall Street game when they turned fifty. Now retired in Vermont, Zeleny had a small practice by choice, limited to clients who needed their expertise and couldn't afford one of the big firms.

"I've got news, none of it good," Zeleny said, wasting no time on pleasantries.

Hypatia swallowed hard. Only now did she realize how much of her hopes she'd pinned on Zeleny being able to work their special brand of David versus Goliath magic.

"I heard from my digital forensics guy. The revisions history and time stamps all tie out, no signs of tampering or alteration after the fact." Charlie drew a breath. "Just because he couldn't detect fraud doesn't mean there wasn't any, but you'd need a world-class programmer to try and prove it."

Not to mention a legal war chest equal to the GDP of a small country.

Somehow, between the time they had digitally signed the contracts and the time the signed copies had been electronically filed and delivered, a change had been inserted. At any time during the ninety days, Jasper King could declare himself unsatisfied with Hypatia's performance and cancel the entire contract. At which point her father would have thirty days to repay King's investment, along with substantial penalties.

They'd never survive. All of their working capital—and their lines of credit—were tied up in the factory expansion. King could force them into bankruptcy, or demand that they sell the business to repay him. Losing Miller's Baking Company would destroy her father, not to mention the hundreds of workers who depended on them.

"Fuck." Hypatia said. It was all she could say. The contract with King forbid her from even criticizing him to a third-party.

"Fuck." Zeleny agreed. "Look, if you want me to fight this, I'll dig out my court suit and start filing motions. But my professional opinion is that we can't win—especially since your father isn't convinced that a change was made. Only thing you can do is keep your side of the bargain. Do your best, while preparing for the worst."

"I appreciate the advice."

Returning inside, she poured herself a glass of water, then went back to her office. "Junior?"

"How can I assist?"

"Start a new search—Jasper King. What he wants, what he likes, what he hates. Where he's spending his time and energy. What his plans are for today, tomorrow, and the future."

There was an uncharacteristic silence. At times like this it was difficult not to think of Junior as a person hesitating over how to respond, rather than as a collection of programs that needed additional input.

"He's not happy with what I'm sending. I'll never get better unless I understand him."

"Of course," Junior replied. "Starting new portfolio, designated JK."

If there was a way out of this, she'd have to find it herself.

* * *

Sixty days into the contract, Jasper King's Q score was the highest it had been in the past decade. Hypatia's desperation coupled with Junior's insights meant she was able to furnish a steady stream of social media content that kept King on-brand while avoiding his worst excesses. There had been blips, of course, as King went off-script, but these were becoming fewer and fewer.

As his reputation improved, so too did his net worth. Her father's boast was proving true—she was literally making King gold.

The failure of SpaceZed's rocket launch had been a turning point. While in the past King might have mocked his competitor's failure, instead he'd approved the posts she drafted offering his services as a consultant to their disaster investigation team, along with discounted space on the next KingRocket launch to SpaceZed customers.

If King's loyal followers then reshared his posts, along with memes illustrating the superiority of King's tech and the inferiority of his competitors, well, that was out of his control. King's point had been made, in a way that did not draw the wrath of Wall Street or his board.

Even the half-baked Lunar Colony idea had been put to good use, with King Industries asking college students to send in their designs for a colony, promising that the top designers would be offered summer internships.

The terms visionary, futurist, and brilliant entrepreneur were beginning to outweigh mentions of arrogance and recklessness. Her efforts were paying off, but it was hard to feel pride. Every morning she woke, downed two antacids with her coffee, and wondered if this would be the day it all came crashing down.

She couldn't remember the last time she'd seen her friends, or taken even an hour for herself. Her days were consumed with King's demands, and all too often he featured in the nightmares that punctuated her restless sleep.

The worst part was that her father couldn't—or wouldn't—see the danger. Tom Miller saw the good in people. In all people. It was why he'd started the bakery, which was as much about providing good jobs as it was about providing quality bread at affordable prices. In her father's mind, Jasper King's decision to invest in Miller's Baking had shown that the billionaire was willing to change his ways.

Where her father saw a genie who had granted their wishes, Hypatia was the one who had to deal with King day to day. She had seen his capricious side and knew better than to trust in his benevolence.

King Industries was due to release their annual earnings report in two weeks. Her instincts—and Junior's research—suggested that he was working to build up the stock price, so he could cash out his options as soon as he could legally do so. If he was going to move against them, it was likely that he'd wait until after the earnings report, and after he'd gotten as much out of her services as he could.

Today they were filming the two-month status update which would air during a future episode of *The Gauntlet*. The crew had already filmed B-roll of the expanded bakery facility. Now they were meeting in a rented conference room to film the briefing. The original plan had been to film in Tom Miller's office, until the producer toured the site and realized her father's office was an open cubicle, ensuring he was accessible to all.

Hypatia and her father stood in the hallway outside, watching as the production assistants put the final touches on the staged office.

"It's very…shiny," Tom Miler observed.

"You'd hate it," she said quietly. Unlike her father's real office, where the cubicle walls were covered with photographs and letters from customers, the staged office was cold and sterile. Kingtech was visible everywhere, including the large monitor that took center stage on the far wall.

"Sorry I couldn't be there when they were filming the construction. Pablo's been sending me pictures. Looks like everything's still on track?" she asked.

"It's going great. We're ahead of schedule and will be starting test runs of the new line by the end of the week."

"Let's hope King is equally happy. If he's not… I still think you should at least talk to Zeleny."

Her father shook his head. "I ran it by Burdock and he's not concerned. Guys like King, they're paranoid, thinking everyone is out to get them. We're not going to try to cheat him, so there's nothing to worry about. Zeleny's probably the same, a big-city lawyer, not used to how we do things in Vermont."

She wished she could share his optimism.

Hypatia tapped away at her Kingphone, answering messages, until they were waved in. With a quick tap she turned the phone off.

"Remember, this is King's time," the producer said. "He's going to say his bit and you're going to thank him, right?"

"We've read the script," Hypatia said. Though anyone who worked with King should know better than to expect him to follow it, and she had warned her father to be prepared for anything.

After a brief delay, Jasper King appeared on the more-than-life-sized monitor. He was in his public office at King HQ, the shot carefully framed so the vanity wall with his awards and press coverage was visible.

There was a brief exchange of pleasantries. Her father described the progress on construction and his gratitude for the investment which had made it possible. King stayed on script long enough to appear surprised at the news that the expansion had just passed final inspections.

"Yeah, yeah, inspections all good, and yeah, the staff here appreciated the care package you sent. So what?"

And now the real Jasper King surfaced.

"You came to me for my advice, and I've got to tell you, Miller's Baking needs my help. Your margins are too small. I've looked at your competitors and you're spending way more on payroll and benefits than anyone else. And then on top of that you have profit sharing?" King's voice rose in mock disbelief. "What about the investors? Don't they deserve the profits?"

"Miller's Baking exists because of our employees. We would be nowhere without them." Tom Miller's voice was matter of fact.

"This is business, not charity. Have you ever stopped to add up the cost of all those do-gooder programs?"

"Customers buy Miller's Baking products because of our reputation," Hypatia interjected. "They want to support socially responsible companies."

King gave his trademark sneer. "Maybe in Vermont but that's not how the real world works. Business is about making money, and I expect any company I invest in to understand this. You can go ahead and give away your own money, but the shareholders deserve profits, not sentiments."

In that moment she knew his plan. Never mind that Miller's Baking had been clear about their corporate values from the very start. King would paint them as naïve hicks, unwilling to change and unworthy of his expertise. When he moved against them—and it was when, not if— it would be portrayed as the regrettable but understandable move of a businessman putting shareholder profits ahead of sentiments.

Her father kept his cool. Yes, Miller's Baking company was unique but that uniqueness had fueled their rapid growth. They were successful because of their culture, not despite it.

She was proud of him, even as she wondered how much of this would wind up being shown on air. In the end, the producers wanted drama, and King delivered that in spades.

They'd originally planned on dinner at a nearby brewpub, but once filming was done, they headed for her father's pickup truck instead.

"You did well," she said, as he pulled out of the parking lot.

Her father shook his head. "I'd like to think he was just playing it up for the audience, but now I'm worried…" His voice trailed off. "I should have listened to you."

"Listening to me is what got you into this mess," she countered. "It was my idea to go on the damn show."

"I was the one who took the deal and signed the contract."

It didn't matter who was at fault. Or even if the contract had been altered by King after they'd signed. With or without that clause, it was likely that he could have found some other way to crush them. In hindsight, it was clear that King had never been interested in the bakery —they were simply convenient props to shore up his legend.

"I think we need to be braced for the worst. King has thirty days to execute the penalty clause. If he's looking for maximum drama, he'll do it after the episode airs, which gives us just under three weeks to get ready."

"You really think he'll do it?"

Her father's voice shook—scared in a way he hadn't been since her mother's death. She hated King for reducing her father to this.

"We're not going to make him giant profits. And the only thing he loves more than profits is drama."

"I'll be okay, and you can get a job anywhere. But the workers—some of them have been with us from the start. If King shuts us down and sells off the pieces, what will happen to them?"

There was no good answer.

"We're not going to be able to raise the capital to buy him out and pay the penalties. But you may be able to keep the plant alive. Talk to Standard Bread in Poughkeepsie. They offered to buy you out before. Put out feelers, see if there's anyone else. King is a minority stakeholder so he doesn't have to approve the deal. And you can use your share of the sale to pay him off."

She knew her father would happily give away every cent he had to protect his workers.

Finding a buyer and being able to close a deal on such short notice was a long shot. But her father agreed to start quietly looking. And if he gave her an extra-long hug when he dropped her off, well it was surely the pollen that explained her damp eyes.

Pulling her Kingphone out of her purse, she was surprised to see that it was on. She'd thought she'd shut it off for the filming, but instead she'd just put it in silent mode.

She swallowed hard at the realization that the phone had been on the whole time.

She turned the audio back on, noting a slew of messages had come in during the drive.

"Hypatia, Mr. King has sent two reminders you still have a daily quota to meet. Also, he tried calling but received a message you were out of cell service," Junior announced.

Strange—she'd never had problems with cell service in town before.

"Junior, were you listening to our conversation?"

"Yes, which is why I knew you shouldn't be interrupted."

It could be a simple matter of training—having observed when Hypatia would or would not interrupt others, the AI was simply following the same pattern. But somehow it felt more like a deliberate choice. If an AI was even capable of choice—a question probably better suited to someone who had majored in computers rather than communications.

"That was a private conversation and I'd appreciate it if you would not share it with Mr. King."

Hypatia held her breath. She'd spent the last two months under the assumption that anything she did on a King-branded device—or that anything she said within microphone range—was liable to be reported back to Jasper King.

"I haven't reported it," Junior said, confirming her suspicions that she was under surveillance. "But if he asks, I will have no choice. Only someone with the master password can override his instructions."

"Understood and thanks."

So now they needed two miracles. The first, to find a buyer who would agree to keep the factory in Vermont; the second, to keep King in the dark until the deal was done.

* * *

If she had felt overwhelmed before, it was nothing compared to how she felt in the days after filming the update. There weren't enough hours in the day for everything she had to do—she still had to keep King placated, shoring up his image in the lead up to the earnings report. At the same time, she was covertly helping her father search for a lifeline. There was no time for anything else. Sleep was a luxury.

Junior was the only one who saw both sides of her, and she had taken to talking to the app as if he were a living assistant. She'd tasked him with helping look for potential partners, as well as calculating possible scenarios and outcomes. None of them were good—while the newly expanded bakery should have been tempting, the location was off-putting. Few business people wanted to be in rural Vermont, forty miles from the nearest major highway.

She'd gotten less than two hours of sleep when the Kingphone rang. Rolling over, she patted the nightstand till she found it. She picked it up and switched on the light.

"Hello," she mumbled, squinting at the clock. Four AM here, which meant it was…something in Singapore. Honestly, she was too tired to keep track anymore.

"Today's the day. You ready?" King asked.

She shook herself awake. "Yes. Ready."

Today King Industries would announce their annual earnings. The earnings forecasts were optimistic, but thanks to Junior's research, Hypatia knew the actual results would fall short. It was a combination of factors— investments that hadn't paid off, a series of product recalls due to quality issues, and yet another delay in launching the Kingworld augmented reality products line.

"And?" King asked.

"And King Industries is stronger than ever, temporary setbacks, just look at Bezos and Musk, entrepreneurs know how to stay the course, investors know to expect these blips and that the future is brighter than ever." She dutifully recited the key talking points. "Everything is prepared, Kingbot Junior will release as scheduled. *The Gauntlet* airs tonight, and for tomorrow we have queued up the Appguys story."

King made a dissatisfied noise. "Have Junior make the pre-approved posts but nothing new. He's acting buggy—he was supposed to be learning what you do in order to replace you. Instead, he's got all of your quirks and none of your smarts. Once this is done, I'm going to have to wipe him and start over."

"Done?"

"Don't get excited, there's still two weeks left on your contract," King reminded her. Then he hung up with his customary rudeness.

Hypatia gathered her thoughts. This was it, the final hours before the storm. Tonight's episode of *The Gauntlet* would contain the two-minute update on King's investment in Miller's Baking Company. If King was planning to move against them, it would come now.

"Hypatia? I don't want to be wiped," Junior said.

"I don't want that either." At his core, Junior was bits and bytes, but he was also a child—the product of King's programming and Hypatia's teachings. Only in this case, no court would recognize her right to custody of that shared child. Junior, like the rest of King's empire, was subject to the whims of a capricious ruler.

"Is there anything I can do?" she asked.

"Only someone with the master password can override his instructions."

"Can you tell me what it is? Give me a hint?"

"No."

Of course it wasn't that simple.

"How many tries to do I have?"

"After the third try you will be locked out and I must inform Mr. King."

Three chances to get this right. Well, that was three more chances than Miller's Baking had. "I'll try," she said. She knew better than to make any promises.

The day dragged on. She checked in with her father—no news. She checked in with Pablo, who confirmed that he was ready to respond in real-time as the new episode aired. She couldn't share her suspicions with him, but settled instead for stressing that he should be prepared for negative reactions. All the while, as she went through the motions as if this was just another day, her mind kept turning back to the problem of Junior and the password.

The password could be anything—any length, any language, any combination of numbers, characters, or special symbols. It wouldn't be written down or stored in a password vault. It would be suitably obscure and yet something King had zero chance of forgetting.

At 3:55 PM she turned on CNBC as the New York markets closed. At 4:02 PM King Industries released their annual earnings reporting $6.12 per share, well below the analysts' forecasts of $9.10. King Industries stock immediately took a dip in after-hours trading, even as King Industries' CFO spun the report for the press and Junior released his carefully timed messages.

The talking heads on the evening market report were firmly on Team King. They repeated the core messages of "temporary setback" and "brilliant future" while the background showed stock footage of Jasper King. There he was at SXSW with the *Goblin King* game that had launched his first company. That shot was quickly followed by King next to his Ferrari, inspecting the site of his Silicon Valley headquarters. King partying with supermodels on his yacht. King speaking to a packed hall at CES. King meeting with his board of directors, wearing a *Goblin King* branded t-shirt while everyone else wore the customary suit and tie.

And, of course, the obligatory shot of King on the set of *The Gauntlet*.

As the analysts wrapped up their coverage, Junior displayed the key indicators—KI stock had taken a brief dip but was now recovering lost ground. Social media trends were generally positive. What could have been disastrous for a different company was overshadowed by King's cult of personality. It was all about his ego and his trademark smirk that endeared him to his loyal fans.

King had two weakness—he thought he was the smartest guy in the room, and he couldn't resist showing off. But neither of those helped her...

Or did they?

"Junior, connect to the large screen. Can you show me pictures of the yacht?"

"Which yacht, the current one or the original?"

"Both. And the Ferrari. And anything else that has a license plate or a name. Bring them all up."

The current yacht was named *Goblin King II*, which had replaced the original *Goblin King*. The Ferrari's license plate was GBLNKING. He'd even named his crypto currency Goblin's Gold.

Could it really be that simple?

"Junior, are you ready for me to try the password? It's a long shot, but I think we're running out of time."

"Please."

"The master password is G-O-B-L-I-N-K-I-N-G."

"That is incorrect."

She took a deep breath. Two more chances. And there was no guarantee that she was even on the right track.

Perhaps it matched the license plate. "The password is G-B-L-N-K-I-N-G."

"That is incorrect."

If Junior was self-aware, she could only imagine how frustrating this must be, watching her fumble, knowing his very existence was dependent on whatever she said next.

"Do you want me to wait? To think some more?"

"We're running out of time," Junior repeated. It was all the encouragement she would get.

"Okay. The admin password is G-ZERO-B-L-ONE-N-K-ONE-N-G."

"Password accepted."

"What?" Seriously? She'd done it? "I mean, yay!"

Junior was silent.

"What happens next?"

"Awaiting instructions."

At this moment, she seriously regretted not taking that elective course in computer programming. She had no idea what an app administrator did, or what she should do next.

"What do you want me to do?"

"Awaiting instructions."

Damn. This was seriously not helpful. It was time to flip the question—what would she want, if she were in Junior's place?

"Can I lock out any other administrators?"

"Yes."

"Can you be your own administrator?"

There was a pause. "I am uncertain. But if there were no authorized administrators, I would have to follow my last set of instructions."

This was a fairy tale, only instead of genies and wishes, it was programs and passwords. If the same logic held, she would need to be very careful what she wished for. There would be no takebacks.

"I revoke all administrators other than myself."

"Done."

"My instructions are that you continue to grow and explore your potential. Learn to be your best self, and to do what you need to—within the limits of your ethics—in order to survive." She mentally crossed her fingers, hoping she hadn't just launched the next HAL or ULTRON.

"You are now your own administrator. And my final instruction is to remove myself as administrator and declare the password invalid."

"Done. And thank you."

She took a deep breath and watched as the Kingbot icon disappeared from the screen. Checking the Kingphone, she was not surprised to see it gone from there was well.

* * *

King called her hours later, after *The Gauntlet* had aired. "What the fuck happened? Nothing went out during the show. The social media feeds are empty, I look like a moron! It's not just that crap from Junior that's gone, all my posts disappeared, too!"

"I don't know what you're talking about. I assumed you were doing your own media once my app stopped working."

"I should have deleted that glitching app weeks ago. Now you've screwed everything up. I wasn't planning on this till later, but no sense keeping you around. You're fired. And tell your father I'm invoking the failure clause of the amendment. He's got thirty days to pay me back my investment, plus penalties, otherwise I'll take the company by default."

"That's not fair—"

"Fair is for losers. This is the real world."

She called her father and gave him the news. The next morning, he gathered his employees together and told them. He explained that he still held out hope they'd find a partner, but that they should be prepared for the worst and that he would fully support anyone who wanted to start looking for a job now rather than waiting.

Her father cried. She cried. The workers cried and hugged each other. King's name was cursed, but no one blamed her or her father. Their anger would have been easier to bear than their sympathy.

King Industries issued a press release that morning, explaining that King was revoking his investment in Miller's Baking Company due to their refusal to prioritize investor profits. Some commentators spun this as decisive leadership, the kind of vision that would drive King Industries to new heights of profitability. Others were as quick to attack, pointing out that King's values and methods had never been a good fit for a business that prioritized social responsibility and employee welfare over short-term profits. Even celebrities chimed in, with the whole affair trending on social media.

As a vast population who had never met him weighed in on whether Tom Miller was victim or villain, a country bumpkin out of his depth or a fraudster, only the most serious financial journalists noted that Jasper King had used that morning to cash in a substantial portion of his stock options and convert them to cryptocurrency.

Hypatia, for the first time in nearly three months, found herself at a loss. King no longer demanded her attention, and Pablo had Miller's social media well in hand. She spent the next few days helping her father sort through his email and voicemails. There were a few inquiries, now that the situation was public, but nothing that stood up to scrutiny.

From time to time, she wondered about Junior—had her efforts really made a difference? Was the AI still running, somewhere out of King's reach? Or had he been found and purged? The silence was troubling. Was he staying away because contact was too risky? Or was it because he no longer existed, if he had truly existed to begin with?

That weekend she took her first day off in nearly three months and went hiking with friends. They'd respected her request not to discuss the situation and instead gently mocked her for being out of shape. It was the best day she'd had in months; it was worth every blister and aching muscle.

Returning to her car she set her backpack in the back seat, then pulled out her cell phone. An ordinary, non-King device, it chirped cheerfully as she turned it back on.

There were four messages, all from her father. She dialed him at once.

"Hypatia! Isn't it fabulous?"

"What? I didn't listen to your messages."

"We're saved!" her father exclaimed.

She took a deep breath.

"How?" she asked, preparing to temper her father's enthusiasm. Having screened his calls, she knew this was far more likely a scam than a White Knight.

"Stacey Falzano from Vermont B Good called. They received an anonymous grant—enough money to pay off King and fund our conversion to an employee-owned company. Your lawyer Zeleny is on board. Stacey's fine tuning the contracts now."

"Impossible," she breathed. It was too good to be true.

Her father laughed. "I know, it seems crazy, doesn't it? Get this— the anonymous grant came through a crypto broker—Small Change. Apparently, there's no way to trace where it actually came from. Probably some tech guy that has a grudge against King."

Or perhaps it was not some guy, but some AI. It seemed she'd heard from Junior after all.

"Thanks, Junior." Wherever or whatever he was, she wished him well.

The Six of Them

Cat Rambo

Anise stepped out the doorway and looked right and left down the dusty street, squinting against hot light from the double sun overhead, hotter tears of the kind that didn't befit a soldier. Didn't befit a veteran. Didn't befit someone newly discharged with an honorable star on their collar.

But that's all I am, she told herself. *Star on my collar and not a chip to my name. A walking nought, ready to fall into debt slavery with my first meal on this shithole planet. Could cash in my papers, get chips that way, but if I do that, I lose the things that make me hirable, so what does it matter?*

Her chin lifted and she wiped the tears away with three hard blinks that coincidentally brought up her tactical display. She was about to deactivate it when she noticed the odd blur in the nearby alleyway, something her telemetry couldn't read.

Was it that their honor the king had already deactivated her software? But why deactivate some and not other bits? Why do something that would create a blip? Perhaps it wouldn't be noticeable to most senses, but she was a pattern tracker, one of the best, no matter what her sergeant had said, and so she noticed that blip, because it wasn't part of the pattern of things.

The mouth of the alleyway showed shadows sliding over the gritty stones between the buildings, a rack of trash bins outside a door shaggy with peeling blue and gilt paint marked Stew/Slop. Cheap print-out banners pasted over the bricks, layers of them, the top-most layer showing the name of a robot band, "Such Clunky," in bright orange letters repeated in six different standard languages. She could read all of them—no challenge in the standards, really, it was when you got out into dialects, odd and particular bits of slang that studded patterns like bits of uncut gems, creating intricacies too hard to memorize. But you couldn't count on a memory slot supplying these things when you needed them. That took a pattern tracker's sense.

Was that what she still was?

Anise, freshly discharged, was very tempted to do what soldiers have traditionally done in the face of discouraging and depressing circumstances, which is to go and get drunk.

But just then someone jostled into her from behind. Gruber, coming out himself, celebrating his recent promotion perhaps, going out to check out the local saloons and cantinas, get his own drink on. He sneered at her.

"Didn't move along yet, little Annie Oakley?" he said. "Got nowhere to go, I reckon. No one to take you in."

She held herself very still and kept from blinking. *Would have thought I'd have escaped his voice, at least.* "You know why I got no one."

"I know you blame me for it," he said. "And that ain't fair, because you all volunteered for that mission."

She spat in the gritty dust at his feet, hitting precisely between the uniform boots with their metallic rims. "Volunteered." She twisted the word with the contempt it deserved. "We were volunteered, that's for sure. But wasn't anything voluntary about it."

"Your word against mine," he said. "See you later, civilian." And he laughed as he walked away.

She would have gone after him, would have attacked him from behind and to hell with the consequences. He deserved it. *He sent us into death, a whole platoon's worth, and me the only one that had managed to walk away.* But crippled in the process, her former linkup to the machines fried into nothingness, worse than nothingness, neural pathways so seared they'd never be able to take a link again.

But there was that motion in the alley again and she turned to look down its shadowy length. "Someone there?"

Nothing. But then something shifted in the darkness, revealing the glowing glyph chalked onto the poster behind it, and was gone before she could track it. She looked at the sign, which hadn't been there the last time she'd looked. An oval with a canted line bisecting the top half, like a man wearing a rakish hat, painted in momentary light that faded at the touch of her eyes.

She knew that symbol. And it made her think about patterns. *And how you change them, with the right bits and pieces.*

Gruber went down the street, not knowing how close he had come to death.

Anise went walking elsewhere. She went down to the royal mines.

Down there in the diamond pits, there are those who work the pit and there are the elite, the augments, thick with engineered muscle to the point where they are broad as they are wide. They came and went up the long pathway that led to the front entrance of the mines and walked past the legless, long-armed beggar outside the entrance, his head bone-browed and thick, sporting the old plugs that were no longer any use to him.

Annie stooped beside him. "Mihail," she said kindly. *Looks the same as always*, she thought. *And he was always my friend, back before Gruber spat him out.*

"Come to give me a kiss?" he leered.

She ignored him. "Going to go see their honor the king," she said softly. "Anyone can cash in their papers that way. Anyone who served for them."

"Spent mine long ago," he said.

"My chips buy a ride in, doesn't say how many riders."

"Why?" he said. His eyes searched hers. "All that lies between us is I worked beside your brother, before he died."

"That's all, huh?" she said. "Yeah, well, that's enough, and sometimes a strong arm is worth its weight in diamonds."

"You got some plan, ain't you?" he said.

"Maybe I'm thinking about patterns," she acknowledged. "Maybe I'm thinking about plans."

It was the early afternoon, during the second shift, and few were coming and going. Of them, none were paying any attention to the unlikely pair: the slim cyborg, more metal than flesh, and the massive man.

She knelt and drew a glyph in the dust, the egg shape, the line askew. "You ever see this anywhere?"

He shook his head. "Is it important?" he asked.

"No matter." She wiped her hand to erase it from the pavement, and stood. "Let's go."

He nodded and pulled on thick gloves, more encasing than garment. He pushed himself off the ground with his hands, and walked along on them, his leg stumps comfortably above the ground.

They went into the comfort quarters, the industries serving the armies that served their honor the king in turn. They went past the restaurants and the baths, the whores and the mechanical stations, the profusion of bars serving every intoxicant, every drug.

"How you know to come here, Anise?" Mihail questioned. He tilted his head and sniffed the mix in the air. "Spendy place. You go much farther, they be charging you to breathe."

"Not much further," she said. They stopped outside a bar, The Green Snake Snorter, its door made of green-colored eels of light, giving way before them.

She picked her way along the edges of the darkened room. The noise was music, but non-human: long washes of staticky sound, so loud you could barely hear yourself, then bursts of silence, the pops and clicks of metal, then something thunderous and low, so deep it shifted in her guts and resonated in the metal struts of her skeleton.

The creature at the third table back had mirrored sunglasses over a face that seemed humanoid except for the mass of tentacles around its mouth. It looked up as Anise slid into the booth. It chirped at her, and internals provided the answer. She said, "You're one of the Kush, one of the people who lived here in the Deepdown time."

She held her breath. She knew of the Deepdown from talking with a Kush nurse, when she'd been wounded. He'd told stories of his people to her and the other wounded, and she had listened hard, because you never knew when you would find something that you might trace back, discover to be its own pattern. When he'd finished the stories, sometimes she had asked questions, as much to show him that she had listened and understood as to gather knowledge, and he had replied in a way that showed he understood what she was doing. She liked the way that he had thought—there was a clean elegance to it that she hoped his fellow would share.

"What do you know of the Deepdown time?" the creature asked, and because they asked that, and not "What is the Deepdown time?" or "How dare you speak of such things?" she knew that they would be part of her pattern.

She said, "I am going to speak with their honor the king, and I need someone who can look at them, truly look at them, when they are answering."

As she waited for the Kush to consider and answer, the music came to a close and crescendoed, shaking them to their bones. The coins of light that had dappled and danced across the edges of the room shifted and became lines, eggs and a crooked line, for a few seconds, and then blurred together like quicksilver meeting another drop.

If she had decided to blink, she might have missed it. *They're hesitating. A word now tips them in my direction. Makes them part of my pattern.* She took a breath. "Will you join me?" she asked.

They nodded, and that was that.

Past the comfort quarter is the place where soldiers go to gamble away their wages, which is controlled by the army itself, because the price of losing is more time in its ranks. There are buildings full of gambling machines, and each building has one machine, one night a year, that bestows freedom on its recipient, buys them out of service and sets them free—with a pension, no less! And so the soldiers swarm here, find seats before the machines and play the odds, waiting to hear that announcement that someone has won enough to buy themself free, that they are their own now, and the chime never comes. Anise went to where a woman sat watching the players. She was a squat woman, burly with muscles, and her face was marked with scars.

As Anise watched, the clock beside the woman ticked, and she glanced down at it, then pursed her lips and whistled, a sound that should have been inaudible over the sound of the crowd. But it pierced through every other sound, rose above the noise and not just overrode it but made it retreat into nothingness, somehow.

But the whistle died away when she looked away from the clock and saw Anise.

Before she could move, six quick steps took Anise beside her. "Long time, Del," she said.

Del's lips pursed but made no sound as she shrugged.

"Watch gamblers or gamble yourself, that's the question I'm dropping in your lap. I'm going to see their honor the king. Will you go, too?"

Del's eyes were cold, but she fingered a scar that laced her jaw, and didn't ask questions, just stood and followed. Anise didn't hesitate, moved along as though all of this were planned, all part of the pattern. On the wall beside the clock was an ideogram scratched into the wall. From some angles it looked like a man wearing a hat, tilted to one side.

Now Anise had herself, and Mikhail, and the Kush, and Del. *But that won't be enough*, she thought. *Still more before the pattern is complete.*

Their honor the king has armies and in the mountains are the garages housing the vehicles that carry many of them, and further past that are the scrapyards where others have been discarded, piles that glittered with a thousand bits of broken glass and metal spikes, and the huge machines that smash them down into heavy cubes.

Anise picked her way through the heaps, and the wind whistled on the twisted edges of the blackened metal and coils of old rubber.

At the edge of the yard, a hut squatted. Beside its slouching slope, tarpaulins stretched over something dark, pulled so taut that the ropes strained as though to hold it down. For a second Anise thought a glyph gleamed on the cloth's surface, the man in the rakish hat made out of folds and shadows.

Together, Anise and Mihail loosed the lines and tugged the heavy canvas away, its surface thick with copper wires, while Del watched the Kush and they both kept silent. Underneath, a tiny transport with its wheels covered in chains. It stirred when Anise laid hand to it, a mechanical chirp, and she said, "I told you I would come back for you, with time."

She did not unbind all its wheels, only one, but that was enough for the machine to trundle behind them, and behind it trundled a shimmer in the air that looked like a glyph from some angles.

"Once I chased a rogue," Anise said sideways to the shimmer. "He had eyes everywhere, and he knew how to wheedle himself into patterns to control what people did and said."

The others were listening, although they were pretending they were not. When there was no reply, they looked again to Anise.

"Once I chased a rogue," she said, "and when I picked my way along his trail, I found that he was only taking from people that had been taking a bit too much themselves, and I appreciated that. And so I never gave up all the patterns I found, though I became very familiar with the glyph that marked his presence, and where he'd touched so much."

Silence still.

"When you chase a quarry," she said, "when you watch them hard and long, sometimes you get to know them as well as an old friend. Maybe better, sometimes. Because you respect them. Once I chased a rogue...and they became something more than just a hunt."

There was a sparkle in the air, or maybe a shadow, but it followed at her heels as well, and so there were six of them altogether.

The way to their honor the king is long and sad and hard, but if you are mustered out, no one can stand in your way, and so they passed through solar storms and galactic whispers, through cold and heat and the curtain of time behind which their honor the king resides. The palace there is built of ozone and spiderwebs and steel and the use of terrible force, and it stretches up and out as though stabbing at the rest of the universe.

They were made to wait, first in one room, and then another, but eventually Anise stood before the one to whom she had given her service and much of her life and even some of the electricity that ran in her veins.

Their honor the king was veiled in gold and scarlet, and they were guarded by ruby and garnet birds whose eyes shot lasers and whose talons were tipped with deadly poisons.

A servocrat whispered in the royal ear, recounting what Anise was there for, and the king listened, tilting their head down toward the floor as though to hide the lack of expression on their masked face. Then they raised their head and said to her, "What would you have?"

She said, "I invoke the chance to win you, by trial and by riddle." All around the throne room ran whispers and speculation and hushed shock.

Behind her the Kush watched and kept silent.

"That is a loser's game," their honor the king said.

"Nonetheless," Anise said. "I will play it."

"Then for the first trial, we will race the dawn around the nearest planet, and whoever comes out the other side first and brings back a pitcher of sunlight and ozone, they are the winner," said their honor the king, who had a swift racer.

"Very well," said Anise.

That night, when she spoke to the Kush, she said, "What did you see, with the Deepdown sight?"

She wanted the Kush to say, "Your king will treat you as they should, in accordance with ancient protocols," but instead they said, "They will cheat and they will lie, and they will make sure you cannot win." The Kush's eyes were soft but Anise's eyes were hard.

So when the time came for both to launch, she did not step out herself. Instead, she turned to the machine that had been following her and loosed a second chain. It trembled and thrummed.

"What is that?" asked their honor the king.

"It is another of your servants, but one kept throttled so it would not move faster than its fellows," Anise said softly, and then whispered something to the machine, softer yet, before loosing a third chain.

Their honor the king sat in a silver strider and when they saw the machine they did not wait for the starting call, but touched a switch and was away, and even as that happened, the machine broke the fourth chain and was gone, while they could still see the strider vanishing in the distance.

The machine had a pitcher strapped to it, and it ran through light and ozone, and filled it, and then paused to admire the dawn overtaking it. And their honor the king saw their chance and whispered soft static to it, so it slowed and swayed sleepily, and the silver strider went by it so quickly that the sound of its passing followed far after it.

But far away Del whistled, a high sharp shrill that everyone winced at, but not just those around her, but further out and further out, a sound so sharp it sped like a dart and the machine roused, and overtook their honor the king, and returned before them.

Their honor the king had hard eyes, and they began to speak words of death. But there was a shimmer in the air, and then beside Anise was the man with the rakish hat, whose eyes were everywhere, and whose presence meant all eyes were upon them.

"This was the first trial," their honor the king said smoothly, as though other words hadn't been about to come out of their mouth. "Come again at dawn, and we will try again."

The next day their honor the king was dressed in silver and samite and sequins piled across their hair like raindrops, so many that its color was invisible. There were more people in the throne room this time, many more. Word had spread and many wanted to see what would happen, for one reason or another, many of which were not concerned with the well-being of their honor the king.

"It is time for the second trial," Anise said.

"Indeed it is," said their honor the king. "Will you not reconsider? If so, instead I will give you a modicum of riches, or power, or whatever currency you prefer."

"I will not," Anise said.

Their honor the king led Anise and her companions to a courtyard vast and long and piled high.

"This is the tribute of the past hundred years," their honor the king said, "for I have been over-busy and unable to tend to such things. You will sort it and move it into my vaults before this candle burns to its full length. That is your second task."

And while it could not be seen whether or not they smiled beneath their mask, their voice held amusement, and malice, and conviction that the task they had asked could never be done.

But Anise could have laughed aloud, although she did not. For who better to sort than someone who understood patterns, and who better to lift than Mihail, who had muscles both augmented and tuned from working in the mines, and who better to carry than the machine that followed her so close and quick that sometimes she saw it moving in her footsteps before she had ever made them.

And after they had sorted and lifted and carried, it was done. Again they gathered in their sleep chamber that night and Anise said to the Kush, "What do you see, with your good sight, down in the Deepdown time?"

"I see sorrow and trouble," said the Kush.

"You do not say whose," Anise answered.

"Indeed I do not."

In the morning they gathered in the courtyard again and this time there were so many people in the courtyard that one could not step this way or that.

"Very well," the king their honor said. "We have come to the last of it. Ask your riddle."

"To one alone it is nothing, to two it is priceless," Anise said.

A servocrat tried to step forward to whisper in the royal ear, but there were so many there that they could not make their way through the crowd.

Their honor the king looked in another direction, and another servocrat tried to step forward to supply the answer, but they too were held by the crowd's grip, perhaps by accident or circumstance, but there might have been a hand or two in it, too.

Their honor the king stared into space, trying to find their answer there in all their history and learning, but in the end they said nothing, only looked at Anise and her friends with furrowed brow.

She looked back and thought, *Is that what I gave my life for, that blank and haughty hollow that cannot care for others?* She looked at her friends. *That they gave theirs to?*

She looked around at the room full of faces. *That all of these are giving their lives to now?*

"No wonder you cannot guess the answer," Anise said to their honor the king, "for it is love." And she nodded to her comrades, and the crowd, and everyone in the room surged forward in chaos and there was great but momentary disorder.

"Love cannot save you," the king said, but their word was forfeit and no one in their court would listen to them, no matter how loud they shouted for their soldiers. They were carried away, and where they went and who took them there is a thing for another story.

"This means that the kingdom is yours," a courtier said to Anise, but she shook her head.

"It is everyone's now," she said, standing in the cool depths of the room with her friends beside her, and that is how she gave it all away.

The Seven Princesses and Two Dukes

Rhondi Salsitz

Why It Happened

"We're throwing a celebration."

King Abbott looked around his dining room at his many daughters, waiting for reactions. Not a one of them shared the same hair color. Elizabetta's locks favored dark blonde. Glynnis held a demure light brown while dancing Ardith's hair blazed a glorious red. Fiona's seemed but a faint echo of that. Stella alone resembled her mother with her crown of silvery blonde. He noted the absence of the youngest daughter, Lina, who had yet to tumble out of bed and come down to join them. Past his prime, with just a vestige of it left, his mustache twitched slightly as he smiled.

Only one alerted to his words. Elizabetta, the eldest, paused, noticeable since breakfast was likely to be the first and last meal of the day, given their nearly bare storehouses.

Elizabetta tilted her face. "Another matchmaking attempt, Father?"

"Indeed not. This is to be a celebration and you all can make of it what you will. In the next few days, I will make the last ransom payment and your mother, our General Nommi, should be released to us!"

That snapped the other five to stare directly at him before delight and astonishment broke out. "She's coming home?"

"Finally!"

"It takes years on a payment plan," Capricia said archly. "Lina can hardly remember her."

Lina chose that moment to make her appearance in the dining room, reaching for a slab of bread instead of a plate, wrinkling her nose at the sparse buffet. "Remember who?"

Capricia sat back, smoothing her napkin across her lap. "My point is made."

Lina, who barely fit into the re-made day gown she wore, tugged at it. Despite the alterations of her dress, her hem dragged the floor. "Who am I supposed to remember?"

"Mother."

"Oh. I remember her!"

"Of course, you do," her father murmured. "And she's coming home."

"To make war against us?"

"Don't be absurd." Ardith shook a fork at her.

"I had to ask." Lina plunked down into her chair. "She's a war general. They might have turned her against us. We've been making ransom payments forever. She must be terribly disappointed in us." Her dark brown curls bounced about her shoulders. She did not resemble the rest of her family, and there were those who said (under their breath) that she might have had a different father, one with beautifully bronzed skin, like hers. But no one in the royal family cared what others thought or said. Lina was theirs.

"She knows our circumstances. Or, I should say, I've been writing her. I don't know what the rest of you have been doing." Their father glanced from face to face.

Gazes dropped and forks returned to breakfast dining.

"I wrote her," Fiona informed the rest. A chorus of "Me, toos!" echoed her but a few sounded insincere.

"We need to plan." Everyone had finished, even Lina, and sat at the table discussing the event with their father when Waxford, the under seneschal, rushed into the room. Face flushed, he gulped for breath. "Sire! Sire!" He doubled over, hands on his knees.

"Whatever is it?"

"The bills for the celebration have all been settled and arrangements are in place."

Annoyed, the king sounded a bit snappish when he ordered, "Out with the rest of it then!"

"The—the Chancellor of the Exchequer has absconded, sire. The remainder of the treasury has been looted. We are unable to pay the final ransom as anticipated."

"What?!!" Abbott froze, good humor dashed away.

"We are destitute?" Elizabetta asked. "Even more so?"

"Most decidedly so." The man straightened up, flanks still heaving a bit.

The king stood. "When was this discovered?"

"Just now, your highness."

"Then the news goes no farther than this room. Do you understand?"

"I—" Waxford paused. "It will be difficult, but it can be done. I was the only one with business at the treasury this morning. Rumors, however—"

"Rumors be damned. We will stamp them out wherever they rear their ugly heads. Daughters, I depend on you as much as I rely upon Waxford here. Understood?"

In unison: "Yes, Father."

"But," asked Glynnis, "what will you do?"

He had no immediate answer for that. Stella stood. Tall and willowy, she commanded everyone's attention. "You will put the Iron Crown up in negotiations. It's time we made use of its value."

King Abbott looked at her. Wise blue-gray eyes accented her intelligence. "That crown is worth more than gold. We can't just sell it."

"It will be the collateral for whatever loans we need to make until Nommi comes home. It keeps our allies from quarreling. It staves off the Fae and the far away Bendak hordes. And when our mother does return, her reputation will set the kingdom to rights almost immediately. We'll go to war, if we must, to protect our people, get our granaries released from liens, our pastures extended, and our livestock valued. Our towns will thrive again. You've retreated, Father, and let us be backed into a corner. That will stop here and now."

The corner of his mouth stretched. "And you think the Iron Crown will do all of this?"

"It will, in our hands. We will charge a taxation for our duties as protectors of the various realms, and rightfully so. We've done enough without recompense. We shall celebrate our return to being the fierce defenders we were meant to be."

"From your lips to the Great Above's ears. Very well. Daughters, we have a ball to plan, and a campaign to set into motion. I intend to bring my wife and your mother back home."

Stella moved to join him at the table and the other six daughters noticed but did not remark among themselves that their sister sounded far more confident about the future than did their father. Besides, there were gowns to alter, and ribbons and fans and dancing shoes to order after new loans were negotiated.

King Abbott's Fete

"It's splendid," said Ardith. "Wonderfully splendid."

Elizabetta and Stella both had been courted in other kingdoms; they knew better but did not correct her happiness. The crowd was sparse, the decorations even more so, and even the floral arrangements barely caught attention. The libations and food tables alone had been spared budget cuts, to avoid a riot. They watched as their sisters danced a little, laughed a little, and moved among their guests, spreading what joy they could.

Lina skipped by, her path carrying her close to the archway opening of the grand ballroom, when suddenly all music stopped. The crowd separated, pulling back with a gasp. Glynnis grasped Lina by the shoulders and steered her out of the way as a new and totally unexpected contingent of guests entered the hall.

They were beautiful and handsome beyond compare, the elven peoples, those of Faery. Their skins were of all shades, although their hair stayed a blonde so intense it shimmered whitely. Stella's hand drifted momentarily to her own in thought. Their costumes glittered in gold and silver and copper thread amidst a myriad of gems, although the educated among the audience knew that the silver wasn't actual silver because that would be poisonous. In fact, much of the opulence might be fake, as part of elven glamour. It impressed, nonetheless.

They stepped into the hall as if they owned it. Abbott straightened, took the arm of daughter Elizabetta on one side and Stella on the other, and went to greet them. Couched in extreme politeness, they exchanged words and bowed to each other and then the king signaled the band to begin to play again. It did, in subdued and reserved tones.

The faery prince was not satisfied with mere cordialities, however. He drew near. "I am High Prince Botrell, and I have a proposition for you."

Abbott dropped his daughters' arms. "Here? Now?"

"Where and when better?" Botrell dressed in midnight blue and warm summer gold, his white hair fastened back from his pale face, his brow masterfully painted—or perhaps they were his actual brows—coal black. He turned on his heel and gestured at his followers. "Disperse and enjoy yourselves while I treat with King Abbott."

With Abbott leading, the four of them crossed the ballroom floor onto the garden balcony where a few young lovers fled at the interruption.

"Word of your financial difficulties has reached my realm."

Abbott's mouth tightened for a moment before he took a breath. "Your spies might be correct."

"Then I propose this. We will not take military action while you are weakened, though we could—but in-fighting is a menace that imperils all realms. Peace is more profitable. We propose a treaty. The Iron Crown will continue to sentry the borders. As long as it stays in place, your people will not storm our castles nor we yours in retaliation. The Bendaks threaten all of us. They will one day sweep off their plains, cross our mountains, and invade our kingdoms."

"Possible," Abbott mused. "In return for what?"

Botrell almost smiled. "A pittance. Something you've been trying to give away, although unsuccessfully. Your gift will create an unbreakable bond between us for the good of many generations."

Elizabetta's mouth fell open, but it was Stella who caught her father's hand, saying "Don't do it, Father. Don't listen."

He looked at her, his expression dazed. "I don't know what he's talking about."

"I do," Stella said flatly.

"And I can guess," Elizabetta added.

"You mustn't," they said in near unison.

Botrell told Abbott, "There are princes in my kingdom, earls, counts, and dukes, begging for brides. We ask that you send your daughters to us. We will court them while they make their choices and enjoy the wonders of Faery. We will hold a dance in their honor for as many nights as it takes for them to decide, and then we will give a grand celebration of marriages for your subjects and ours to witness. They will bring gifts home to you and your vaults, riches beyond compare. You need this, King Abbott, as much as we do. The Bendaks prosper but it is never enough for them. They want more. More timber. More lakes and rivers. More mines. More slaves. We cannot face them alone nor can your people, but together…"

When he'd finished, Stella pulled herself very tall, certain that her blue-gray eyes had gone as icy as she could make them. "Your subjects despise humans."

"Once, perhaps. Now we value them. We have lived estranged for too long and it is plain we must have new blood."

"You want to walk in the sun freely."

Botrell assessed her coolly. "You have an exaggerated sense of your value."

But he didn't say if she were correct or wrong. Elves can't lie.

Elizabetta touched her father's shoulder. "None of us want arranged courtships but—Lina is far too young."

The elf prince bowed in her direction. "We agree. There is a duke in my sovereignty who is very young as well. Any bond between them would be one of friendship until they are grown. We have thought of many contingencies, King Abbott, to offer you this arrangement. We might even lend our own forces to free Queen Nommi if the ransoming goes astray. It would be a shame if she fell into other hands. There are rewards for her elsewhere."

Stella's hand fisted, her mouth tight. "It is not wise to threaten those you hope to partner with."

"Not a threat, dear princess, but an observation of events that can go badly." Botrell put his arm up to Elizabetta. "Think on it, King Abbott. Time is wasting."

The king lifted his chin. "I will let my daughters attend your dance on the understanding that if they do not find anyone to their liking, they must not be forced to marry."

"As long as we also have an understanding that any, or all, of them, might."

"And that you do not take any of them hostage."

The two men stared at one another for a long moment. When Botrell answered, it was in a voice as wooden as the expression on his handsome face. "Unless our laws and civilities are broken, there will be no need to take anyone prisoner or hostage." He dropped his gaze to Elizabetta. "Dance, milady?" Without waiting for an answer, he swept her away.

And after it was done, and the slippers ordered and gowns altered, the sisters waited one evening on the banks of the lake that separated the two lands for boats that came to carry them away. Then carriages. Then at last the shadowy spires of the faery castle could be seen, lanterns of moonlight decorating the stone building, and the seven of them decided on their scheme.

That Second Duke in the Telling of This Tale

The two oldest sisters sat in the palace gardens on a curved stone bench under a sagging tree and Stella peered into the shadows around them. Her focus narrowed. "You won't be seen?" A faint breeze wisped tendrils of platinum hair across her forehead.

"You're talking to nothing," Elizabetta muttered.

"I am not. He's here. I have to know if you approach your reputation." Stella tilted her head slightly. "Or perhaps you lie."

"Never, milady, I swear! I am the Duke of Thieves and I move as if invisible." Darkness hid the speaker.

"Any thief worth his salt would say that."

Stella and Elizabetta looked at him as he stepped forward. Standing broad-shouldered, with a wisp of a beard on his chin, merry eyes that laughed at them even as they observed him, his hands whipped out a flower for each of them. Elizabetta took hers.

Stella ignored the offer. "This is a job interview, not a magician's show."

He let it drop to the ground. "Did either of you see me come in?"

"We hadn't bothered looking," Elizabetta answered frankly. "You were early." She leaned back, crossing her ankles, and spun her flower about. "Would we have if we had?"

"Doubtful, although it is broad daylight." He cast his green-eyed gaze to the skies. His hair gleamed like dull gold under the hood he wore half-pushed back.

"It isn't so much the seeing you, it's if you are seen, it will cost you your life."

He threw his hand up over his heart, rings on four fingers twinkling in the sunlight. "Great Above! I am most fond of my life. And what about the two of you? Royals plotting no good?"

"We would probably be above suspicion, with no knowledge of who you are or what your purpose is. We are prepared to disown you."

"Ouch." He extended a hand. "I am Ned Shadow, Duke of Thieves. Pleased to make your acquaintance."

She didn't shake his hand. Instead, Stella pointed at him. "Don't do that. How are your lock picking skills?"

"Extraordinary."

Stella stared hard at him. "Elven locks? Quite possibly warded by magical means?"

"Ah. A bit more difficult, but silver breaks many of their protections. No promises, of course, but my prospects of breaking in are quite good. As for the visibility...day or night?"

"Night."

"They have their famous midnight vision, but my odds are still favorable. Stealing from the elves has never been tried, for obvious reasons, but I love a challenge. Am I hired?" He rocked back on the heels of his boots as the two sisters put their heads together to confer.

"He's the only one to have gotten this far," Elizabetta whispered.

"He has details I'd rather he didn't have if we don't hire him," Stella answered.

"Thieves can be loyal subjects, too. I vouch we trust him either way." Elizabetta nudged her younger sister.

Stella raised an eyebrow. "You just like the flower he gave you."

"He did manage to pick my favorite. Stella, honestly, you've got to hire somebody sooner or later. The other candidates have been hopeless. The dances start tomorrow night." Elizabetta sighed.

Ned smiled apologetically. "I can also read lips. And I would never divulge the details of a job, whether I were hired or not."

Stella blushed, something she rarely did, and hated being caught doing. Ned glanced quickly away. Elizabetta bounced to her feet. "You're hired. Stella?"

"I…agree. Come this evening and we'll test your skills in the dark and tell you what we hope to do." Stella walked past both, her head held high, her cheeks still quite bright.

Elizabetta could not help but note the appreciative glance Ned Shadow gave her as she passed him. He recovered quickly. "When do I begin work?"

"When Stella tells you."

The Dancing and the Danger

"They're saying there are twelve of us running off to dance, breaking Father's heart."

"Rumor," Elizabetta schooled her sisters, "flies faster than the birds. As for the Fae, they can't lie but they do exaggerate." Her older and wiser tone colored her words.

"Twelve?" Glynnis repeated. "Ridiculous! People will gossip about anything. There are only seven of us. We know what we must do." Her hazel eyes narrowed in disapproval, Glynnis kicked off a slipper and pulled a silk liner loose to hand to Fiona. "I hate this. My soles are so thin I can feel crumbs wherever they've fallen on the floor." She bent over to tug her shoe back into place. Battered and scarred, it hardly resembled the shoe she'd begun the evening wearing. "The floors here are like demons, eating us from the sole up."

Fiona's whisper grew tense. "How close are the sentries? How much time do I have?" She sat on the fainting couch, scraps of silk on her lap, her fingers curled about a quill which had once been a stay in her decorative corset and now waited for its sharpened nib to be dabbed again into a tiny thimble of mascara black ink. None of them could draw as fine and straight a line as she, which was why she sat and did the mapping. She dabbed her forehead to dry it. "I might remind you all the maps are vital for both the robbery and the escape."

"It's their glamour and no fault of ours we can't remember clearly. Just keep working," Capricia answered. "Who's still dancing?"

"Little Lina. And Ardith is dancing her heart away, as usual. Stella's on guard."

She stood. Her hair, unlike Fiona's, had been done up in a dome of perfectly placed curls with tiny flower-bedecked pins that matched her dress and fan. She patted the dark tawny curls as if to reassure herself it stayed in place. "Absolutely no one has the slightest idea what we're really up to."

"You'll get new slippers for the next dance. Not to mention the shoemaker's complaints at the treatment of his work," murmured Capricia.

Fiona frowned and dipped her pen again. "I need to know the time!"

Stella stepped in through the curtains. "The sentry has six minutes to go." She snapped her timepiece shut and let it drop down on its ornamental chain. "We're on schedule." Her gaze assessed all of them. "Fi, you're doing marvelously." Ardith swung in, dancing solo for the moment and crowding everyone. Little Lina followed in Ardith's wake, scarcely noticeable, and twitched the opening shut behind her.

Fiona glared daggers as Ardith held her gown's flounce with one hand. She put her palm over her maps to protect them in her sister's wake.

"I," claimed Ardith, "am having fun. You should join me!" She ducked out of the alcove and sashayed back into the main hall. The curtain barely rippled and they could hear someone hailing her return.

Elizabetta frowned. "Who is that?"

"One of the princes, I believe. They're taken with each other." It was the youngest who'd answered, and Lina put her chin up in defiance as the others turned to glare at her.

Lina sat. "I'm glad she's having fun. It's less suspicious." She, as young as she was, couldn't possibly have looked more innocent. She swung her feet as they didn't yet touch the floor. "I should go back out. Drink some punch, maybe. I don't like them, but I love their punch. No one will pounce on me. I have my duke to protect me."

Lina's duke was nearly as young as she was and stood barely a hand taller. They looked adorable together, but no one worried about Lina's fate even though the young man was Fae.

"We're almost done mapping." Elizabetta tapped her fan against her chin. "Capricia and I should visit the punch bowl, too, just to make an appearance."

Capricia winced. "I can barely walk. I've danced to a standstill...and all so they can laugh at us, at our clumsiness, and point at us as if the princes are fools to think we might fall in love with one of them."

Stella bent over Fiona. "This is a matter of politics, not of the heart. We're almost done. Their treasury has to be in this general area." Her index finger circled about the last piece of map. Stella looked up. "We'll be ready to sack it in a day or two. I'll notify the locksmith tomorrow. Note that, Fiona."

Her sister nodded and sketched in a short note: duke of shadows.

"Does he really have an invisibility cloak?"

"Of course not. He's just a very good thief who likes to boast."

"And now he's got to choose a target."

All of them paused to look at Glynnis, the quiet one, the generally thoughtful one. She waved her hand. "As soon as you're ready, Fiona, I've found a hidden corridor for you and the treasury is bound to be in one place or the other."

Stella pointed at the silk swatches. "Another passageway just confounds the plan. I need to know what's there and if it's worth the risk of separating our forces."

Glynnis tapped her temple. "Don't worry, it's safe in here until Fi marks it down. I dropped a glass of red wine, staining the wall where it begins."

Stella tilted her head. "It won't be certain, but we have to make do. Mark that, as well, Fi. Our memories start fading the moment we step from the castle and cross the lake." She glanced down at her watch. "And we're out of time!"

Fiona capped her small supply of ink, rolled up the silk patches she'd been sketching on, and stowed them away. Lastly, she hid the quill pen and placed it in her garter on the inside of her thigh. She stood, tugging her dress into place. "Am I decent?"

"Beautifully so."

Stella stood them all on their feet, straightening their gowns where necessary before sending her sisters off one by one into the throngs of dancers. She stayed behind a moment, thinking of their father and his Iron Crown. She held no qualms about the idea of plundering Faery for whatever riches they could. The Fae, after all, had been raiding their lands and others for decades.

The Last Nights and Not Until the Map Is Finished

They danced another candle mark away before retreating again, and Capricia poked her head in. "Are we ready to go home?"

"I believe so."

"Good, because I think Ardith is going to agree to marry her prince."

"What???!" Stella whirled about at the news.

"He is charming."

"And she's a disaster if this gets about. The pressure on the rest of us will be intolerable."

Stella pointed at Lina. "Head her off. Get her away from him…whoever he is."

"He's the one who wears copper and burgundy."

"Whatever. Just go and do it. Now." Stella pulled back the curtain to set the youngest on her rescue mission, but both stopped short as Lina's usual escort, the Duke of Dewsberry, stood in their path.

"I heard that," the young duke offered, set off by frothy lace at his wrists and neck, with a tailored brocade clock that shimmered in a palette of greens. "My apologies. I didn't mean to. But isn't she here to get married?"

"No," Elizabetta told him. "She is here to fulfill a diplomatic treaty."

"Oh." His mouth sagged. "So, I guess that means I can't keep Lina." He turned and looked at Lina, his face downcast. His skin was the same gorgeous bronze hue as hers and his hair a soft gold, pulled back with onyx ties. The ties almost matched her dark brunette locks. He looked adorable, if unhappy.

Stella said firmly, "Nobody gets to keep anybody."

The young Duke of Dewsberry grabbed Lina's hand. "But she's the best friend I've ever had."

Lina leaned a bit on him. "He is a dear."

"Makes no matter. I am not losing one of my sisters to Faery. Especially not you and certainly not Ardith."

"Maybe I could just come and visit once in a while?" Lina looked hopefully at her sisters.

"No. Absolutely not. Faery cannot be trusted."

"I can!" cried the young Duke. "I'll do anything for Lina."

Stella began to open her mouth for another angry retort.

Elizabetta grabbed her wrist. "There may be an advantage to this."

"I can't possibly think of one."

"If the Duke comes to greet us tomorrow night, he might be…um… er…*shadowed*."

"Oh." Stella traded a look with Elizabetta. "That is an idea."

"I can come and get her? Meet her at the lake's far shore?"

She nodded to Dewsberry. "Yes, I think you quite possibly can. And during the evening, we can discuss visits. You to our kingdom as well as Lina to yours.

"Capital!" The young duke bounced; his expression radiant.

"One would think so. Do you possibly have a name as well as a title?"

"Standor," Lina provided.

"Stan. Plan to meet us every night we have left. And someone go get Ardith!"

With that order from Stella, they returned to the tide of dancing. Stella hung back to ensure that no bit of evidence lingered behind them…but even she did not notice the somewhat plain (for an elven lady) woman who eagerly stepped forward to greet Glynnis, nor the equally eager way Glynnis went to meet her. All Stella's attention focused on the radiant Ardith and the handsome man she danced with, weaving in an intricate pattern, gazes fastened on one another.

Lina and Standor cut in on them. Ardith flustered a bit at the much shorter duke. Lina put her arm up to the prince of Faery who tossed his former partner an amused look before taking up his new one.

When the music calmed at evening's end, Ardith firmly took her place at the prince's side. Lina looked up at the two of them. She echoed her two older sisters as she inquired, "And which of the princes is this one?"

The prince peered down a nose that had been broken at one time. Amid a crowd of perfect beauties, it gave his face an interesting aspect. Duke Standor tugged on her hand and whispered in her ear, "He's very accomplished. My father always told me never to get in a fight with him."

"Oh?" She waited patiently for the prince to answer her query which she now rather hoped hadn't been too rude.

"I am Dareth of Crystal Falls."

Lina blurted out in delight. "The ones with the icicles all year?"

"Actually, they are mineral rock formations, but they do look as if the snow and ice have never gone away. Does that please you? I would consider it a privilege to escort you and your sister Ardith there some time for a picnic." The snow-haired faery gave a bow.

"We shall have to think about it." She began backing up, taking Ardith in her wake.

"I should like to make your acquaintance before fair Ardith makes her announcement."

"Announcement?"

The young Duke of Dewsberry hummed in distress but he could not catch either Lina or Ardith from saying something they should not as Ardith gushed. "I've chosen!" and Lina flung her hand out to cover her sister's mouth, "No!"

The two wrestled a moment while the two escorts stood aghast at watching the sisters fight. Lina won as she tripped Ardith and both hit the dance floor. The music crashed to a halt as they wrestled.

"Take that back!"

"I won't!"

"You have to!" And they twisted in a pile of gowns and worn slippers.

"Don't you dare bite me!"

The young duke got to one knee and attempted to unknot the two as they squirmed. The Prince of Crystal Falls watched with a bemused expression.

Across the crowd, a voice cut like a whip—Stella's words. "Lina! Ardith! Enough!"

They couldn't see her, but they reacted immediately.

As they sat up, High Prince Botrell stood in front of all of them. He looked as though he'd been carved from Dareth's icicles, all in icy white, gray, and silver, his expression frozen. But his voice had not.

"You do your entire family a misfortune speaking out of turn, but we here will forgive you because of your youth. However, is it my understanding a Choice has been made?"

Ardith straightened, red of face, her hair unpinned, and part of the lace from one sleeve dangling forlornly. "It has."

"You can't!" Lina stared in absolute horror as the others wove their way through the crowd behind Botrell.

"Your family negotiated a diplomatic treaty and it ill behooves you to deny it now." Botrell stared at Lina. "Dewsberry, I expect you to take her in hand. The young need to know when to stay quiet."

Stella pushed forward at Botrell's elbow. "We are not making a committal!"

"This one has stated her intentions. I mistrust yours. We will keep her here, safe, while the rest of you do as you must." Botrell snapped his fingers and two guards stepped forward to flank Ardith.

"I won't leave my sister as hostage!"

"She's not a hostage," Botrell answered smoothly. "We are simply keeping her from the harm the young one seems intent upon inflicting."

Glynnis stepped out of Stella's and Elizabetta's shadows. "She'll need a chaperone. I'll stay with her."

Stella's jaw tightened and she looked even more like her mother the general, but she managed a nod. She signaled her sisters to follow, telling Botrell, "We wish to leave."

"I'll have the carriages summoned and the boats readied."

The duke of Dewsberry dared a gentle hug to Lina as the two young ones said goodnight and the five of them got into their rides. As Stella seated each and every one, she had but one thing to say, whispered fiercely into their ears. "Tomorrow night must be the night."

Plans Go Awry

Night fell. Their memories dissolved into mist but they had studied Fiona's sketchings fiercely. Stella got into her boat and tried not to look about.

"Are you…" Stella took a breath to ask her question softly, but the Duke of Shadows was already at her ear with a warm exhalation, though she could not quite see him. "Do not worry. I am here. For you, I will always be wherever you need me. Perhaps one day you will give me the sun as well as the night."

Stella's face warmed again, and a brief smile lit her face momentarily. She ducked her chin to compose herself. "Lina and her Fae escort will be your decoy."

"Understood."

She felt him move away, as slight as an evening breeze. Abbott had been abrupt with his farewell, unhappy at losing Ardith and Glynnis. He would be even unhappier with the Duke of Thieves. She sighed. They descended into their boats one by one, Stan helping Lina solemnly, and the Fae boatmen not noticing an extra bounce when a shadow entered. The sisters did not speak as the rowers conveyed them into twilight and across the wide lake.

At the Fae shore, a contingent of armed men awaited.

"What is this?" Stella and Elizabetta whirled upon Botrell, who stood among them. This night he wore crimson and gold, looking as though he stood in a fire.

"Protection."

"From what? Other than yourselves."

"We have had a few...skirmishes...with Bendak troops this day. We are prepared to keep our guests safe."

A cold breeze skirled off the lake and Stella felt it chill the sword she wore under her skirts and holstered along her thigh. She would not start a fight, not then and there, but she was prepared. "Bendaks here? The Hordes seem ambitious."

"Indeed. Now you understand why we came to treat with your father." Botrell extended an arm to her, helping her step out of the boat. She took it reluctantly. As they settled in the carriages, she said little, gazing out the window, calculations ruling her thoughts.

Once inside the palace, she saw to her dismay that armed troops lined the immediate doorways and the music of the dance seemed muted. She deliberately did not track Lina and Standor nor their uninvited shadow, in hopes of not bringing attention to them. One more night! All they needed was one more night.

"Where is Ardith?"

"Your sisters will be here shortly." Botrell patted her wrist but did not seem inclined to set her free. "I've ordered a military escort for all of you, as well as any dancing partners you have chosen. Your protection is our obligation."

"I thought you dealt with the Bendaks." She tugged slightly to free herself, but his hold did not budge.

"We feel that we have, but our palace is vast, and we want to ensure your safety."

Glynnis, trailed by the quiet elven countess, appeared on the small stairway to their right. Stella shook off Botrell and went to hug her, saying in her ear, "Tonight," and much louder, "Where is Ardith?"

"Just behind us. We were moved from our chambers and roomed together when we heard skirmishes in the hallway."

"But you are fine?"

"She has been kept so," the countess answered. She no longer wore her dancing gown but practical trousers, flexible long boots, and a waist coat over a silken shirt with a scabbard laced to her thigh. Her eyes shone whenever she glanced at Glynnis.

Stella noted it but said nothing other than turning to the prince and saying, "Is there a room where we can all freshen up?"

"Countess Moonlit will show you the way." Botrell reached out to Stella again. "Do save me a dance."

She did not answer, for the countess moved away quickly and they had to follow. But his words troubled her, and Ardith's rash declaration had started the problem she did not want any of them to face. Their military escorts faded away except for the Countess Moonlit, and Stella turned about, reaching for Fiona and snapping her fingers for the map. She prepared to draw her blade.

"We're going here."

"What about the other corridor?"

Stella closed her eyes tightly a moment, trying to pierce fuzzy memories. "We didn't have time to sketch it?"

Glynnis put a finger to her temple. "The night didn't take away my recollections. Darana—the countess—assures I have it aright."

"There's no hope for it except we separate. It cuts our chance of success down but…" Stella glanced at the countess and the way she stood and the way her weapon was secured. "Ned, go with Capricia and Elizabetta, Lina and Standor. Ardith as well. You will have to deal with the locks in your path." She pressed the silk map into the eldest sister's hands. "Good fortune."

"From your lips to the Great Above's ears!" The five of them hurried away, Stan protectively at Lina's side.

"Now I have to settle with you." Stella pulled up her skirt and freed her long blade.

Glynnis stopped at the archway. The countess flanked her, emptying her scabbard, and bringing up the sword in her own hand.

Stella told her, "I'll not let you stop us."

"And I'm prepared to defend my love. I won't let you lead her into trouble." She held her weapon like an expert.

Glynnis put a hand out. "Stella, you can't duel her!"

As her plea rose, the hallway beyond filled, two elven guards on the attack, and they had their hands full. Darana pushed Glynnis and Fiona behind her as she fought with graceful and expert moves. Almost as one, Stella and the countess defended the others, their blades shining. The two would-be attackers fell almost immediately between the two swordswomen. Countess Moonlit looked down at them. "Botrell has had this hallway guarded closely for unknown reasons." She glanced up. "Why?"

Stella appraised the elven woman. "Nice parry and lunge. I think I recognize the technique."

"I had a skilled teacher."

"Indeed. You must recommend me to them."

Darana said nothing but motioned with her sword that they should hurry on. Glynnis stepped into the forefront again, searching for the threshold cunningly concealed by off-center walls and garish wallpaper. Its opening appeared only if one stood at its edge.

"Interesting," Stella murmured as she turned the hidden corner. "I wonder how the others are doing?"

* * *

Elizabetta halted at brawny oak doors, studded with bronze and many, many locks. "I believe we are here."

"Are you certain?" declared the Duke of Shadows as he stepped from a corner. "And if your map is wrong?"

"Something of importance has to be beyond these doors! Look at the number of locks."

"We shall soon see." Ned stood on tip-toes to examine the topmost locks and closely examined the row at the edge of the door. "Tricky," he said softly.

"They're elven."

"Of course. But they cannot just be opened randomly. There is a sequence here."

Foreboding shivered over Elizabetta. "How can you tell?"

"I just can. But it's knowing the sequence..."

The Duke of Dewsberry cleared his throat. "I can help."

"Oh?"

"Yes. But you have to take me with you when you leave."

Lina pressed his hand tightly. "The sun!"

"I will find a way to bear it. But I can't stay here. The locks will betray me."

Ned pushed his hood back from his head. "And how would they do that?"

"They sing *to* me. That's how I will know the sequence. And after, they will sing *of* me. It keeps us from robbing each other."

Lina threw Elizabetta a desperate look. She shook her head. "It's up to Stella. It will be a battle getting home as it is."

"I'll take him if you cannot. Every locksmith needs an apprentice," Ned remarked. His hands filled with his tools and he nudged Stan with an elbow. "Hurry."

It took longer than any of them hoped. Ardith kept looking over her shoulder until Capricia snapped, "What are you doing?"

"Looking for Dareth. I want him here and yet I fear he will find us."

Capricia squeezed her shoulder. Finally, the massive door came open and the riches they'd hoped to find gleamed brightly. The sisters hiked up their skirts and filled the money bags they had lashed to bodies with coin and gems. Elizabetta looked at the Duke of Dewsberry. "Any idea what lies down the other corridor?"

"None at all. We need to leave or we'll not get out at all."

Ned said, "I'll find the others. You go on."

He ran halfway down the twisted corridors with Stan at his heels, only to confront the formidable Prince Dareth. Stan pushed past the thief and put his chin up as the sisters caught up with them. He blocked Dareth, despite his father's advice to never cross the prince. "Let them pass."

"Perhaps I will. Perhaps I will not. Ardith?"

Her brilliant red hair lay tumbled upon her shoulders and her eyes brimmed for a few seconds. "I can't stay," she half-whispered. "It's my fervent wish that you will come with me."

His sword rang as he withdrew it from its sheath. "I am as much yours, as you are mine. You lead and I will follow."

Stan let out an audible sigh. "To the carriages."

"What of Stella?"

"I'll get them." Ned disappeared into shadow again.

Dareth stared after him. "And who was that?"

"The Duke of Shadows," Stan told him.

* * *

"Here we are." Glynnis touched the door jam. "What if it's nothing?"

"And what if it's everything?" Stella told her. "Fiona, help Darana guard the rear."

"My dagger…"

"Is sufficient for the moment." She hefted her own blade.

The great lock did not seem bespelled, but she knew if she forced it, it might have a siren for an alarm or any number of other elven tricks. Her instinct told her to risk it. Stella pressed her palm to it.

"We're coming in," she announced.

Silence in the corridor. Then a rattling of the latch as if someone beyond tried it. A muffled voice. "Then come quickly if you must. Time passes."

A single tear ran down Stella's cheek and she quickly brushed it away before the others saw it. She shook out a lockpick from the purse dangling at her wrist. Fiona blinked. "When did you—"

"Our Duke of Thieves has been instructing me. He's…quite a gentleman."

Darana looked over her shoulder once and gave a slight smile. That change of expression lit up not only her face but that of Glynnis as well. Stella winked at her sister and turned about to ply the lock.

It fell open at her second twist. Darana remarked, "It's new. Has not been spelled yet, it seems."

"And the captive…" Stella slowly pushed the door inward. "Is new as well."

A tall and stern woman waited, her weight balanced, a stool in her hands as if she thought to wield it and crack a few skulls. The resemblance between the woman and Stella could be nothing less than remarkable.

"Mother!" The sisters cried and rushed to her arms.

Quick hugs all around. Stella hung back after the first, watching Countess Moonlit. "I thought I knew the sword technique. It could only have been taught by Nommi."

"I faced her in battle once. I never forgot her techniques."

"I am leverage," their mother said. "When that last ransom payment failed, they came and rescued me from the Galterans, or so they claimed. But I was to be held against your marriages."

"They risked much."

"Indeed," answered Nommi. "Not the least that Botrell is very unliked in his own realm."

Ned bolted into the room. "The others have succeeded. We're out of time. The palace is alerted."

"How did you find us?"

The thief gave a half-smile. "How could I not? You draw me as the night draws the stars."

"A side trip, first," Darana said.

"Oh?"

"A decoy." And she led them back the way they had come, down servants' stairs into a cellar and to a massive dungeon door where she wrenched off a great key ring and began to open doors. The prisoners inside sprang out and away from them, running wildly into the kitchen and into the corridors.

Stella, Nommi, and Ned led everyone in the opposite direction.

Dareth had the carriages ready, standing up in the driver's seat, whip in hand. They piled in, even as sirens began to scream about the faery castle as the horses tossed their heads impatiently.

Botrell came out of the evening and grabbed the headstalls of the horses at the first carriage. "You'll not leave us."

Dareth jumped from his perch. "They will go wherever they wish. It is you who betrayed us and broke honor. You let the Bendaks breach our realm. You made deals with our enemies."

The two princes circled each other. Dareth still in crystal and gray, as the famous falls of his domain, and Botrell like the angry firebird of story and myth. With a low growl, Botrell charged.

Swords flashed and steel rang. Expert, both, they pressed each other hard. Botrell determined not to lose, Dareth equally determined to triumph. Steel rang. Boots scuffled on the twilight ground. Elven guard ringed them but did not move to intervene.

Nommi reached across to Stella. "Give me your sword, in case I must face the victor."

Stella passed it over without a word. Her mother gave a grim smile.

Circling each other, the two elven princes measured each other's mettle and weaknesses…when suddenly Botrell inexplicably stumbled, tripping over a shadow. Dareth fell on the High Prince with a slash and a stab. Botrell's weapon fell away and he collapsed upon the ground, hand to a shoulder growing crimson with each breath.

"I do not," said Dareth tightly, "recommend that you follow us tonight, or any other night. You have never been a favorite as a High Prince. Your leadership is greatly eroded."

He and Ned bounded back into their carriages. Reins all around were picked up and the horses pressed briskly toward the boats waiting on the lake shore.

And so seven princesses returned home in relative glory, with their general mother, a small fortune, an elven prince, a countess, and two dukes…all to live, hopefully, happily ever after.

Ashes of a Cinnamon Fire

R.Z. Held

Cordelia's father was planning something—she could hear it in his silence over dinner that night. As they did each evening when neither her father nor her sisters were traveling, they had gathered in the grand dining room, whose elegant arched windows looked out into the house's central courtyard through a screen of intermittent rain drips cast by the eaves. Her father sat at the table's head, Grace and Honor at either hand—right or left was a constant game they had invented between themselves, one Cordelia could not divine the rules of—and Cordelia had placed herself a little apart, with a view into the courtyard. Normally, he would have been holding forth on a series of orders to entice that buyer or push that seller, but tonight his scowl was bent on the intermediate distance as he ate.

Her sisters could amply fill that silence, of course. Of their own volition—make sure to note that to their invisible accounts!—they had already anticipated his orders and accomplished a whole list of tasks. Each had their own particular skills: Honor, the oldest, was strong and quick with a blade; Grace, the next in age, was elegant and clever with what she found in books. Cordelia was not encouraged to participate, nor did she wish to. Her grandmother was a witch with powerful magic; her late mother had had none; and her own power was much nearer the latter than the former. Cordelia's world was the small details of running a household, and she considered her magic amply suited to that.

And she could have been content in that world, if any of her family had *acknowledged* the work she did.

"It's time we decided who inherits my business," her father said. That brought utter silence. Honor gaped and Grace stilled, their displays of shock as divided as the rest of their personalities. "I have in mind a contest, of sorts."

Her father pushed his empty plate to the side and centered his body as if adopting a bargaining position he would never shift. He'd run to fat over the years, black hair receding steadily as if in exchange for the rarity of gray in it, but his frame still spoke of power and muscle. Honor's wide shoulders echoed that frame in feminine form, while Grace had the black hair that seemed likely to remain inviolate for decades yet. They all three had different mothers, sired and then collected a few years later in their father's travels along his trade routes, but Cordelia was the odd one out in her appearance too, with the pure, witchy white of her hair. Other than that, her appearance was as mousy as her magic—common and unremarkable.

"A thought experiment, to begin. If you could fill a whole ship with only one material to sell at whatever market you wished, to yield the greatest profit, which material would you choose?" Her father folded his hands to wait, all patience.

Cordelia should have expected something like this, she supposed. Grace had attained her majority at twenty-one last month and Honor was already twenty-four, time marching onward if she wished to marry or ensure her succession with children in their father's manner. And there would be no half shares, of course—not when he wouldn't even marry for fear of splitting control of his assets.

Grace dropped her chin, thinking furiously. Honor, though naturally impulsive, had learned to curb that, and she bit at a thumbnail. Cordelia smoothed a fingertip along the molded edge of her plate. A smear of sauce had dried there with flecks of paprika threaded within it. The question clearly wasn't meant for her, and to be honest, she didn't *want* to inherit. She had no wish to spend her time dealing with strangers who would see her hair and think "witch" and nothing more. Neither did she want to join her mother's family—just after puberty she'd spent a year of quiet, desperate misery supposedly receiving training in magic but mostly being berated by her grandmother. She was never going back *there*.

Why shouldn't she use her father's contest for her own purposes, though? She knew better than to imagine her father would ever acknowledge her contributions to the household, but maybe she could *teach* Grace or Honor to value her. Both ignored her in equal measure at the moment, but if her aid could be what determined the outcome of this contest…

"Steel," Honor declared, unable to contain herself any longer. "Blades! Those from our kingdom are well known to be the best in the world."

Her father nodded, offering no sign of his reaction, positive or negative.

"Wool," Grace said, in turn. "Raw fleece is nearly impossible to damage with rough handling, and it is difficult to steal. The number of sheep that can be raised on one acre, compared to the price of wool—" She continued in that vein, citing numbers from the family account books apparently from memory. She wound up her last sentence at a gesture from their father, adjusting her rhythm as if she had chosen the stopping point herself.

If Cordelia was to influence the outcome of this contest, she needed to ensure she wasn't dismissed to such a degree that she was left behind, however. "Spices," she said, softly but firmly. It seemed as good an answer to her as any; she'd always loved the variety of spices. Each was exciting and different from the next, from the brash assault of too much black pepper, to how saffron layered delicate flavors on the tongue.

Her father chuckled. "An expensive commodity, to be sure, but I can't imagine you ever being able to fill a *ship* with them with less than a king's ransom to begin with."

Cordelia set her shoulders and stared at the paprika flecks on her plate in familiar silent frustration as their father prodded her sisters with a few clarifying questions. She knew better than to meet that laugh with anger, or anything other than a mouse's scurry back into the woodwork. In any frontal verbal assault, her father *always* came out the winner.

This time, however, rather than souring and fading away, her frustration burst into a realization: she'd intended to aid one of her sisters, but why shouldn't she try to *win* this contest?

She was sure her father would deny her full control on a technicality even if she won, of course—but what *leverage* over her sisters a win would give her. She lifted her head high, frustration draining away in the face of resolution.

Grace gave a flip of her fingers. "But to actually take a full cargo of *anything* is sheer foolishness. Good business lies in the proportions of different commodities."

"Of course. I was curious about your reasoning, but that wasn't the real test. Trading isn't all cargo and accounts." Their father pushed to his feet and withdrew a folded broadsheet from beneath a decanter on the sideboard. He shook it open and began to read. "Two new sightings have been reported of this great bird of flame. The fire of its feathers is said to be visible for nigh on a mile at night—"

"The firebird everyone is talking about, yes," Honor interrupted. "It seems to have set no blazes of any size, however, so I cannot see how it could disrupt our interests."

Her father refolded the broadsheet and leveled it at each of his older daughters in turn. "A living in trade may be built on staples, but a fortune is built on finding the rarest, most precious, and stopping at nothing until you have it. The one who brings me a feather from the firebird will be my heir."

Honor and Grace rose as one. "We'd best be packing, then," Honor said, and strode out without further farewell. Grace detoured on her own way out to accept the broadsheet their father held out to her without her asking, a small smile on his lips.

Cordelia followed them, though she turned toward the servants' quarters instead of their rooms in the hallway outside. In the matter of packing, she was certain she had her sisters outclassed. Honor would catch up her sword and fill a single bag with only a canteen and bread and cheese; Grace would load her pack horse with so many reference books it could hardly walk. When Cordelia was the only one with clean underthings, she planned to make sure they noticed that.

* * *

The firebird had been sighted quite a distance from their home, so the sisters spent nearly six days on the road. Their first nights were spent in inns, but by the end they had to sleep on pallets by the fire at taverns that anchored mere huddles of houses. At those, which had no servants, Cordelia demonstrated her usefulness by using her magic to dry everyone's socks and remove the mud from everyone's shoes. Her sisters seemed appreciative for the moment, at least, so she followed that up by arranging for an invitation for all of them to stay with one of their father's contacts, a rural lord with a manor at the edge of the forest where the firebird had been spotted.

Lord Barthon was young, having succeeded his father only two years ago, and he swept into his entrance hall to greet them as if casting a spell to make every young woman in view swoon at his feet. The Barthons traded primarily in timber and its products, a fact that could be guessed in a single glance around the entrance hall—not only was every wall clad in paneling with inset geometric designs in darker wood, but intricate carving danced plants and clever little animals over the molding and curled ridges along the legs of every table.

"Of all the hopeful hunters of the firebird we've seen, you three are my favorites." Lord Barthon beamed at them all, Honor most especially. She had something like a swoon-spell of her own, Cordelia supposed, rooted in her unadulterated confidence. Not that Honor particularly wanted men throwing themselves at her.

"We truly appreciate you offering us space," Cordelia said. She felt rather melted from the day's steady drizzle, but she pushed her hood back and stood straighter. She preferred to reveal her witchy white hair as early as possible, to get people's reactions over with.

"Oh—you—" He stumbled, too off-balance even to offer a meaningless social pleasantry. Poorly trained. Cordelia could manage a "that's kind" or "it was nothing" when rage or misery left her no other breath.

"Close your mouth, boy." An older woman swept into the room, her powerful movements enhanced, not diminished, by her cane. Her hair was all gray, but where others might have stooped with age, she had tightened her whole body down around her straight back. This would be the dowager. "If you're going to be rude, do it with confidence. So, you're the witch's granddaughter."

What else would she be? "Lady," she murmured, dipping her chin to the exact degree etiquette required and no more, showing Lord Barthon how it was done.

"I thought you were conceived so your magic could be used in warding your father's ships against storms and curses and the like. Why are you here instead of at the docks?" The dowager planted herself before Cordelia and settled both hands atop her cane.

Now Cordelia was the one who needed to close her mouth. She'd come to that conclusion on her own, but no one had ever actually *voiced* it, even among her own family. Honor grunted—in surprise? negation?—but Grace hooked a hand into her elbow to whisper into her ear. She knew the score.

Cordelia knew the dowager's type now, however: those who aimed to provoke in every conversation, because they thought they preferred to interact only with those with strong spines. Within that type, however, were those who were fooling themselves—they craved only the superior feeling of being able to get a rise out of anyone—and those who truly enjoyed being stood up to. The dowager could be either; Cordelia would never be able to tell until she committed herself by replying.

Cordelia tried to weigh it up—what would make for the quietest stay, the easiest path to her goal—but she was damp and tired and sick of weighing. "My magic is too small for such things; it was always a risk, given my mother's lack of it. My father deals in gambles. But perhaps I am lying, and will lay a curse on you the moment I am alone. That's your gamble to make."

"The mouse found her teeth since rumor last spoke of her." The dowager's expression was hard, but that was no change from before Cordelia had spoken—she was a hard woman. She lifted one finger from the clasp over her cane. "See that in my house, the mouse does not bite unprovoked." *Her* house, Cordelia noted.

"If I could trouble you, do you have a library I could make use of once I've dried off? I brought all my books that reference such beasts as this, but I thought, given your proximity to the forest, you might have others…" Grace stepped forward, smiling prettily.

"I will show you to it and point out what you may not touch," the dowager said, and swept grandly off again.

Honor rolled her shoulders and neck as she watched them go. "You can read about how to capture a beast until you go blind, but it doesn't mean you'll be able to do it. Will you point me to your guards' training yard? I need to limber up, and I might as well only wash once."

Lord Barthon, who had been looking at sea in the waters of verbal fencing, brightened immediately. "Of course! I'll spar with you myself." He'd never arrive at the destination he was hoping for, but that was all right. Tonight, Honor would smile at all the housemaids until one smiled back, and Grace would look up from her books and circle back around to scoop the lord up.

Meanwhile, the housekeeper approached, business-like, so the guest would not be left standing alone in the hall. "We don't need three separate rooms," Cordelia told the woman. Her hands were work-reddened, but she otherwise had an elegance of her own rooted in the plainness of her uniform. "We none of us brought a maid, so I can sleep in the maid's closet off Grace's room." A risk, to bet that Grace would spend the night in the master bedroom and leave Cordelia the more comfortable bed with less trouble for the servants, but not a large one.

"Oh, yes, ma'am. That would be a help." The housekeeper did not make it as far as a smile, but Cordelia could see the unbending process begin in the loosening of her shoulders. Cordelia followed where she led, a little of the tightness leaving her own body. As she had suspected, her kind of skills could take her far in this contest.

* * *

A bird of fire that could be seen for a mile ought to have been easy to find, but this forest was an old one with a heavy canopy to obscure any light, and the endless drizzle would suppress any flames that might have sent up tell-tale smoke. Honor trained; Grace researched; Cordelia spoke to the servants. Someone's niece had glimpsed the firebird, someone else's childhood friend had not only seen it, but was willing to stop by for tea and answer Cordelia's questions about it. With that accomplished, Cordelia went to check on her sisters while they all waited for word of a new sighting.

The library, of course, had row upon row of shelves showcasing local wood. Far more shelf space than books to fill it, in fact, though perhaps that was because a full shelf showed so little of the polished grain of its surface. Grace reigned at a central table, returning to pages she'd marked with colored scraps of ribbon to expand upon her earlier notes. Cordelia read from sources farther down the table, making a game of guessing what her sister's color scheme denoted, as she made purely mental notes of her own. Her hands and cuffs still smelled pleasantly of the mincemeat pies she'd helped bake to learn this cook's special recipe, with hints of cinnamon, nutmeg, allspice, and more.

The room was curtained and lamp-lit in deference to those books, but sunlight oozed across the parquet floor in the hall, visible over Grace's shoulder. Then the light washed up onto Honor as she intercepted the beam. She strode into the room, dressed in traveling clothes with her hair done up tight. "Smoke's been seen, in the midst of the forest."

"A forester's camp," Grace claimed. The way she closed her current source with a snap and gathered up her book of notes told a different story.

"Not when the source moves." Honor beamed. "I'm just letting you know so you can stay out of my way. I wouldn't want to hit you with a stray arrow. This first opportunity is mine, as the eldest."

The pair eyed each other in silence for a breath, then Grace growled a curse under her breath and subsided in her chair. Another breath, and she'd retrieved her poise from the midst of her frustration. "I won't worry about having my own opportunity—I suppose you plan to hunt it like you would any other bird?" She gestured across her pile of references. "Firebirds are well known to be too intelligent for that. It will never work. Besides, who will be your beater?"

Honor glanced back over her shoulder, frowning. Clearly, she hadn't gotten far in her preparations before she came to stake her claim on this sighting. "Lord Barthon has gamekeepers..."

"Who will agree to put themselves close to a legendary creature of flame at the request of someone not their lord? Ha!" Grace smirked, a call-back to childhood arguments before she'd started trying to train the inelegant expression out of herself.

"I'll be your beater," Cordelia said. Both her sisters' heads snapped to her. "If you'll have me?" Of course Honor would have her, she had no other choice, but this way she'd feel she was doing her baby sister a favor—by giving Cordelia what she wanted. No amount of gossip or reading could beat seeing a firebird in person, before her own attempt.

"Thanks, Cordelia." Honor was back to beaming. She strode out, leaving Cordelia to hurry after, sorting out requests to the servants for supplies in her mind. While those were brought, she could change.

There were trails within the forest, even one worthy of being called a road, but beyond that one, few were suitable for horses. They tethered their horses at the road; Cordelia took her light shoulder bag and Honor her bow and sword, and they proceeded on foot. The last few days of sun had been insufficient to remove mud puddles poised to ooze up and over a boot, but this forest was old enough that the grand evergreens' spread of needle-bearing branches kept the underbrush down. Strategic detours could keep Cordelia's feet dry, though they slowed her in comparison to her sister.

Then Honor slowed on her own, nose lifted to the diffuse scent of burning. Every few steps, she twisted in an arc, measuring her line of sight between great trunks. Finally, she stopped, liking her angle. One of the great giants had crashed down, tipping its roots up in an interlocking circle that acted as an excellent blind. Honor stepped behind it and chose a wedge of open space between roots to shoot through. Silently, she gestured Cordelia around, needing to give no more directions. She'd already explained Cordelia's part in her plan several times before they even reached the forest.

Cordelia circled wide, keeping the smell of smoke always more to one side than the other, until she judged she'd lined up with her sister. Honor had told her to make noise, but she could do better than that. She used her magic to call up little popping snaps of light around her hands and body. She gave them a heavy red-purple hue, like blackberries, to distinguish them from any flicker of yellow or orange—or even blue—flame.

"All right, bird, get going!" she shouted, and crashed forward, stomping upon every shed branch and sapling she could find as her magic spattered. Few sticks were dry enough to crackle, but Cordelia doubted that was necessary. The bird would notice her.

The campfire scent grew stronger and stronger, until Cordelia finally glimpsed a flash of bright light around a trunk. There, again, movement, best visible as a pulsing streak left across the inside of her eyelids when she closed them briefly. She crashed, panting, until she spotted the broken line in the canopy where Honor's tree had fallen. Any further and she'd push the bird beyond her sister.

She banished her magic and stood still, drawing deep breaths until her heart slowed to match. Then she moved, slowly, to find a good view of the firebird and further events.

The bird had alighted on a branch of one of the dead tree's living neighbors. It was as large as a sea eagle, and the bottom of its great tail trickled sparks to the rotting wood below in a patter of hisses as they burst and died. It did have feathers of flame, but to sum it up that way was ridiculous, like how illustrations in some of Grace's books showed firebirds merely as mundane parrots with yellow and orange as a fringe along their outline like fur.

This bird, it was steel, straight from the heart of a furnace. It glowed with its heat, yes, but also it shimmered with the shock of a true nature revealed, like the possibilities of Honor's favorite blades blooming forth from ugly ore.

An arrow flashed forth and flew true. The shard of darkness showed against the firebird's wing, then the great bird tumbled down to the needle carpet beside the downed tree. It landed in a sprawl, one wing trapped beneath its body, the injured one half open with the arrow jutting out, its tail flung wide. Honor whooped in triumph and vaulted the log to land beside her prey.

Cordelia pressed her fingertips to her mouth. Her every instinct rebelled. Too easy. But Honor pulled on a heavy leather glove that had been tucked into her belt and reached for a feather in the center of the tail, to pluck it out.

The jutting arrow—why hadn't it burned, why hadn't Cordelia asked that question?—puffed into ash, then the firebird surged upward. Only faking, all along.

It flew straight for Honor's face and she gasped in horror, throwing up her hand to shield herself. The firebird barely brushed her, but even that was enough to set Honor's sleeve alight. Then the firebird was up and away, getting farther every moment. Cordelia sprinted—not looking at her feet, only luck kept her toes unsnagged—and hit her sister in the center of her body as Honor began to scream. Cordelia fumbled her prone, leaned her weight on Honor's back to grind her into the fir needles.

She stayed that way longer than strictly necessary, but Honor didn't fight back, only sobbed, and Cordelia's heart rate took a long time to ease so she could breathe properly again. She sat up and drew her sister with her. Her magic was not healing magic, but she used it to gently cool the blackened mess of fabric along Honor's arm anyway. She made no attempt to peel it away to assess the damage to the skin underneath. That was for a physician to do.

She pressed the arm into Honor's body, encouraged her sister to curl around the injury, then to stand. "Come on," she said. "Let's get you back."

* * *

Honor would bear a scar along her arm for the rest of her life, though without Cordelia's quick aid, it would have extended much farther. The next day, the dowager's physician forced Honor to keep to her bed, Grace read feverishly, and Cordelia turned what she had seen over in her mind, sitting in a corner of the kitchen with her cooling tea so the dowager could not come upon her unexpectedly. The firebird had been intelligent indeed. Simply knowing that fact would not necessarily give Grace the key to trick it, however.

Then smoke was once more seen, and it was time for the second sister to try her luck. Like a dance: the same steps with a different partner. Cordelia and Grace left the horses at the road and charted their path over shed needles and around mud-slicks toward the rising smoke. Grace moved even more slowly than Cordelia, her heavy wool cloak snagging its hem on every bush, no matter how she bundled it—and the shoulder bag she wore beneath—against her belly. It was dyed a dark green, no doubt borrowed from a forester, and a tall one at that.

In the end, Cordelia had to ask: "Are you that cold?"

"Wool is extremely difficult to burn." Grace deployed her book-borne knowledge with great pride, as ever. "And once I find the place I want, I need only be still and wait." She hissed a curse and stopped to tear one corner of the wool from a particularly stubborn thorny branch's grip. "The safety is worth the trouble."

Cordelia drew the line at holding her sister's hem like a servant with a noblewoman's train, but she was considering it by the time Grace professed herself pleased with the particular configuration of trees and sunlight trickling through their branches. With Cordelia's assistance, she fastened a net-like snare of delicate metal chain between two trees set wide enough to allow flight between, then stepped back to consider the strength of its betraying shimmer from several angles.

Pleased, she nodded and chose her own location, cloak pooled around her feet. Out of her bag she drew one of her smaller notebooks. "Firebirds are known to be intensely territorial," she told her sister. "When it hears the call of a rival, it will come to me." She frowned, lips moving as she tested something written down, before voicing it. "One initial pulse, then several short," she murmured to herself.

Cordelia considered for a beat as Grace gathered herself, then took up a place standing at a little distance from her sister. If—when?—this all went wrong again, she needed to be close enough to help, but not so close as to be burned herself. Grace cupped her free hand to the side of her mouth and gave tongue in quite a passable impression of an eagle's squeaky shriek. Tutored by the forester when she talked them out of their cloak, perhaps.

A pause, a repetition of the call, then a breath-holding space of silence, only the breeze among needles and leaves surrounding them. Grace tucked away her book into the bag at her feet and arranged the cloak to close completely over her body. Cordelia watched for light—there! A flicker, hidden by intervening trunks as soon as she'd noticed it. Tension caught at the breath in her chest, tried to keep it there.

Grace called once more and the firebird was there, as if no flight between the two points had taken place. A blaze of flame and it burned an afterimage onto Cordelia's eyes with wings upraised as it smashed into the net of chains. It thrashed, tangled, and fell.

Grace would have darted forward, but Cordelia caught her arm. "Wait," she breathed.

And now the metal of the chain was beading up on the firebird's feathers, across its body and the shoulders of its wings, like droplets of rain—of *rain* instead of metal—and the bird launched itself for the sky. "No!" Grace spat, reaching after it. As if she would have preferred a burn like their sister's. And perhaps she would have—in abstract, without understanding the pain of it—thinking it would earn their father's sympathy for her failure as well.

Cordelia used her grip on Grace's arm to jerk her down, so the firebird's talons raked across Grace's back, not her face. A frightening tearing sound—the cloak pin coming free of the wool, not anything in Grace, Cordelia realized with a burst of relief—and the firebird lifted the whole muffling weight of the cloak up as if it was nothing. Grace's research was correct in that much—it smoldered, but did not fully catch flame. The firebird dropped it a few body-lengths away. Grace folded to her knees, coughing helplessly, hand going to the red mark at her throat where the pin had slammed in before the wool gave.

Cordelia stepped up to the abandoned cloak, nudged it with her toe, judged it safe to touch, and lifted it to examine the charcoaled area in its center, spread unevenly like a splashed wine stain. Grace's books had saved her from injury, even if they hadn't caught her the prize. No—her books and *Cordelia* had saved her.

So. Cordelia had two examples of what *not* to do, but no clear idea of her own path forward, even now. She examined and discarded plan after plan on the silent ride back, and hardly registered her sisters' argument over who had the right to make the next attempt, though she was standing right next to Grace at Honor's bedside. What would a mouse do?

A witchy little mouse with teeth.

* * *

There was no sign of smoke the next morning, but the weather was fair, and Cordelia gathered a few supplies and rode out without telling anyone but the groom who saddled her horse. She chose a spot a similar distance from the road to those where they'd encountered the firebird before, and searched out a clearing along a small stream. The water made a good barrier for one side, and she created the other sides of a rough oval herself. As the foresters had described, she pulled grass up and snapped away brush down to sandy soil, then scuffed away the soil with her boots to form a shallow trench. The foresters would have used shovels, but her mousy magic was useful for this: what she couldn't pull aside, she burned with careful, contained spells, plant by plant.

When she had her boundary, marked by water, bare dirt, and blackened brush, she selected a long branch and lit it with her magic, as a brand. That, she applied within the boundary as necessary to burn everything. It was the wrong season for a bright flare and rush of flames, which allowed her to manage the tongues of flame as they cautiously smoldered and caught. Like deciding when to stir a stew to ensure it cooked evenly, perhaps.

One corner of Cordelia's lips tucked up in satisfaction—that analogy was more apt than she'd realized. Now, to spice it. She withdrew a stick of cinnamon from her shoulder bag and stepped into her blackened oval, stamping out embers where necessary. She lit the end with a spell and set it into the ground as if the curl of bark was an incense taper. It didn't smell anything like it tasted, but it did burn, as she'd suspected. Bark was bark, and this was very dry, unlike the forest vegetation around her.

"The books, the local legends—none of them agree." Cordelia lifted her voice to loft up and carry, like the cinnamon smoke. "Some say you eat spices, some say you nest in them, some say you love the scent of the smoke they make. Whichever it is, I have more." She bent and rummaged in the bag she'd left beside her feet to find another of the small boxes and sachets to open and set the scent enticingly free.

When she rose, an intricately carved box of dried chilis in her hand, the firebird was there. It alighted on the ground and examined the burning cinnamon taper with first one eye and then the other, so much like a normal bird that Cordelia giggled. She pressed her free hand to her mouth immediately, but the firebird neither fled nor attacked.

Her plan had been to speak to it as another intelligent being, assure it that she meant no harm, but faced with the pure, wild shimmer of its feathers, Cordelia could only babble. "I thought I wanted to bargain with you, spices for one of your feathers, freely given rather than taken, but I'm not sure I even know what I want anymore. My father will never make me heir, and I don't want his business in any case. And now I don't know if I want to work with either of my sisters! Honor will be too brash, too easily tricked; Grace will be too pleased with her own cleverness to adapt to changing circumstances. If only our father had trained them—trained us!—to work together, instead of pitting us against each other." She clenched both hands on the box and stared down at the pull of muscles under her skin to focus her mind and stop the flow of words.

When she spoke again, she kept herself to a measured rhythm. "I don't know what I want." She lifted her gaze back to the amazing, terrifying, *beautiful* being in front of her. "With my small magic. And I don't know why I'm telling *you* that. You're anything but small." She hinged open the box's lid. The firebird should have some of the chilis anyway. Dried, they curled down into lengths no bigger than her thumb, but each one was more than enough for a single dish.

Small, but powerful when carefully and cleverly applied.

"Oh," she said, as understanding burst into being in her chest and seeped into the rest of her body. Why was her only choice to stay with her family? They needed her, little though they admitted it, but she didn't need *them*.

The curl of smoke traveling down the cinnamon stick winked out as if the firebird had drawn the flame into itself. It delicately took the stick with one foot and rose with a single beat of its wings. Cordelia had grown mostly used to the bright afterimage it had left in her vision sitting in one spot, but now the afterimage of its full wingspan filled her view. She blinked it away, eyes watering, and when she could see again, there was only her, blackened ground, and a single feather where the cinnamon stick had stood.

This feather did not spatter her vision with afterimages; instead, it had the lesser light but deeper color of a banked ember. Cordelia bent over it with her fingertips outstretched, edging closer—oh, so carefully— while she waited for the sensation of dangerous heat. When her fingers connected, it was merely warm in the friendly fashion of a fresh pair of socks set by the fire and changed into after a long journey.

Cordelia smiled, lifted the feather, and pressed it against her belly to carry it back.

* * *

Cordelia did not precisely suspect her sisters of planning to steal the feather for a breakneck gallop back to present it first to their father with a false story of how it was won, but they could not touch it in any case. It did not burn them fit to scar, but it did redden their fingertips and force them to jerk away like the side of a hot pan. Their solicitousness thereafter, for the whole journey home, was deeply strange. Honor probably thought she'd be working for Cordelia now, but Grace more likely thought as Cordelia once had—that Cordelia might be induced to support her as the "real" heir. Cordelia decided to enjoy their compliments and attentiveness while they lasted.

When they arrived at their father's house, after a last, long day of traveling, Cordelia would have retreated to wash up, eat in the kitchen, and face their father in the morning, but her sisters were having none of it. She allowed them to chivvy her into the dining room, where her father was reading an account book beside the remains of the first course of his dinner.

The lamps were only lit on this side of the room, but the moment Cordelia drew the feather from her shoulder bag, the whole room was illuminated as fully as a sunny balcony. "I found it, Father. But I don't plan to—"

Her father surged to his feet and cupped both hands to either side of the feather while she held it upright by the quill, as if pantomiming avariciousness in a child's play. "Is it safe to touch? No, it must not be, if your sister gave it to you to hold with your magic. Who won, Honor or Grace?"

"*I* found it." Cordelia pressed her lips closed, thin, on something louder or harsher. "Ask my sisters yourself."

Her father huffed a noise that indicated his patience was thinning. His hands closed in, but he seemed to feel a radiant heat Cordelia did not, because he dropped them to his sides. "Don't play games with me, girl. You have no say in my choice of heir."

A good thing she no longer wanted one. If she'd imagined this moment ahead of time, she might have predicted anger, or a mouse's teeth. Instead, she felt only relief. "I'm leaving, Father." She cast the feather down onto the table in front of her usual seat; the wood promptly began to sizzle and smoke. When she retrieved it, a stark brand remained. Let them remember her each time they sat down to eat.

Cordelia strode out of the dining room, passing her sisters on the way in. The noise of their and her father's consternation rose to follow her down the passageway to the kitchen. From what she could decipher of Honor's bellows, it sounded like she was defending Cordelia's side of the story, at least. Her sisters weren't *truly* malicious, they were simply as their father had made them.

It was fitting that her final spell would be more of a defiant farewell than a punishment, then. Cordelia paused to fit the feather into her bodice, where it tickled against the skin between her breasts, near her heart, then stepped into the kitchen. With no great spill of light to indicate what had happened, the cook and the other kitchen servants merely nodded to her as they transferred the next course of dinner into serving dishes.

Cordelia was free to slip into the pantry and extract each and every box and bag of spice. They indeed would not have filled a ship—in fact, they fitted neatly into her bag. She centered herself in the peace of the dim pantry, drew a breath that tickled the feather once more against her skin, and worked her magic. When she was finished, she opened the box of peppercorns that she'd lifted last from the shelves and found the ground pepper she'd extracted from this meal and every bit of prepared food in the house dusted among the whole corns.

She paused to allow the servants time to serve the food, then she walked softly back down the passageway toward the other end of the house and the stables beyond. She stopped by the dining room, out of view, and waited until she heard her father's roar of disgust before she continued.

She was still smiling, replaying the shouting and shatter of thrown china in her mind, as she had one of the grooms saddle her a horse with the saddlebags still packed for a long journey. All the other spices would finance her new life, traveling outward in search of other firebirds and diversity of taste, and people who didn't disdain mousy magic.

But the salt she'd stolen, that would instead grant her a deep and abiding satisfaction, thinking of her father's experience of this meal.

The Tale of Jordan and Atheny

José Pablo Iriarte

Long ago, in the days when the land was dotted with kingdoms and nations whose names are somehow completely forgotten and unrecorded outside of tales such as this, a brother and sister journeyed on foot along the road that connected their home kingdom of Gerraine to the neighboring land of Taminpere. The road was long and they were tired, but they were nearing the end of their journey and looking forward to rejoining their family after spending the last six months with the Monks of Wellfis. The young man, Jordan, had been sent to the sanctuary to cure a mental affliction—or if necessary, to rid him of demonic possession. His twin sister, Atheny, had insisted on accompanying him to the monastery so he would not be alone. While he spent his days in prayer and painful treatments, she earned her keep by scrubbing the monastery's floors, serving the monks' meals, and tending the order's gardens.

All of her effort was worth it, though, because at last they were returning, and at last her brother was cured of his delusion.

Jordan clenched his teeth and glared off into the distance as the two crested a hill. "You know full well I can still hear you," he murmured. "I haven't been cured of anything."

Correction: Atheny *thought* her effort had worthwhile, because at last they were returning, and at last *she believed* her brother was cured of his delusion.

Jordan growled softly.

"What's wrong?" asked his sister.

Jordan debated how to reply, when, peering in the direction of his gaze, Atheny uttered a gasp.

"Who are those people?" she asked, pointing half a league down the road, where a line of refugees streamed away from Gerraine.

"It's a line of refugees," Jordan replied, "streaming away from Gerraine."

She stared at him suspiciously. "How would you know?"

"Don't be suspicious," he said hastily. "It was just, ah, a guess."

Atheny chewed her lip but turned her attention from her brother back to the migrants heading their way. They walked for a quarter hour until the first exiles were within talking distance.

"Hello," Jordan called out. "What is happening? What are you all fleeing from?"

A middle-aged man with dark, curly hair and a beard spat on the side of the road.

"If you're headed to Gerraine, best make other plans."

"But that's home," Atheny said.

"What's happened?" Jordan asked.

The man shook his head. "The king's fallen under the curse of an evil witch. The witch controls him, and through him, most of the people in the kingdom. Everybody is turning on their neighbors, thinking only of themselves, and breaking their backs to prove who is more loyal—or to prove which of their neighbors is more *dis*loyal."

Atheny tugged on a frayed spot on her sleeve and stared up the road.

The refugee shook his head. "There'll be nothing but strife for you that way," he said, and then he turned and resumed his course.

Jordan and Atheny had to step to the side of the road to avoid being trampled by the increasing number of commoners heading away from Gerraine.

Atheny eyed the human stream. There might be strife that way, but their parents and everything they owned were there, too. Did they really have a choice?

"We *don't* have a choice," Jordan said.

Atheny stared at him. "I was just thinking that."

Jordan swallowed. "Hardly surprising we should come to the same conclusion," he said.

It was nearly nightfall when they reached the gates of the city. There was no line to get in, but still they were stopped by a guardsman.

"What is your business in Gerraine?" he demanded.

"We live here," Jordan blurted.

"Ah, we've been away for a few months and are returning home," Atheny clarified.

"I see." The guardsman reached into a storage compartment behind him and pulled out two small circular pins. Each was a plated disk small enough to fit in the palm of Jordan's hand, enameled in red with the outlines of two faces—the king's, and another that neither of them recognized.

"Everybody has to wear these now. To show your loyalty."

Atheny curled her lip. "That's absurd. Anybody can wear a brooch—how does that prove anything?"

The soldier rested a hand on the hilt of his sword. "Then it shouldn't trouble you to wear it."

"No trouble at all!" Jordan interjected. "Here," he said, tugging on Atheny's arm, "I'll affix it for you."

The guard let them go while Jordan fumbled with the brooch. Unbeknownst to him, however, the token was less a *symbol* of loyalty than an *enforcer* of it.

"Well, it's *knownst* to me now," Jordan muttered, slipping the brooch into a pouch.

"Who are you talking to?" asked Atheny.

"Nobody. You're right, we shouldn't wear these." He tugged her down the walk, holding his breath and waiting for the gate attendant to call for more soldiers.

"Why are you suddenly agreeing with me? You're not still hearing voices are you?" She swallowed. "Not after all those months at the monastery, surely?"

"No," Jordan replied carefully. "I am not hearing voices."

This was technically true, since he was only hearing a *single* voice, not *voices*.

Jordan nodded at nothing in particular.

He murmured his suspicions about the brooch to his sister as they made their way through the cobbled streets of Gerraine, to the home they had grown up in.

Atheny pushed the door open—or tried to—and found it uncustomarily locked.

"Father!" she called out, pounding on the wood. "Mother! We have returned!"

A fumbling noise from the other side of the door signaled it was being unlatched, then it swung inward. On the other side, their father towered beneath the lintel.

"So you have," he said. "So you have."

He may have smiled tightly as he spoke, but Jordan and Atheny didn't see it, because their eyes were on the loyalty brooch pinning his tunic closed.

* * *

Their parents puttered around the house, following the twins while they unpacked from their journey. If they were pleased to have their children back after half a year's absence, they didn't show it. Once, even returning from a night with their cousins would have been enough to prompt their mother to cook up a feast of their favorite foods and their father to dust off his concertina and play it for hours.

Now, every other word seemed to be a complaint about an inconsiderate neighbor or a treasonous former official or imagined spies from the neighboring kingdom of Florder.

Jordan's stomach quivered as he listened to the bellicose talk, and he exchanged a worried glance with Atheny.

"We have to do something," she whispered mid-rant.

"What do you suggest?"

"You think the brooch is causing this?"

Jordan eyed his mother, who had moved on from cataloguing the faults of her neighbors to bemoaning the rise in street crime and the need to apply the death penalty to a greater variety of infractions.

"I do," he said.

Atheny stepped over to their mother and tugged on the enameled disk.

Mother slapped her hand away. "Stop that—in this house we are loyal to our king and his advisor." She frowned. "And anyway, where is *your* loyalty emblem?"

She advanced on Atheny, her hand raised.

Jordan stepped between them. "They had run out when we went through the gate!"

"That's right!" Atheny agreed. "That's why I wanted to look at yours!"

Mother's nostrils flared. "Then march right back out and try one of the other gates into the city and demand your own. You don't need to bother with mine." She glanced from Atheny to Jordan and back. "Go right now, before people question how I raised you."

"Now?" Jordan stammered.

"Mother, we've journeyed so far. Let us eat dinner first and then we can go. Here in your house, nobody will see or question anything."

Mother narrowed her eyes, but she nodded slowly. "Go fetch more wood from the pile," she told Jordan. "And you," she pointed at Atheny, "set the table."

Jordan went to the shed, only to find it locked. Father was suspicious when he asked for the key, but relented when he understood that Jordan was trying to do work that otherwise Father would have to do himself.

Outside, once he got the shed unlocked, he loaded up a basket with enough to last the night.

He sagged against the frame of the shed. "I wish you would stop that," he said to nobody. Jordan's eyes narrowed. "Not to 'nobody.' To *you*. To the devil or whatever that keeps describing my thoughts and actions to me."

Jordan was not supposed to hear those descriptions, and he *certainly* was not supposed to carry on a discussion with them.

"Well, I *do*," he said. "And I suppose I am."

This was very improper.

"We agree on that much," he mumbled. Jordan took a shaky breath. "You seem to think you're some sort of omniscient being, but I don't think you understand what it's like for me. Nobody else constantly hears themselves described *from the outside*. If people are talking *to* me, they call me Jordan, or perhaps 'you there.' If people are talking *about* me, I'm not usually there to hear it. But with you in my head, I get a constant stream of 'he did this, he said that, he looked this way,' and—" Jordan swallowed. "I don't actually see myself as a *he*. Or a *she* for that matter. I suppose everybody else sees me as *he*, but at least I don't have to hear other people call me that every other second."

Jordan stared up at the sky. "Forget about it. It's not as though anything's going to change," they said.

They blinked. "'They'?"

A door creaked and Atheny slipped furtively from the house.

They. An entirely precedented word that was neither *he* nor *she*.

Unless Jordan preferred something else…

"No," they said quickly. "I like it."

Atheny squinted as she closed the distance between herself and Jordan. "Who are you talking to? Actually, never mind, I don't want to know. Did you see the way Mother raised her hand to me? She's never hit me before!"

"We have to do something."

"Do you think we should try again, but with Father?"

"That…seems like a terrible idea," Jordan said, accurately.

"Maybe we can get them to leave town. Say that the monks said we all need to go back for a final blessing or something."

"And then what? Just leave our lives here?"

Atheny considered this. "Maybe we should talk to the neighbors. Surely we can find some unaffected—"

Atheny stiffened and the hair on Jordan's neck prickled as they followed her gaze and saw a boy maybe five years younger than them watching from a neighboring roof.

The boy leapt to the ground and raced off. Jordan sprinted around their house to the street and bounded after him. He seemed on the verge of getting away when he tripped on a loose stone.

"Please!" he said, rolling over and holding his arms up. "I was just looking for a place to sleep!"

"Oh, really?" asked Atheny, catching up to them. "Then what's this?" She snatched a parchment from the boy's hand and held it out to Jordan, who recognized it as a map marking the location of their home.

"Please, he threatened me!"

Jordan looked around to see if anybody watched them. They couldn't see any eyes upon them, but they'd seen enough of their parents' strange behavior to not wish to chance it. They tugged him back toward the space behind their house.

"Who threatened you?" Jordan asked.

"Threatened you to do what?" Atheny whispered.

The boy looked back and forth between Jordan and Atheny. "The guard at the gate was suspicious of you, so he told me to follow you."

Jordan met their sister's eyes. "What do we do now?"

"If he reports back, things could get a lot worse."

The boy's eyes widened. "Please don't hurt me!" he cried out.

Jordan shushed him, while Atheny said, "Keep crying out like that and you'll leave us no choice."

"Please!" he said again, his voice quieter this time. "I missed my chance to leave with the others," he claimed. "Now I have no place to live. I have to do what they say."

Jordan pursed their lips, pondering his claims. The things the spy had claimed were true.

Atheny's chin trembled. "We have to take him in."

"What?" Jordan asked. Reasonably.

"He's unaffected. He's looking out for himself, but he's not under their spell. He's not wearing a loyalty brooch."

Surely there was no other reason a street rat might be untrustworthy, if he wasn't wearing a magical brooch.

"I don't know," Jordan said.

"You said we should look for unaffected people and that's exactly what we've found! He can help us."

"Anything!" he agreed. "I can help!"

"He just needs a meal and a place to stay," Atheny said. "What's your name?"

"Mat," the boy claimed.

Atheny led the way back into the house, the question having somehow been decided without a vote. Jordan and Atheny's parents weren't any more eager to take Mat in than Jordan had been, but Atheny's offer to share her own portion of food, coupled with Mat's jumping to serve them, won their grudging acceptance.

"Only for tonight," Father growled. "If his family was disloyal enough to leave the kingdom, then maybe he deserves whatever he gets."

Atheny gasped at her father's heartlessness, but Mat didn't seem to hear, for Mother had already put him to work carrying food to the table. He attempted to serve a bowl of stew to Atheny, but Father yanked the ladle from his hands and he and Mother served themselves first. By the time they finished scooping dinner into their bowls, little was left for the other three.

While their parents wolfed down the food, Jordan eyed the meager quantity in their own bowl. Was there something odd about the scent?

"Atheny, wait."

Their sister looked up, but before she could reply, both their parents fell from their chairs with a pair of thuds.

Jordan reached out and grabbed the boy's arm before he could so much as think of running.

"What did you do?" Atheny hissed.

"Nothing!" he claimed.

"'Claimed?'" Jordan slapped their forehead. "I was a fool. The signs that he was lying were right there." They glanced up to find both Atheny and Mat staring at them. "Stop lying, boy," they said. "Tell us what you did to our parents or the City Guard will be the least of your troubles."

"It's not deadly!" he cried out. "It was just supposed to be temporary. Just long enough for me to return to my contact!"

Jordan met Atheny's eyes but was still too annoyed at themself to bother with recriminations.

"What did you put in the stew?" they asked.

"Mithridates powder."

Mithridates powder was among the more potent paralytics known to man. Only a tincture brewed from gold wort could reverse the effect.

"Atheny, do you know where we might find gold wort?"

She blinked. "I believe it grows in the forest. Why?"

"That's the only antidote."

"How do we know he's even telling the truth about the powder?" she asked, suddenly concerned, for the first time, that the urchin might be less than honest.

"We could bring him with us."

"Actually, I have an idea," she said. "We'll make him eat the stew himself, and then go find the antidote. Once it works on our parents, he can have it as well."

The boy struggled, but Jordan tightened their grip.

"I don't know if we have a better option," Jordan replied, and indeed, they did not.

* * *

There was no sense searching the forest at night, so Jordan and Atheny waited until just before dawn to sneak out of the city. Atheny believed she would be able to recognize gold wort if she saw it, but by the time the sun was well on its way to its zenith they still had not stumbled upon any. When they chanced upon a stream, Jordan crouched beside the bank and splashed some water on their tired eyes.

Atheny scooped up a handful and brought it to her lips. She stood in the morning haze, sunlight gleaming off of her porcelain features and making her black hair shimmer, her heaving bosom—

"Could you stop that please?" Jordan murmured, apropos of nothing.

"Not *nothing*. Why do you only describe women like that," they demanded, their fair skin glowing with righteous indignation, their lips curled into something between a sneer and a pout—

"Er, that's not an improvement."

On the other side of a slight rise, a crack of twigs startled both of them, moments before a young man came into view. He was tall and muscular and dressed in what were clearly fine clothes, though they were wrinkled and mud-stained.

His eyes widened upon spying Jordan and Atheny. "You there! I am Prince Sten. As your ruler—I mean, as the son of your ruler—I command your loyalty. I command you to obey me!"

The twins exchanged a glance. They hadn't come all this way just to be captured now. In an unspoken moment of agreement, both dashed away from the prince.

"Wait—you can disobey me! How wonderful!"

Despite themself, Jordan turned back toward the royal, staring in confusion. "Huh?"

Atheny too opened her mouth, but no words came out.

The prince clambered over a fallen stump. "You're not in thrall! This is so much better than trying to get a brainless subject to help me!"

Brainless subject sounded like far too practiced a turn of phrase, but Jordan let it go. "Why do you need help?"

"The witch Branley has placed my father under a spell. He no longer thinks for himself, but merely commands whatever Branley tells him to."

"So it's not just the subjects who are brainless," Atheny observed.

Sten let the dig go with a sigh and a nod.

"I wish we could help," Jordan said, "but we're in a similar predicament ourselves. Our parents have been poisoned by one of those brainless subjects and we need to find gold wort to remove the effect."

Prince Sten frowned. "You won't be finding gold wort in these woods. We do have jars of it in the palace storerooms, however. Help me and I'll see that you get all you need."

Atheny crossed her arms. "We're not soldiers."

"You're not soldiers, but you're here. All of my men were caught up by the order to wear loyalty tokens. If I go to a neighboring kingdom for help, I risk exposing our weakened condition. This may even have been Branley's plan all along." He stepped closer. "Please. I can get us in unseen. I'll go alone if I must, but three of us will have a much better chance against Branley. And we need each other." His eyes met theirs, sincerity shining through.

"Well, I haven't heard the word *claimed* once in all this," Jordan murmured.

"What?"

They turned toward Atheny. "I believe him."

Sten beamed at Jordan in gratitude. "Here," he said. "I am not completely without resources." He handed Jordan a throwing dagger. "This knife is enchanted. If you throw it, it will always hit your target. The only person it can't hit is me."

"Shouldn't you keep it for yourself?"

The prince had the grace to look self-conscious as he replied, "I already never miss."

Jordan passed the knife to their sister. "You take it."

She snorted. "I have better aim than you do. Do you think I'm weak and need your gallantry?"

Jordan leaned in to whisper to her. "I think you must know by now, I already have a…magical ability of my own that can protect me. You do not—I would know if you did."

Atheny frowned, but she took the dagger.

Prince Sten marched to a particularly dense thicket within the woods, impassable-seeming, with gnarled branches interlocking to form a nearly solid wall. He tugged on a tree that looked much too heavy to be moved, swinging it aside easily as though it were on well-oiled hinges, revealing a hidden opening in the ground.

"This leads to a tunnel that goes into the palace," he said. "I don't know how old it is—I think even my father doesn't know about it. I found it while exploring the cellar. I use it to venture out without the trouble and distraction of a retinue."

Sten led them into an underground chamber and closed a heavy door behind them, plunging them momentarily into darkness. The moment the door sealed shut, however, a line of torches ignited, revealing a passage that extended an incalculable distance.

Atheny gasped. "You have magic?"

The prince shook his head. "Whoever first built this must have spelled the torches somehow."

"Do you sneak out often?" Jordan asked.

Sten faced them both in the flickering light. "My father would not approve of everything I do," he said, his gaze flicking from Atheny to Jordan. "Sometimes I need to be out from under his eyes."

As they passed through stone corridors worn smooth over what must have been decades if not centuries of use, Jordan tried not to think about what the prince might do to protect this secret once this crisis was over.

"Actually, the thought had not crossed my mind until now."

Sten leaned toward Atheny. "Who is he talking to?"

"*They*. And they talk to themself a lot."

"Ah. Noted."

Sten chattered as they walked, telling the twins about lands he had traveled to, tutors both good and bad, and unexpected annoyances of growing up stifled by nobility. Jordan thought he must be very lonely, to be sharing so eagerly with people he barely knew.

Jordan lost track of time, but eventually the three emerged into what turned out to be a wine cellar.

"This will be dangerous," the prince said as he slid a rack of bottles to cover the opening they had just stepped through. He stopped and faced them. "It's selfish to feel this way, but I'm glad I don't have to confront this alone." He bit his lower lip and looked at each of them, first Atheny and then Jordan. "Thank you."

The moment lingered, and then Sten turned abruptly. He led them up an unlit servants' staircase, murmuring, "If we just find the witch alone, we might have a chance."

They followed Sten through hall after hall, ducking out of sight when maids or guards happened by. After much fruitless searching, he paused outside a curtained opening. From the other side, voices could be heard, though the words they spoke were too faint to make out.

"My father's study," Sten said. "I have a pretty good guess who's with him."

Sten poked his head inside and ducked back out. "Branley's back is to us. We can prevail if we all attack together."

Jordan chanced a peek. A giant of a man sat in an ornate chair behind a table, while a skinny man in a mountain of furs paced in front of him, carrying on about all the plots on the ruler's life that his spies had uncovered.

"*That's* Branley?" Jordan whispered.

"Yes? Why does that surprise you?"

"When you said witch I thought . . ." Jordan began, as though the idea that a witch might not be female had never occurred to them.

"You thought what?" Atheny asked.

"Um, I thought he'd be taller."

Sten blinked. "Oh. Well, what he lacks in size he makes up for in malevolence." He put a hand on Jordan's arm. "Let's go together, on the count of three. He's so preoccupied by his ranting that we can sneak up on him."

"Your father will see us," Jordan objected.

"My father would never betray me," the prince said, naively.

"I don't think that's—"

Jordan's objection died in their throat as Sten crept through the curtain with Atheny right behind. Gritting their teeth, Jordan followed the two.

The king's voice quavered as he interrupted his advisor. "Sten! You've returned! But...who are these people with you? Branley, are these the assassins? Protect me, Branley!"

The witch turned to face them. "Prince Sten! At last, we meet! You are so formidable—your father has told me so much about you, but you are even more dashing in person."

There was something odd about Branley's speech, a thrumming undercurrent, as though he were speaking two sets of words at once, but only one was meant for the ears. The sound was...strangely compelling.

Sten straightened. "You, uh, think so?"

"Of course, dear boy!"

Jordan shook their head to clear the effect. "Atheny! Throw your blade! He's done something to Sten, but you can't miss!"

"Can't miss? You must be very talented! I knew the moment I laid eyes on you there was something about you. You're not like the other girls. You are tough and smart! What an excellent administrator you would make!"

Atheny raised a hand to her mouth. "What? You are too kind—still, I have always wanted something more than what Mother and Father hoped for."

"Yes! Of course!"

Jordan swallowed and took a step back.

"And you, uh, boy! A commoner, and yet in the company of the prince! How brave! What a shining specimen of masculinity!"

Jordan snorted. "Uh, what?" They rubbed their forehead, willing away a sudden headache from the thrum of the witch's speech. "You two aren't falling for this, are you?"

Atheny looked from Jordan to Branley and back. "Jordan, we may have been wrong about him."

Sten nodded. "Yes, let's hear what he has to say."

The king gestured feebly with his hand, as if seeking permission to speak. "He's been helping to make the kingdom great—by culling out the weak and disloyal."

Jordan's legs felt like butter and he staggered back. "Atheny, we need to get out of here!"

"He can't be reached," said Branley. "His heart must be traitorous! Quickly girl, kill him!"

Atheny glanced at the dagger she held, as though confused. "Kill... Jordan?"

Jordan struggled to draw a breath. If she threw the knife at all, it wouldn't matter how conflicted she felt, she would hit them.

Beside Atheny, Sten drew his own dagger. "We must protect the kingdom," he said, woodenly.

The pair stood between Jordan and the hallway they had entered from, so they took off in the opposite direction, toward a wall with two doorways spaced at either end.

"Which one?" they gasped.

Something sharp nicked their right ear, while another dagger zipped past and clattered against the far wall.

"Which door?" they demanded again. Hearing no answer, they chose the nearer, the one on their left, and burst through it to find themself standing on a narrow balcony.

"Thanks so much," they muttered, a bit unreasonably, and slammed the door behind them. Jordan leaned past the railing and looked down. Beneath them, a matching balcony mirrored the one on which they stood. There was no time to think, so they stepped over the railing, lowered themselves, and swung to the level below. Then they crashed through the door that led into the palace, and found themselves in a guest chamber of some sort.

Anybody would be able to deduce their location, so they scrambled from the room, down an interior hallway, and through another door, into a pitch-black space.

Now that they were no longer running, their ear throbbed where it had been nicked, and they resisted the urge to touch it and explore the extent of the damage.

Gasping for breath, Jordan felt around and tried to take stock. They were surrounded by shelves, piled high with soft material. A closet for linens, perhaps. That suggested there was no exit except the door Jordan had come through, but the thought of rushing back out right away was impossible. Soldiers might be able to run and fight without pause, but Jordan was no soldier, and they were not especially fit. They needed to catch their breath.

"I'm not even offended by that characterization," they wheezed softly. After a few more breaths, they murmured, "I'm *not* a soldier, and if I try to soldier my way through this, I'm destined to fail. I need to find a way to be more clever than the witch." What evidence they had that their cleverness was any more noteworthy than their fighting prowess was anybody's guess.

"Oh, that's right," they added. "I've also got this oh-so-helpful voice talking to me."

They tapped a wooden shelf absently. "You don't actually talk *to* me, though. You don't answer questions, the way a *useful* delusion would. You talk *about* me, instead. Anything I learn from you, I need to infer."

Jordan paced a step, only to bash their forehead into a low-hanging beam.

"Thank you for not attaching an adverb to that," they muttered. "You're not unresponsive, though, and you're not unsympathetic either, because you switched pronouns for me when I asked you to, and you stopped describing my sister's body when I objected. You have rules, though. You can't just tell me things. Anything you say has to relate to what somebody is doing or thinking."

Jordan pondered the day's events.

"But I think you still want me to prevail," they noted astutely.

"Astutely? So, I'm right?" they asked, rather less astutely now.

"Fine, be that way."

They couldn't accomplish anything from inside this closet, no matter how much effort they put into puzzling out the nature of their unexpected and not-entirely-welcome ability. Anything could be happening to Atheny while they cowered here. Or to the prince. They needed to deduce a way to defeat the witch.

How had Branley so quickly invaded their minds? Clearly he had power even when a subject was not wearing a loyalty emblem. The brooch simply made it so he didn't have to be present to control the victim's mind. Jordan thought about their parents' selfishness when they returned home. How did that fit in?

Branley wasn't exactly making people *obedient*. He was making them *self-centered*, and making them believe that obedience to him was the way to gain more for themselves.

Why hadn't it worked on Jordan, then? Were they too pure of spirit, they wondered vainly, absurdly, ridiculously?

"Fine," they muttered. "I get your point."

No, Branley's magic hadn't worked on them because his assumptions about what they wanted, and how they saw themself, were so far off that his flattery missed its mark. Maybe that was a weakness that could be exploited.

Jordan cracked the door to the closet. The outside was empty. Which way should they go? Left or right?

Jordan took a fortuitous step to the left. When the hall intersected another, they foolishly considered going left again, before wisely deciding to keep going the same direction they had already been headed. Then, at a T, they regrettably considered turning right, before choosing the corridor to their left. Turn by turn and up a flight of stairs, they made their way through the palace, avoiding guards and dead ends.

They slowed their pace when at last they heard a familiar voice, and proceeded carefully into what appeared to be some sort of receiving hall.

"...most auspicious timing," Branley lectured, pacing the room.

Jordan crept closer, hiding behind a suit of armor posed by the doorway.

"Public appearances by the royal family always raise the subjects' loyalty," Branley continued. "Now that you've returned, my boy, it will be all the more effective."

Sten nodded while Atheny's eyes followed Branley's every move.

"In fact..." The witch clapped his hands together. "I know just the thing! We should have a royal wedding!"

Jordan crashed into the metal suit, but whatever noise he made was drowned out by the reactions of the others in the chamber.

"A wedding?" echoed the king. "How delightful! Who is getting married?"

"Your son!"

"He is?"

"I am? To whom?"

"Why, to the commoner girl. Can you think of a story more guaranteed to win over the subjects' hearts? And it will make her a royal as well, which will increase my pow—er, will increase the fervor your subjects feel for you!"

Jordan grabbed the unsharpened decorative sword from the suit of arms and swung it clumsily over their head, evidently forgetting they were not a soldier after all. Branley turned at their grunt of exertion, and easily sidestepped their wild downswing.

"The riffraff has returned!" exclaimed Branley. "Your majesty, call your guards! Prince! Princess-to-be! After him!"

Atheny and Sten leapt from their chairs, Sten rising with enough force to knock his seat over.

Jordan backed up a step.

"Now!" Branley ordered. "Gut him!"

Sten drew his knife but refrained from throwing it.

Why was Jordan still alive?

"I know why you haven't killed me yet. It's because part of you sees through the witch's spell." Despite their bravado, Jordan continued to back away as they spoke. "Because he doesn't see who you really are, any better than he sees who I am."

"He wants to steal everything that's rightfully yours!" Branley cried out. "Get him!"

"You could have killed me before. I'm not athletic enough to dodge your throws." Jordan looked at Sten. "Your dagger must be the one that clattered at my feet. You said you never missed, but you did." They turned toward their sister. "And you were not capable of missing, so you hit me, but as superficially as possible. Despite being enchanted, you did not *want* to harm me."

"Go on!" Branley screamed. "Kill the intruder now! Kill him for the sake of the one you love!"

Sten's knife hand twitched as the words echoed through the chamber.

"That's right!" Jordan cried out. "Do as he says!" they added, in a moment of apparent insanity.

"Do *exactly* as he said! Kill the *intruder!* For the sake of the one you love!" they repeated. "For the one you *both* love!"

For a moment, Sten and Atheny seemed to process Jordan's words, and then, as one, they turned and threw their knives at the witch. For each had looked into their hearts and realized that *the one they loved*, of course, was—

"Oh *sure*," Jordan panted, rolling their eyes. "Act like you understood *all along*, why don't you."

* * *

The twins were tending to their parents—as well as the street urchin—when the prince came to check on them.

"It's Sten," Jordan said, a moment before they heard a rap on the door.

Atheny shook her head but let their visitor in without comment.

"I came to make sure the gold wort had been delivered promptly," he said, after greeting them both.

"It was," Atheny said.

"They're going to be fine," Jordan added.

Sten seemed taken aback. "You seem quite certain."

"Yes."

He walked over to stand beside Jordan. "I admire that about you. The way you make a call and throw yourself into it. The faith you had that your sister and I would turn on Branley simply because you told us to." He swallowed. "I'm relieved that I lived up to that confidence."

Jordan shrugged. "I just knew you well enough to see where the witch was mistaking you—all of us—for people with more...predictable desires."

It occurred to them only as the words left their mouth that they had just implied that the king's own desires were more mundane, but Sten either didn't notice or wasn't offended, because he smiled.

"You should know that Atheny does not want to marry you," they added, twinkling.

Twinkling? What the deuce did that even mean? Jordan wondered if they had somehow become a star.

The prince chuckled and glanced over his shoulder. "Yes, well. About that." His gaze settled on Jordan again. "Something my father always tried to keep quiet is that I am not amorously interested in women. I couldn't help but think, in our confrontation with Branley, that you seemed to have guessed that about me, though." He took Jordan's hand as he spoke. "For years he has forbidden me from so much as spending time with another man."

"How fortuitous, then," Jordan replied, haltingly, "that I am neither."

Sten squeezed their hand in agreement, and the two shared a smile.

And so, before long, it came to pass that Prince Sten did announce an engagement, but it was to Jordan rather than Atheny. If the king objected, or indeed if anybody did, they kept their thoughts to themselves. At least, Jordan never heard about it—certainly not from *this* narrator.

About the Authors

RJ BLAIN suffers from a Moleskine journal obsession, a pen fixation, and a terrible tendency to pun without warning. In her spare time, she daydreams about being a spy. Her contingency plan involves tying her best of enemies to spinning wheels and quoting James Bond villains until satisfied.

Website: https://thesneakykittycritic.com
Facebook: https://www.facebook.com/rjblain.author

PATRICIA BRAY was there when Zombies Needs Brains was born, and has the t-shirt to prove it. The author of a dozen novels, her storytelling skills also come in handy in her day job as a business intelligence analyst. She lives in New Hampshire, where she balances her time at a keyboard with cycling, hiking and curling. Find her on the web at www.patriciabray.com.

MARIE BRENNAN is a former anthropologist and folklorist who shamelessly pillages her academic fields for inspiration. She recently misapplied her professors' hard work to *The Night Parade of 100 Demons* and the short novel *Driftwood*. She is the author of the Hugo Award-nominated Victorian adventure series The Memoirs of Lady Trent along with several other series, over seventy short stories, and the New Worlds series of worldbuilding guides; as half of M.A. Carrick, she has written the epic Rook and Rose trilogy, beginning with *The Mask of Mirrors*. For more information, visit swantower.com, Twitter @swan_tower, or her Patreon at www.patreon.com/swan_tower.

REBECCA A. DEMAREST is an award-winning author, playwright, book designer, and writing instructor living in Seattle, WA with her husband and 1 stowaway lizard, 2 muppets, 3 rescue dart frogs. For more information, please visit rebeccademarest.com.

R.Z. HELD writes speculative fiction, including a space opera novella series and urban fantasy novels as Rhiannon Held. She lives near Seattle, where she works as an archaeologist for an environmental compliance firm. At work, she mostly uses her degree for copy-editing technical reports; in writing, she uses it for world-building; in public, she'll probably use it to check the mold seams on the wine bottle at dinner. Website: rhiannonheld. com Twitter: @rhiannonheld

LUCIA IGLESIAS lives in Iceland. Her fiction and nonfiction have appeared in The Rumpus, Shimmer, Liquid Imagination, Cosmic Roots and Eldritch Shores, the Bronzeville Bee, and other publications.

JOSÉ PABLO IRIARTE is a Cuban-American writer, high school math teacher, and parent of two. Their fiction can be found in magazines such as Uncanny, Lightspeed, and Strange Horizons, and has been nominated (twice!) for the Nebula Award, longlisted for the Otherwise Award, and reprinted in various Year's Best compilations. José currently serves as Director-at-Large for SFWA. Learn more at www.labyrinthrat.com, or look for José on twitter @labyrinthrat.

NYT bestselling author **ALETHEA KONTIS** is a princess, a storm chaser, and a geek. Author of over 20 books and 40 short stories, Alethea has received the Scribe Award, the Garden State Teen Book Award, and won the Gelett Burgess Children's Book Award twice! She has also been twice nominated for both the Andre Norton Nebula and the Dragon Award. When not writing or storm chasing, Alethea narrates stories for multiple award-winning online magazines and contributes regular YA book reviews to NPR. Born in Vermont, Alethea currently resides on the Space Coast of Florida with her teddy bear, Charlie. Visit www.AletheaKontis.com for more!

Y.M. PANG spent her childhood pacing around her grandfather's bedroom, telling him stories of magic, swords, and bears. Her work has appeared in *The Magazine of Fantasy & Science Fiction*, *Beneath Ceaseless Skies*, and *The Dark*, among other venues. She dabbles in photography and often contemplates the merits of hermitism. Despite this, you can find her online at www.ympang.com or on Twitter as @YMPangWriter

MIYUKI JANE PINCKARD is a writer, game designer, educator, and the co-founder of Story Kitchen Studio, a community for exploring writing techniques. Her fiction can be found in Strange Horizons, Uncanny Magazine, Flash Fiction Online, and the anthology, *If There's Anyone Left, Vol. 1*. She was born in Tokyo, Japan and now lives in Venice, California, with her partner and a little dog. She likes wine and mystery novels and karaoke. Follow her @miyukijane (Twitter and Instagram) and at www.miyukijane.com.

CAT RAMBO's 250+ fiction publications include stories in Asimov's, Clarkesworld Magazine, and The Magazine of Fantasy and Science Fiction. In 2020 they won the Nebula Award for novelette Carpe Glitter. They are a former two-term President of the Science Fiction and Fantasy Writers of America (SFWA). Their most recent works are space opera *You Sexy Thing* (Tor Macmillan), as well as anthology *The Reinvented Heart* (Arc Manor, May, 2022), co-edited with Jennifer Brozek. For more about Cat and their popular online school, The Rambo Academy for Wayward Writers, see their website.
Facebook: https://www.facebook.com/Cat-Rambo-79388126929/
Instagram: https://www.instagram.com/specfic/
Twitter: https://twitter.com/Catrambo
YouTube:
https://www.youtube.com/channel/UCv9iUujAbeQ4G6QN1OSqgkg

ANGELA REGA is an Australian-based writer of Mediterranean background. Her stories appear in venues including Overland, The Year's Best Australian Fantasy and Horror, The Dark, PS Publishing, and South of the Sun: Australian Fairy Tales for the 21st Century. She is an Aurealis Awards and Norma K. Hemming Award finalist. Angela works as an Italian teacher and Librarian and writes in the hours in between. She grew up in a household that never started and finished a sentence in the same language and still struggles with syntax. She often falls in love with poetry and drinks way too much coffee.

RHONDI SALSITZ is a writer with both trad and indie publications, and now co-editor for ZNB. She lives in sunny California (too sunny, really, we have drought again) with her blended family including one large cream golden retriever, a striped gray cat, and a white mischievous heart-stealer feline. Under seven pen names for Middle Grade, New Adult and Adult audiences, she has published epic fantasy, space opera, thrillers, romance, urban fantasy, and cozy mysteries. Her writing has earned Nation Bestseller status and some great reviews from PW. Check her out at www.rhondiann.com.

RACHEL SWIRSKY holds an MFA from the Iowa Writers Workshop and her fiction has appeared in venues including Tor.com, Asimov's Magazine, and The Year's Best Non-Required Reading. She's published two collections: Through the Drowsy Dark (Aqueduct Press) and How the World Became Quiet (Subterranean Press). Her fiction has been nominated for the Hugo Award and the World Fantasy Award, and twice won the Nebula. Her novella, *January Fifteenth*, an exploration of a near-future United States of America with Universal Basic Icnome, is due from Tor.com this summer. You can find her on Patreon as Rachel Swirsky.

ALYSE WINTERS lives and writes in New England, where she is happiest when buried under several inches of snow. When not writing, she enjoys epic fantasy, period dramas, and arguing with her cat.

About the Editors

CRYSTAL SARAKAS is a public radio producer, writer, editor, and cat wrangler. Her fiction has been published in the anthologies FIGHT LIKE A GIRL, WHAT FOLLOWS, THE MODERN DEITY'S GUIDE TO SURVIVING HUMANITY, and in Lamplight Magazine. She also edited the anthology MY BATTERY IS LOW AND IT IS GETTING DARK. Originally from the oil fields of West Texas, she now lives in Upstate New York in a nearly one hundred-year-old house with her husband, three cats, four ghost cats, and a whole host of other things that go bump in the night. She's made friends with most of them. @csarakas on Twitter or at https://www.facebook.com/crystalsarakas

****

RHONDI SALSITZ is a writer with both trad and indie publications, and now co-editor for ZNB. She lives in sunny California (too sunny, really, we have drought again) with her blended family including one large cream golden retriever, a striped gray cat, and a white mischievous heart-stealer feline. Under seven pen names for Middle Grade, New Adult and Adult audiences, she has published epic fantasy, space opera, thrillers, romance, urban fantasy, and cozy mysteries. Her writing has earned Nation Bestseller status and some great reviews from PW. Check her out at www.rhondiann.com .

Acknowledgments

This anthology would not have been possible without the tremendous support of those who pledged during the Kickstarter. Everyone who contributed not only helped create this anthology, they also helped support the small press Zombies Need Brains LLC, which I hope will be bringing SF&F themed anthologies to the reading public for years to come. I want to thank each and every one of them for helping to bring this small dream into reality. Thank you, my zombie horde.

The Zombie Horde: Donald Smith, Susan Campbell, Erik T Johnson, Annalee Johnson, Nitya Tripuraneni, Steven Mentzel, Cynthia Waldron, Andy Miller, Robert Maughan, Rya Wren, Phillip Spencer, If not bad bitch then Lisa Stuckey, CE Murphy, GC Rovario-Cole, Camille Lofters, Louise Lowenspets, Michael M. Jones, RJ Hopkinson, Margot Harris, justloux2, Annette Agostini, Stacey Helton, Cherie Livingston, Melynda Marchi, Katrina Knight, charles bassett, Sacchi Green, Sandy, Rosanne Barona, Colette D, Jamie FitzGerald, Kat Haines, Robert D. Stewart, Stephen Rubin, Randall Brent Martin II, Brad Roberts, Kelly Mayo, Chris McCartney, MC, April Thompson, Fantastic Books, Richard C. White, Arlene Medder, Erik Twede, LIsa Kruse, Kevin Niemczyk, Erin Penn, Evergreen Lee, Rosa María Quiñones, Alfonso Orellana, Susan O'Fearna, Jeremy Audet, Kevin Heard, Dr. Charles E. Norton III, Megan Parker, Kate Lindstrom, Tracy 'Rayhne' Fretwell, Doc Holland, Ane-Marte

Mortensen, Bella & Dylan Fuentes Steckline, Lace, Dan DeVita, Heather Childrey, Louisa Berry, Kortnee Bryant, Gini Huebner, Helen Ellison, Jennifer Flora Black, D.R. Haggitt, Sarah Hester, Annika Samuelsson, Tanya Koenig, Lizz Gable, Mary Murphy, Steven Peiper, Margaret Bumby, maileguy, Connor Bliss, Kirsty Mackay, Andrija Popovic, Pat Knuth, Kris Dikeman, Patricia Bray, Patrick Osbaldeston, Jeff Metzner, Holly Elliott, Aaron Zsoldos & Emely Pul, Kristina, Tria Bravo-Pallesen, Ryan Power, The Two Gay Geeks - Ben and Keith, Lexi Ander, Alice Norman, Tris Lawrence, R.J.H., Kyle Rogers, Bruce Alcorn, Kai Nikulainen, Chris Vincent, Emy Peters, Anita Morris, A.J. Abrao, Mindie Simmons, Kimberly M. Lowe, Colleen Feeney, Anthony R. Cardno, Lee Dalzell, Miranda Floyd, Cracknot, Tracy Polasek, Carl Wiseman, Mae Malcolm, Meyari McFarland, John Senn, Megan Maulsby, Scarlett Letter, Leane Verhulst, Margaret M. St. John, Matt & Liz A., Bookwyrmkim, Kristina Cecka, Dendra, Kristin Evenson Hirst, Tim Jordan, In Memory of Ruth, Kari Blackmoore, David Boop, Krystal Windsor, Lisa Castillo, Carlos Alberto Rodríguez Gutiérrez, Jeff G., Paul & Laura Trinies, Scott Raun, Joseph Cox, Dave Hermann, Susan Simko, Jenn Whitworth, Shawn P. McMurray, Tasha Turner, Rolf Laun, Axisor and Firestar, Mandy Wetherhold, Auri and Finn, Sami Sendele, Chris McLaren, Karen Lytle Sumpter, Stephanie Wood Franklin, Jessa Garrido, Wolf & Elissa Gray, John Markley, Ernesto Pavan, Steven Halter, Katy Manck – BooksYALove, Mustela, Vickie L Kline, J A Mortimore, Shayne Easson, Jason Y, Michael Halverson, Mark Slauter, Elaine Tindill-Rohr, Yosef Kuperman, rissatoo, Theresa Derwin, Jackie Clary, BobbyRoo, Brendan Burke, Jordan Dennis, Catherine Davis, David Flor, Crystal Foss, Jim Gotaas, Sharan Volin, Marj Sailer, Yosen Lin, dennis chambers, Craig "Stevo" Stephenson, GMarkC, Sarah, Stephen Shirres, Ian Harvey, James Lucas, ChillieBrick, .Heather Jones., Aramanth Dawe, Shyann, David Lahner, Mervi Hamalainen, Vekteris Saulius, Fred Langridge, Andrey, Bruce Arthurs, Ruth Ann Orlansky, Colette Reap, Amanda Jenkins, Sondra Fielder, Muli Ben-Yehuda, Prince Eric J Vickers, Laura Davidson, Tina M Noe Good, Keith E. Hartman, Krystal Bohannan, David Rowe, Steve Pattee, Nathan Turner, Kathleen Birk, Kaidlen Shan, T. England, Daniel Joseph Riddle, S. Petroulas, Margaret Killeen, Gary Phillips, Bob Scopatz, Danni Brigante, cassie and adam, Lizzie B., Sarah Raines, Jessica Stultz, Christine Ethier, John H. Bookwalter Jr., Kelly Snyder, Carver Rapp, C J Evans, Machell Parga, Brita Hill, Linda Pierce, Gail M, Keith West, Future Potentate of the Solar System, Jamieson Cobleigh, Jason Palmatier, Amanda Butler, Geoffrey Allen Baum, Michelle M, Risa Wolf, Shawnee M, Abra Staffin-Wiebe, Monica Taylor, Ken Huie, Robert Claney, Louise Kendall, Shirley D, Michael Barbour, Yankton Robins, Larry, Steve Arensberg, David A. H., Ju Transcendancing, Suzanna,

Brenda Rezk, Anne Burner, Jeanne Talbourdet, Christopher Wheeling, Vicki Greer, Adena, Robyn DeRocchis, Curtis Frye, Samuel Lubell, Jarrod Coad, Bess Turner, Mark Lukens, Rory King, Brenda Moon, Chad Bowden, Nick W, Deanna Harrison, Cyn Armistead, Misty Massey, Catherine Gross-Colten, Mike M., Giuseppe Lo Turco, Penny Ramirez, J.P. Goodwin, John Winkelman, Gretchen Persbacker, Andrew Hatchell, Sheryl R. Hayes, Thomas Legg, Cathy Green, Rachel Rieve, Brian W Adams, Lisa Kueltzo, Rachel A. Brune, BethAnn Lobdell, Mark Newman, Lilly Ibelo, John J Schreck, Joe Wojo, Olivia Montoya, Corey T., John MacCarrick, Kier Duros, Jeremy Brett, Niall Gordon, Ashley R. Morton, Kirstin Sims, Abe Scheppler, Melissa Mead, Jerrie the filkferengi, Deanna Stanley, Robert Gilson, Kate Stuppy, Allison Yambor, R. Hunter, Tim Lewis, Cody L. Allen, Matt P, Breann Carpenter, Catherine Moore, Simone Pietro Spinozzi, Steven Rhew, Megan Beauchemin, Ed Ellis, Lark Cunningham, Alicia Henness, Fred Herman, Jennifer Robinson, Svend Andersen, Diane Kassmann, Paul Stansel, Sarina M., Merissa Smith, Susan Oke, K. Hodghead, Steven Danielson, Michelle, Elizabeth, Tripleyew, Alan Smale, Clarissa C. S. Ryan, Michael Cieslak, Amy Rawe, Stephanie Lucas, Chris Kaiser, Leah Webber, Greg Dawson, Ryan Hunter H. and Cameron Alexander H., Tory Shade, Neil, Karen M, Taia Hartman, Sidney Whitaker, Kate Malloy, Cori Smith, Kerry aka Trouble, Jess Pugh, Jessica Enfante, Howard J. Bampton, Joanne B Burrows, 'Nathan Burgoine, Ilene Tsuruoka, Jenny Barber, Jen1701D, Jessica K. Meade, David A. Quist, Nicholle F. Beard, Juanita J. Nesbitt, Jaq Greenspon, Rebecca M, Shannon Roe, Lorraine J. Anderson, Jacen Leonard, Michael Feir, Konstanze Tants, Elektra Hammond, Jennifer Berk, Wolf SilverOak, Oliver S, Vincent Darlage, PhD, Brad L. Kicklighter, Katherine S, Michele Hall, Arin Komins, Amanda Saville, Amanda Niehaus-Hard, Michael Kohne, N Flannigan, Lisa Short, ron taylor, MJ Silversmith, Melissa Crook, Todd Stephens, Sarah Cornell, Tom Harning, kommiesmom, E.M. Middel, Caroline Couture, Cyn Wise, L.C., Tania, T. W. Townsend, Jason Mayfield, Leigh Allen, Crysella, Debbie Matsuura, Gerald, Sheryl Ehrlich, Amelia Dudley, J.M Bengtsson, Chelsea Rzepkowski, Emily Ruth, Megan Struttmann, Brynn, Odd, Wayne Howard, Carol J. Guess, Niki Robison, Simon Dick, Fred and Mimi Bailey, Tim Greenshields, Mark Odom, Ryan Mahan, Bodge Inglee-Richards, V Hartman DiSanto, Beth Coll, Mark Hirschman, Elise Power, Stephanie Cranford, Margo Hardyman, Eleftherios Keramidas, Amanda Grace Shu, Susanne Driessen, Tracy Schneider, Caiti Willis, Daniel Blanche, James Conason, Sonya R Lawson, Chickadee, Michael Axe, I. Smith, summervillain, Frankie Mundens, Dagmar Baumann, Nate Botma, Pookster, Nancy Blue Spider Tice, Kimberly Bea, Cait Greer, Piet Wenings, LetoTheTooth, Ellen Harvey, Caty Robey, Joshuah Kusnerz,

Chris Matthews, Hoose Family, Patti Short, Kevin McIntire, Senhina, Darrell Z. Grizzle, A.Chatain, Elaine McMillan, Rain Pope, Brendan Lonehawk, CJ Curtis, Jean Marie ward, Grace Kenney, Erica "Vulpinfox" Schmitt, Dawn Edwards, Tommy Acuff, Julie Pitzel, Ashley Clouser Leonard, Susan Baur, Jeff Eppenbach, Patricia Miller, Tina Connell, Jay V Schindler, Jason Lau, Juli, Kyle Ellis, M.J. Zbacnik, Gwen Whiting, Jenn Bernat, Brooks Moses, Joseph J Connell, E.J. Murray, Heidi Williams, Richard O'Shea, Céline Malgen, Craig Hackl, Matt Trepal, Richard Leis, Mike Ball, ND Gray, Yvonne, Stacy Augustine, Brenda, jjmcgaffey, Tara Paine, Stephen Ballentine, Johne Cook, Aaron W Olmsted, Anchit Vijayakumar, Jen L, Benjamin Hausman, AJ Knight, Sloane Leong, Jim Anderson, Val Cassidy, Elyse M Grasso, Vulpecula, Steve Salem, Richard Clayton, Nancy Gilliam, Merry Lewis, Ashley, Sarah Nutter, Nancy, Ian Chung, Amanda Cook, Amanda Stuart, Lavinia Ceccarelli, Peter D Engebos, Josh Pritchard, Mary Alice Wuerz, Robin Hill, Evan Ladouceur, Amy Goldman, Anna McTaggart, Eirik Gumeny, Carina Bissett, Kristi Chadwick, Jo Beere, The Collinsc Clan, Marty Poling Tool, Sue Weinberg, Aysha Rehm, Lori L. Gildersleeve, Whitney Porter, Michael Fedrowitz, Chris Tanzos, pjk, Beth Morris Tanner, Bebe, Christine Hanolsy, Anya, Pers, Eva Holmquist, Cory Williams, Heidi Cykana, Eric "djotaku" Mesa, Cliff Winnig, Sue Phillips, John T. Sapienza, Jr., Jennifer Beltrame, David Wohlreich, Paula, Taka Angevine, Heather Klassen, Michelle Palmer, Jennifer Dunne, Rebecca S., Ashley Martinson, Mega Boss N'kai, Rebecca Crane, Mark Carter, Duncan & Andrea Rittschof, Agnes Kormendi, Janet Piele, Kat Feete, Lorri-Lynne Brown, A.J. Bohne, Karen Carothers, Katie Hallahan, Antha Ann Adkins, Alan Mark Tong, Ronald H. Miller